T0022262

THE MYSTERY OF
THE CAPE COD PLAYERS

PHOEBE ATWOOD TAYLOR (1909-1976) was one of the most beloved and most successful mystery authors of the 1930s and 1940s, writing under her own name and two pseudonyms, Freeman Dana and Alice Tilton. The Asey Mayo character, first introduced in *The Cape Cod Mystery*, went on to star in 24 novels in a series informed by the author's generations-long family history in Cape Cod.

OTTO PENZLER, the creator of American Mystery Classics, is also the founder of the Mysterious Press (1975); MysteriousPress.com (2011), an electronic-book publishing company; and New York City's Mysterious Bookshop (1979). He has won a Raven, the Ellery Queen Award, two Edgars (for the *Encyclopedia of Mystery and Detection*, 1977, and *The Lineup*, 2010), and lifetime achievement awards from NoirCon and *The Strand Magazine*. He has edited more than 70 anthologies and written extensively about mystery fiction.

THE MYSTERY OF
THE CAPE COD PLAYERS

PHOEBE ATWOOD
TAYLOR

Introduction by
OTTO
PENZLER

AMERICAN
MYSTERY
CLASSICS

Penzler Publishers
New York

Published in 2024 by Penzler Publishers
58 Warren Street, New York, NY 10007
penzlerpublishers.com

Distributed by W. W. Norton

Cover image: Andy Ross
Cover design: Mauricio Diaz

Paperback ISBN 978-1-61316-493-8
Hardcover ISBN 978-1-61316-492-1
eBook ISBN 978-1-61316-494-5

Library of Congress Control Number: 2023918549

Printed in the United States of America

9 8 7 6 5 4 3 2 1

INTRODUCTION

OSTENSIBLY TOLD in first person by Victoria (Vic) Ballard, who has some of the accoutrements of an amateur detective, *The Mystery of the Cape Cod Players* has so many colorful characters that poor Mrs. Ballard, bullied by her son, has less time on the stage than numerous other players in this baffling mystery.

Although only fifty-five years old, Vic is treated like a frail old lady by her son George, who arranges her summer vacation, even picking the little cottage where she'll stay, for how long, and with whom—which is when she puts her foot down and insists that she'll pick her own companion and it won't be her cousin Mercy, who she calls a moron.

The novel quickly becomes delicious when a group of actors gets lost in the fog and are invited to the lonely cottage to get warm and fed. Just as snowstorms and broken bridges can isolate a group of people, so can a good, heavy fog help to create a relatively closed circle of suspects when murder strikes.

The victim is Red Gilpin, a performer with the impecunious troupe, who seemingly is the most beloved of the players. And, apparently, the most beloved of a long string of women whose hearts have been broken by the handsome Lothario.

The actors have their quirks and eccentricities, as do the members of the little household, but none can touch Asey Mayo, the amateur detective known locally and to readers as "the Codfish Sherlock."

Mayo's first appearance was in *The Cape Cod Mystery* (1931), which sold out its first printing of 5,000 copies, an exceptionally strong sale for a first novel during the Great Depression (and not too bad in the present day). No one wrote more mysteries, nor more popular ones, nor better ones, set on Cape Cod than Phoebe Atwood Taylor (1909-1976), best-known for her series of twenty-four novels featuring Mayo.

In the words of the English novelist Nicholas Blake (the pseudonym of C. Day Lewis), Mayo is "an eccentric individual" who Taylor describes as "a typical New Englander . . . the kind of man everybody expects to find on Cape Cod and never does."

A former sailor who made his first voyage on one of the last clipper ships, Mayo lives on Wellfleet, where he is the handyman/chauffeur for the local tycoon but still finds time to solve an inordinate number of murders.

He is tall but unimpressive in appearance as he walks with his long, lean frame hunched over. Variously described as "wily, ornery, and homespun," he relies on his profound, albeit practical, knowledge of human nature for his success as a sleuth. "Common sense" has been the tobacco-chewing Mayo's hallmark since his first episode.

His speech is "impossible for a student of phonetics to record on paper," writes Taylor. "It resembled no other dialect in the world. Let it suffice to say that he never sounded a final *g* or *t*. His *r* was the *ah* of New England. His *a* was so flat . . . you couldn't get under it with a crowbar."

Mayo uses his speech to share his homely wisdom, such as

"they ain't many *whys* without *becauses*." Other characters in Taylor's books are also convincingly Yankee, particularly such aptly named figures as Tabitha Sparrow, Phineas Banbury, and Aunt Nettie Hobbs.

Taylor was born in Boston, descended from the *Mayflower* Pilgrims, and received a B.A. from New York City's Barnard College before returning to live and write in Massachusetts. She uses her intimate knowledge of New England for the settings of her novels, notably such Cape Cod communities as Wellfleet, Orleans, and Provincetown. While these and other nearby towns are recognized as summer resorts, most of the books deal with the people who live ordinary lives there after the tourists have gone home.

Humor plays an important role in the Asey Mayo series, as it does in the eight books she wrote under the Alice Tilton pen name, all of which featured Leonidas Witherall, known to his friends as "Bill" because of his uncanny resemblance to portraits of William Shakespeare. A New England prep school headmaster, he supplements his modest income by writing thrillers. He also hunts for rare books for "the wealthier and lazier Boston collectors."

In his first case, *Beginning with a Bash* (1937), Witherall attempts to prove the innocence of a former student who he encounters on a below-zero evening in Boston, running from the police in a gray flannel suit and carrying a bag of golf clubs. The novel had previously been published in *Mystery League* magazine in 1933 as *The Riddle of Volume Four* under the Taylor byline.

Anthony Boucher was a fan of Taylor's "well-ordered farces" and praised her ability to recreate such historical moments as the Great Depression and the early years of World War II, including blackouts, gasoline rationing, and wardens. The everyday life of those times and more peaceful ones gave readers a window to view Cape Cod as she knew it.

Country auctions, local politics, cake sales, teas, ladies' clubs, gardens, petty disputes among neighbors—all served as the background for Taylor's detective novels, produced with a keenly observant eye and a rich helping of amused and gentle humor.

Otto Penzler
New York, May 2023

THE MYSTERY OF
THE CAPE COD PLAYERS

NOTE

All of the characters in this book are entirely imaginary;
so is the town of Weesit, even though it bears the name
of an existing neck of land on Cape Cod.

1

IT WAS George who was responsible for the whole business.

It was George who made me go to Weesit in the first place, and it was at Weesit, where I was supposed to undergo a quiet and peaceful convalescence, that everything happened. I want to make it clear from the beginning that the next time I recover from pneumonia I'm going not to Cape Cod, but to Sarawak or Tibet or some remote spot where you might reasonably expect people to be killed outside your bedroom window.

I'd been home from the hospital just four weeks when George came in one Monday afternoon in late June and announced peremptorily that I was to spend the summer in Weesit. It was a nice placid little Cape Cod town and Dr. Burnside had particularly recommended its bracing sea air. That I had no desire to go away from Boston had no effect on George.

"You've got to go somewhere for the summer," he pointed out. "You can't stay here in this barracks. I've hired a summer cottage for you, small enough so that you can't possibly invite a lot of guests. Now listen to my plans."

I groaned a little to myself. So many of George's remarks are prefaced by that statement, "Now listen to my plans." Of course his executive ability and passion for detail have made him a huge business success at thirty, and I'm enormously proud of him and his achievements. I couldn't be prouder if he were really my own, instead of my adopted son. But once in a while his plans become tiresome and I wish that my husband were alive to cope with the boy. Adin understood George perfectly. I've always remembered what he remarked to me just after he was taken sick.

"Vic," he said, "if I don't get over this, for Heaven's sakes don't let that boy manage you the way he manages Janet, and Ballard and Company. He's competent, but he hasn't a scrap of humor. Don't let him bully you and tell you he knows what's best for you!"

And I never had until I was taken sick. Then, I must admit, I fully appreciated his capacity for taking charge of things. But now his plans were beginning to bore me. It occurred to me, too, that possibly Weesit without George around to make me do what was best for me might be better than Boston with him. I didn't feel strong enough to argue the matter, anyway. I half started to appeal to Janet, George's wife, and then I decided it would be useless to ask her aid. She was listening dutifully, with an expression of habitual resignation, to George's details.

Privately I've often wondered how Janet happened to marry George. She's a dear girl, but she's not his type at all—and as the most beautiful deb of her day she had a wide choice of husbands. For my own part, even though I admire George's ability, I have my doubts as to whether I should enjoy being married to him. Once in a while lately, I've thought I detected signs that Janet was beginning to have doubts herself. He does supervise her a lot.

But for all that, George is really very kind and thoughtful. As

Adin said, you always had to admit that his ideas were usually much better and much sounder than your own.

"Finally," George was winding up, "you'll need a cook—I've decided on Mrs. Tavish—and a companion of some sort. Cousin Mercy has very kindly offered—"

The mention of Cousin Mercy Cabot affected me as George should have known it would.

"I'll go to Weesit," I told him hotly, "because I haven't the energy to debate about it. But not with Cousin Mercy! Not that—that moron! She'd wear me out. I simply couldn't bear to spend the summer listening to her tales of the sick Ballards. I'll go to Weesit, but I choose my own servant and companion!"

"You don't seem to realize," George announced, "that you're in no condition to make your own plans. Or any plans, for that matter."

That statement, coming on top of Cousin Mercy, goaded me beyond words.

"I'm fifty-five," I said when I was finally able to speak, "and I'll admit that I've hovered over the brink of the grave these last few months. I'm grateful for the way you made plans for me while I was sick. But I've no intention of having you superintend all my affairs now. And," I added as an afterthought, "on your way to the office, stop in at Stephen Crump's and tell him I'll look after my own business in the future. Have your power of attorney revoked."

"You can't, mother! You're in no position to handle things! You'll be away and—"

"I'm perfectly capable, George, of taking care of the few stocks and bonds I have left."

"Few," George spluttered. "Few! Half a million!"

"I managed twice that before you were born or thought of," I returned, "and I survived very well. Now run along. You're tiring me. I'll see you in September."

"September? But I intend to go to the Cape with you and of course I'll come down weekends," George protested. "Janet's leaving for Maine tomorrow to stay with her mother and I'd planned on spending my spare time with you—"

"You said it was a small cottage," I reminded him tartly, "and that I couldn't have visitors. Now, George, go along to Stephen's. It's time for my nap."

George cleared his throat and got up from his chair. Janet looked at me nervously. I knew she knew what the gesture signified. George was going to lose his renowned temper.

"Conditions," he began, his face already growing red, "are changing daily. I absolutely refuse to let you take the responsibility of—"

"Stop acting like a school boy," I said, as calmly as I could. "I've explained to you that I'm grateful for the plans you made and the things you did for me while I was sick, but now that I'm well, I'll take care of things myself. That's all there is to it."

"Of making your own plans," George continued, speaking more loudly and ignoring me entirely, "You'll be away from town, you're out of touch with things. You're not well!" He banged his fist on the table. "I shall not agree to seeing Stephen nor to letting you choose your own companions at the Cape!" He banged the table again, so hard this time that an ash tray bounced to the floor.

"You shall agree and you will agree," I told him, "and *please* don't bang the table so, George. The Ming vase—"

"Damn the Ming vase," George yelled, snatching it up from the table. He raised it, and if Janet hadn't gripped his arm, I truly believe he would have dashed it on the floor. He looked ashamed the next moment, but that did not alter my feelings.

"No," I said as he started to speak, "don't try to apologize. You know that vase is the gem of your father's collection. I've had enough of this scene. I shall take whom I please to the Cape, go when I please, and I shall call Stephen within the hour."

George's face was literally purple as he walked toward the door. "Come, Janet," he said. "Come!"

"In a moment."

George opened his mouth to speak, then apparently thought better of it and left the room. He slammed the door very hard behind him.

"Vic," Janet said, crossing quickly over to the couch, "I'm tremendously sorry! I don't know what to say. He's been—well, he's not been himself since the Janson and Carter Trust went to pieces. And you know how he is when his plans are interfered with—"

"I do," I said, kissing her. "And I know he'll be very sorry for this outburst. Don't antagonize him by making him wait—and write me. There's no harm done. I understand."

But I didn't entirely. George hates to have his plans go askew and opposition of any sort usually irritates him, but I'd never seen him lose control of himself before. Probably it *was* due to business worries. I stared at the ceiling and wondered about him and tried to figure out whom I'd take to the Cape with me.

At that point Rose, my good-looking if slightly hit-or-miss housemaid, brought me in Elizabeth Houghton's scrawled note.

"Sorry to bother you," she wrote, *"but I need your help. The girl I'm enclosing with this is Nelly Stone's daughter Judith Dunham. She fainted from hunger yesterday on Boylston Street and they brought*

her here to the hospital. She's far too decent just to put up any place and I can't keep her here. We're full. Can't you take her on as a companion till she gets on her feet? She's broke. She has a lovely voice and she could read to you. Won't you do something? I'll call later."

I felt rather more than shocked when I finished the note. I'd not seen or heard of Nelly Stone for thirty years, but she'd been my best friend at Miss Owen's Seminary. Hazy recollections of pickle limes and "Trilby" and taffy apples and horse cars and Harvard class days rose before me, and with them all a picture of Nelly, tall and brown-eyed and smiling. Now her daughter fainted from hunger on Boylston Street!

"Send the young woman up," I said, thinking quickly. "And wait, Rose. Should you care to go to the Cape for the summer? Clean, cook, and all that? I'll pay you what Mrs. Tavish gets."

"Is it lonesome, Mrs. Ballard?"

I smiled. Recitals of Rose's love affairs had considerably lessened the tedium of the last few weeks.

"I presume that the town has eligible young men," I told her. "You don't have to be lonesome."

"I'll go."

"Good. Now, what does this girl downstairs look like?"

"She's pretty. Sort of like Sylvia Sydney. She's got a nice smile. I'll bring her up."

I liked Judith Dunham the minute I saw her. She was about twenty-five, and her clothes were good, if somewhat limp from too much pressing and cleaning. She must have known what was in Elizabeth's note, but it didn't bother her. Even if she were penniless, she was carrying her head and chin high.

"I knew your mother," I said. "You look like her. Same brown eyes and hair."

"I'm afraid I haven't mother's figure," she answered.

That was perfectly true. She was excruciatingly thin and looked as though she hadn't eaten regularly for weeks. I learned later that she literally had not.

"I'm going away tomorrow," I went on, "and I wonder if you'd like to come with me and act as my companion? Read to me, order meals, play cards and all?"

"I thought you were going to say," her voice wavered, "say that you'd love to give me something to do if you weren't going away. I—I really don't think I could have stood being turned down again. Thank you, Mrs. Ballard. I'd love to go."

"You can drive a car? Have you a license? Good. Then we'll drive to the Cape tomorrow. Now, what do people call you?"

"Judy."

"Well, Judy, run along and get your trunks and things and by the time you get back, there'll be a room ready for you."

"I'm sorry," she spoke hesitantly, "but I've nothing to get. My last landlady took my trunks for back rent. She's probably pawned everything by now. I've nothing but what I've got on."

"Then bring me my pocketbook," I said briskly, trying to hide the effect of her calm announcement. "Thank you. Here, take this and call it an advance. Get what you need."

"I've not seen so much money in months," she admitted with a little laugh. "Ought you to let me loose with it? You've not seen my references—"

"You're Nelly's daughter and that's enough. Run along and get some clothes." I stopped a moment. Perhaps it wasn't wise to take this girl into the family without someone else's stamp of approval. I didn't want to question her as though she were a charwoman, but in spite of George's complaints to the contrary, I'm a cautious person. "Wait," I said. "After you're through shopping, go to my son's office. Rose'll give you the address. Tell him you're my new companion and that we're leaving tomorrow with Rose. He'll probably raise a rumpus."

She nodded and grinned. From the glint in her eyes I knew she understood that it was more than a casual order.

Just as I downed the last of my five o'clock buttermilk, George phoned.

He considered my new companion headstrong, wilful, and unduly flippant. So I knew then that I'd made no mistake. Judy was firm, self-reliant, and she had a sense of humor.

We set off the next morning, stopped for a leisurely luncheon and reached Weesit just before three in the afternoon. While we hunted for the real estate agent, I took stock of the town. My first impression was of white paint. All the houses were shining white with green blinds. There were tall stately elms along the main street and from the general air of spick-and-spanness, I gathered that the people of Weesit took pride in their village.

Finally we located the agent, an amiable man by the name of Bangs. His garrulousness and appearance reminded me of a peddler who had once attempted to sell me fake diamonds on the installment plan. He guided us over the three or four miles of rutted sandy backroads to our cottage, a small modern reproduction of a Cape Cod house.

It stood in a clearing among scrubby pine trees on the top of a high bluff. Below, at the foot of the bluff, stretched the ocean.

I got out of the car and looked around critically. Although an unsuccessful attempt at a lawn had apparently been made, tall beach grass grew in clusters about the house. It was a perfect location for a summer place. The view was marvelous and there were no neighbors. But the air of wildness and loneliness didn't please me at all. I'm a sociable creature.

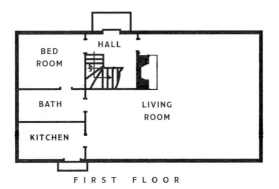

FIRST FLOOR

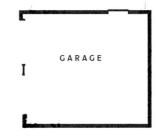

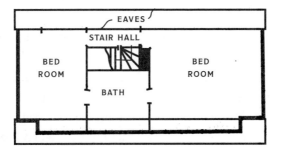

SECOND FLOOR

It annoyed Mr. Bangs that I was not more enthusiastic.

"It's the first summer the Hendersons ever rented this place," he said earnestly. "It's just as they left it, too, except for bein' cleaned an' opened. You got things in this place no other house in town's got. Three nice bedrooms, a nice kitchen, electric lights, electric pump an' a two-car garage." He paused for breath. "Wild roses outside your door, chintz coverings on your chairs, a fireplace, an' Persian rugs. And," with a gesture, "two p'latial bathrooms. Two. Don't you think that's pretty fine?"

"Yes, indeed. But aren't there any people near? I can't see a house and we didn't pass one after we left the main road. It's so lonely!"

"Your son wrote he wanted me to get him a nice quiet place," Mr. Bangs said defensively. "I got it. I told him in my letter that the nearest house was two miles off."

Judy laughed at my woebegone face. "We've got the car, Mrs. Ballard. We can always find people. Listen to the surf. Isn't it grand?"

"Sounds damp to me," I remarked. "I'll probably get pneumonia all over again and I'm sure you can't get over it twice in one life."

"Don't you worry, Mrs. Ballard. I'll bundle you up. Mr. Bangs, what about ice, coal, wood, milk, groceries and all those things?"

"All set," Bangs told her. "Mrs. Ballard's son told me to arrange for everything an' I did. Ice man'll be here this afternoon. So'll the grocery boy. He sent a list, your son did. Coal an' wood'll be here before supper time. Sorry there ain't no phone. Henderson managed electric poles, but I guess phone poles would of busted him. Guess you'll have to run into town in your car when you want anything quick. Glad to help you out when I can."

And with that, Mr. Bangs departed hurriedly. I suspected that he had some doubts about my keeping the cottage after all.

Rose was frankly dubious. "It's lonesome. I bet there's rum-runners an' smugglers. Bet we'll all be shot," she said lugubriously.

"Cheer up," Judy advised. "There are no end of wandering males."

The ice man arrived just then and took forty minutes to fill our diminutive ice box. Rose was whistling when the grocery boy came, and by the time he and the coal man had departed, she burst into song.

"Just the same," she said when she brought in the soup at dinner, "Toby—he's the ice man—he says there still are rum-runners here. And smugglers, too. He said Mr. Henderson that owns this house slept with a gun."

"Uncomfortable, I should think," Judy commented.

"And Toby says this house was broken into four times this last winter. I've put a burglar-proof catch on both the kitchen windows. I brought 'em from home."

"Then," Judy said, "you're safe. Why worry?"

"Just the same," I remarked later while we were having our coffee before the fire, "it's very lonely here. I don't like being without a phone. What would we do if anyone tried to break in?"

"Why, Mrs. Ballard—"

"You can't," I interrupted, "go on Mrs. Ballarding me for ever. My name is Victoria Alexandra. My friends shorten it to Vic. I hope you will."

"It's a bit regal, but it suits you, somehow. Vic, I think you're safer here than you are in Boston. It's so calm and settled. I'm happy for the first time in months."

"I'm glad for you, my dear, but just the same I'm nervous. I've a feeling that I'm being watched from outside that window. I'm sure someone's—"

Promptly the front door knocker beat a tattoo and I looked at Judy.

"There! Hear that? And I saw no car light, did you?"

Judy shook her head and started for the door. I noticed that she eyed the poker reflectively as she passed by it.

I followed her to the door. A harassed looking young man in white flannels and a polo coat stood on the door step.

"Sorry to rouse you, all that—" he said politely, "but can you tell me where I am? Are you the Guilds?"

His broad 'a' and pleasant voice allayed my fears.

"Come in," I said, "but we're not the Guilds."

"I thought as much. You didn't look expectant," he said regretfully as he crossed over to the fireplace. "Maybe you could tell me where to find them?"

"I can't. We've just arrived and there's no phone."

"Gee! Oh, I'm Richard Edson, by the way. Punch Edson. I run an itinerant Punch and Judy show. My gear's in a truck down the road a bit. Lights gave out and the fog stopped me completely."

"Fog?"

"There's quite a lot rolling in. I say, no others have wandered out this way, have they? The Allens—they're a song and dance outfit I've been travelling with—they had the same directions. We were supposed to give our show for these Guilds."

"We've not seen them."

"What a week, what a week! Rain, four flats and more engine trouble than I've ever seen outside a repair shop. Now this! Well, I still can't see how I went wrong. I took the turns as Dan gave 'em to me. Well, I'll pop along. Thanks ever so much."

"Perhaps you'd better wait," I suggested, "and see if your friends don't turn up. Are you professionals?"

"By necessity. I was an engineer. Dan Allen is a customer's man turned barytone. His wife Edie used to dance for charity benefits and now she does it for a living. Harriet, Dan's sister— well, Hat used to teach and now she's a pseudo-Ruth Draper. Our latest addition used to have an automobile agency. Now he pulls rabbits out of silk hats. That's Red Gilpin."

"Did you say Kilpin?" Judy asked in rather a strange voice. "Funny name."

"No, Gilpin. You know, 'John Gilpin was a citizen of credit and renown'? Old man Cowper."

I laughed. "I haven't thought of that poem for years. I recited it once in school. 'Away went Gilpin—dum-de-dum—and sore against his will—'"

The knocker banged again. Punch rushed to the door and ushered in three people.

"Mrs. Allen, Miss Allen and Mr. Allen," he said. "No, Dan, don't start a speech. This isn't the right place. There's no phone, these people have just come and don't know the Guilds, and the truck's lights have gone out."

Dan Allen groaned. He was thirty-odd, stocky and dark, and his eyebrows fascinated me. They met in the middle of his forehead.

"What a life," he said disgustedly. "And the van just got a flat. Red's fixing it."

"Inside tire," Harriet Allen added. She was dark like her brother and she wore a lot of make-up, vivid brown powder and plum colored lipstick. I felt sure that her eyebrows grew naturally like her brother's, though now they were hair lines. "That means two hours!"

Punch shook his head. "That's shot the Guilds' show. Well, let's go help." He bowed to me. "Sorry to have bothered you."

"Wait," I said. "Why not leave the women here till you get things fixed?"

They looked at me gratefully. "We'd like nothing better," Mrs. Allen said. "Run along, boys, and call us when it's over. Hat and I were pretty chilly."

She perched on a footstool before the fire and pulled off her smart, tight fitting red cap. A shock of blonde curls fell almost to her shoulders and in the firelight she looked like a small girl, though I learned later that she was thirty, just three years older than her sister-in-law. I smiled as I remembered an expression of Adin's that covered her exactly. She was a "half-pint beauty."

"Isn't it grand to be warm, Hat? Ooh. You've got the same chintz pattern we had in our sun room in Winchester. The dear, dead days!"

I laughed, for there was no sadness in her tone.

"How long have you been doing this?" I asked.

"Dan and I've been at it two years. Hat and Punch a little over a year, and Red about six months. It's fun except when it rains or the truck or the van breaks down."

She and Hat Allen chatted on about their experiences till the men came back around ten-thirty. They brought John Gilpin with them and I liked him better than either of the other men. He was, I thought, exactly the sort of person I'd have wanted my own son, who died when he was a baby, to be. He was big and tall and pleasant and full of life—and humor. And he had the most cheerful red hair I've ever seen.

"Everyone's mad with me, Mrs. Ballard," he announced. "And by the way, is it B-a-l-l-a-r-d? Punch's hot potato accent is so difficult."

"It is," I told him. "Why are they mad?"

"Because I can't fix the truck lights. I can't seem to grasp the short circuit."

"What are you going to do for the night?"

"That's just the point. I wondered if you'd let us park the cars in the turn off on the left, below the house? We found it just now. Followed the ruts and had to do an about-face. Then we wouldn't be blocking the road. You see, we can crank the truck and use a flashlight to get it there, and then in the morning I can fix everything. But we couldn't possibly get to town in all this fog."

"But where will you sleep?"

Red Gilpin laughed. "Where we always do. Punch and I in the truck and the rest in the van. We won't park up here if you don't want us to, Mrs. Ballard. We'll understand if you say no."

"But of course you may," I said. "I was just trying to figure out if some of you couldn't stay here."

"I could take the couch, Vic," Judy spoke up, "and then Mrs. Allen and Miss Allen could have the two beds in my room."

"Bliss," Edie Allen said, "sheer bliss! A bed. Hat, I'm as excited as a girl! Haven't seen a bed for years!"

Dan went out and brought in a suitcase of night things for them, then Rose served us coffee and sandwiches. It was exactly twelve when we settled down for the night—the Allens and Rose in the bedrooms upstairs, the men out in the cars, Judy in the living room. I occupied the downstairs bedroom.

It was after one o'clock before I went to sleep. As I dropped off I heard the mantel clock strike, and shortly after it seemed I heard a car backfiring—four times. In my drowsy state I thought I was home on Beacon Street and muttered to myself that the police should stop those banging trucks at night.

I woke shivering a little later—three-fifteen by the luminous dial of my travelling clock. After much wavering back and forth as to whether or not I really needed an extra blanket, I decided that I did, and so I got up and went into the living room.

A few charred logs glowed feebly in the fireplace and I could see the outline of my steamer rug and its strap handle on the floor near Judy's couch. I didn't want to wake her, so I picked it up quietly and hurried back to my own room. I wondered sleepily where she'd found that white blanket. I hadn't remembered any but colored blankets in the Henderson chests.

It took some time to undo the rug strap, but at last I got everything settled and with my teeth fairly chattering, I hopped into bed. I was glad all those people were around. Somehow I wasn't at all nervous or lonely with them at hand.

Again I dropped off to sleep and again it seemed that I heard a car backfiring. Louder, this time. Almost like the report of a gun. Maybe, I thought, the men were still trying to fix the truck.

I awoke in the morning to the sound of Rose's pans clinking in the kitchen. The sun poured in my window and outside the ocean was sparkling and blue. I put on a sweater suit and top coat and tiptoed out. I peeked in at Judy, still asleep on the couch. A brisk walk along the bluff, I thought, would give me a fine appetite.

But not three feet from the steps that led to the beach, I stopped short in horror.

I don't think I ever understood the phrase "rooted to the spot" before that minute. For there at my feet, lying in the tall sea grass, was Red Gilpin. Curiously sprawled. Rigid.

His red hair was wet with dew—but his face! I turned away from the sight.

Suddenly it came to me as I looked out over the white flecked rolling waves that those sounds of the night before had not all been car exhausts. They had been gun shots. Someone had shot and done away with Red Gilpin.

Ironically the old tag line of the poem pounded in my ears along with the crashing of the surf:

"Away went Gilpin—dum-de-dum—and sore against his will."

2

"KNOW WHO that feller is?"

I whirled around to find a tall lanky man dressed in corduroy trousers and a canvas coat staring at Red Gilpin's body. I must have looked as frightened and terror-stricken as I felt, for he reached out a hand and steadied me.

"Didn't mean to scare you," he said more gently. "Here. Lean on my stick a minute."

Slipping off his coat, he laid it over Red Gilpin's head and shoulders, then led me some forty feet over to a rustic bench that faced the ocean.

"Sit down here. Don't think about all this for a second, Mrs. Ballard."

"How'd you know my name?" I demanded.

"Got a telegram for you."

Instinctively I put out my hand, but he shook his head.

"It ain't written down on yellow paper. They phoned it to Sylvanus Mayo an' I told Syl I'd deliver the message myself. It said 'Let me know immediately how you stood trip' an' it was signed 'George.'"

"My son," I said. "Thank you."

Involuntarily I started to turn and look again toward that still figure in the grass, but the stranger sat down beside me and cut off the view.

I wanted to cry, but I have nothing but scorn for women who weep at crises. I've always felt they were tremendously selfish, for their tears automatically relieve them of all responsibility and give others only an added burden. So I turned to the stranger as composedly as I could, intending to ask him what should be done.

"Even that telegram," he remarked conversationally before I could speak, "don't answer how I knew you. Last time I seen you was when Miss Prue Whitsby got married to Denny James. Last fall. You had on a black dress an' a lot of pearls."

"You—you were at Prue's wedding?"

"Yup." He chuckled. "I was best man. Oh, I know I don't look now like I did then. Had on city clothes—"

"I know you now," I interrupted. "You're Asey Mayo! Bill Porter's friend."

He nodded. "That's right, I am. Mrs. Ballard, you got a little color in your cheeks now an' you seem to be breathin' easier. What's the name of that redheaded feller yonder? What's been goin' on here?"

"I'm sure I don't know," I answered helplessly. "The man's John Gilpin. Red Gilpin. He—oh, what'll we do? Who shot him? Can't you help? Prue's told me how you saved Bill Porter when that novelist was murdered. You're a constable or something, too, aren't you?"

"Used to be. Look, who's in those trucks on the entrance to the lane?"

"Some—players." I told him about the Allens and Punch. "This Gilpin was one of them."

"I see. Ain't no phone, is there? Nope, I see there ain't no wires. Now, here's Syl Mayo comin' along the beach. When he gets here I'll call down an' have him hop back to his house an' do some phonin'. Anyone up?"

"Only the maid."

"Well, it's just seven an' it won't do any good to rouse the rest just now. I'd have one of them go to town in a car an' phone, only I don't favor the idea of turnin' anyone loose just now. I'll stay here with you till Syl can phone an' the p'lice get here."

"But won't you help? Can't you—?"

"I ain't an arm of the lawr no more. Used to be constable over to Wellfleet, but they had two murders there an' I sort of felt the place'd used up its quota for the next hundred years. B'sides, I had a lot of luck an' I didn't want to take no chances on a third, havin' got to the bottom of the other two. I quit. Just happened to be stayin' over here in Weesit with Syl."

"But, Mr. Mayo, won't you stay and help anyway? I—well, I'm confused. I know these things mean trouble. Police. All that. And I don't know a soul in town. I got here only yesterday afternoon. And Red Gilpin—I saw that young man only an hour or so, but I give you my word, Mr. Mayo, I couldn't be more upset about this if he were my own family. Last night when I saw him I—well, I wished my son would have been like that if he'd lived and grown up. He was just one of those people who come into a room and make you feel—"

"Like the lights had all gone on an' a band was playin' outside?"

"That's it. How'd you know?"

Asey Mayo smiled. "I talked with that young man last week in Hyannis. At a garage where he was tellin' a couple of mechanics how to fix that truck yonder. I liked him. But I thought you had a son, Mrs. Ballard."

"I have. George is my adopted son. My husband and I—we couldn't bear it after young Adin died, and we adopted George when he was a tiny baby. But won't you stay here and help, Mr. Mayo, if the police will let you?" I hesitated to hire him in the sense of offering him money. It was not because Prudence Whitsby and the fastidious Denny James considered this blue-eyed man a friend and a social equal. Even if his friends had not been mine, I think I should have known better than to treat him as an ordinary hired man.

"Well." He considered. "Well, I—guess—so. Yup. I guess so. Here's Syl. You wait."

He scrambled down the cliff with the ease of a chamois. I wondered as I watched him just how old he was. He didn't move like an old man nor did he look old, for all the network of lines in his face. He might have been forty-five or sixty. I couldn't tell. There was an air of calm assurance about him that made me feel I could depend on him and I needed someone on whom I could rely.

I thought of George's message and experienced a sinking sensation. I could almost hear what he'd say when he learned what had happened.

"I told you that Dr. Burnside said you were to have no visitors! Then you go and pick up the first ragtag and bobtail of humanity that presents itself! It's all your own fault!"

For once in his life George was going to have a legitimate excuse for I-told-you-so-ing all over the place. At last he had adequate grounds for losing his temper as thoroughly as he had Monday afternoon. And he probably would. I shouldn't have taken in those people the night before. Yet, after all, they'd been decent and pleasant enough. What had happened had not changed my mind on that point.

Asey scrambled up over the cliff. It must have been forty feet high but he wasn't even panting.

"Watch Syl run!" he said. "He'll call Barnst'ble an' get things started an' then drive back here. He's all het up. Reads a lot of these fool detective stories an' you'd think to hear him talk that he could make even Sherlock Holmes look sort of peaked. Now in the meantime, I wonder if you'd tell me who's around here, in the actin' crowd an' in your house. If you really want me to help you, I guess I can get Parker to let me stick around. An' I'd kind of like to get a head start."

"I think," I said impulsively, "that you'd have helped anyway, Mr. Mayo."

He smiled and tipped his broad brimmed Stetson back on his head. "Guess I would of at that," he admitted. "An' say, call me Asey, will you? Handles make me nervous like. Now, if you'll begin."

I explained briefly about Punch Edson, the Allens, and Gilpin.

"Then I have Rose, a maid, and Judy Dunham, my companion. In case you've wondered how I happened to come here," I added, "I'm supposed to be convalescing from pneumonia."

"Seems's if 'twas goin' to be a kind of lively conv'lescence," he remarked. "Hm. Listen. That feller's got four bullet holes in him that I saw. Didn't you or any of the others hear the shots?"

I told him about the noises of the night before.

"I thought they were cars backfiring," I explained apologetically. "I live on Beacon Street and somehow I was so sleepy that I thought I was back there."

"I know how it goes. There's so many noises that sound like guns an' ain't that you don't think it's a gun shot when it is. That's kind of complicated like, but you see what I mean. You say you heard two sets of noises?"

"The first shortly after one, and the second—let's see. After quarter past three sometime. The last ones were louder. Don't you suppose that was the gun?"

"Seems sensible, but you can't tell."

"Look here," I said, "even if I was sleepy and didn't think much of the noises, why didn't they wake the others? Why didn't anyone else hear them?"

"Maybe they did."

"Then why didn't they get up?" I persisted. "Why?"

"Well, maybe they didn't hear 'em. Or else just dismissed 'em like you did. Where'd you sleep?"

"In the downstairs room. Front."

He got up and squinted at the house. "Huh. Dormers only in the back. Guess people in the upstairs bedrooms wouldn't of been so likely to hear anyway. Who slept where?"

"Dan Allen, Punch and Gilpin were out in the van or the truck. I don't know which. The two women were in one upstairs bedroom, the maid in the other. Judy was parked on the living room couch."

"Huh. Let me see. Fog begun to pour in last night around eight. Around ten, the wind shifted from east around to the north'ards, an' the fog begun to blow out. Later it shifted to the north-west. Y'see," he added by way of explanation, "Syl's dog was sick yesterday an' I sat up doctorin' him most all last night. That's how I know so much about the weather. Now, from one till three, 'bout the time you heard those noises, the wind was blowin' pretty strong out to sea. So it's dollars to doughnuts that you're the only person who heard the noises, unless the livin' room windows was open where your c'mpanion slept. Upstairs they wouldn't of heard anything, not likely, nor in the cars there. They're a good hundred an' fifty feet behind your window an' it's a good likely distance from where Gilpin is even to your window. The wind would of carried off the noise of the shots an' the surf was boomin' plenty last night. Maybe that might explain it. I don't s'pose you heard anyone movin' around, did you?"

"No, but when I sleep, I sleep hard. You could beat a bass drum beside my bed and I'd never hear it."

"Well," Asey said philosophically, "it'll all come out in the wash, as the feller said about the tomato soup spillin'. Who's this?"

I turned to find Judy coming out of the house. She walked over to us without glancing toward the grass clump by the steps.

"Early riser," she said cheerfully. "Vic, don't you feel well? You look—oh, so white!"

"This is Asey Mayo," I said. "I'm not sick, Judy. I've just had a terrific shock. Did you hear any noises during the night?"

"Why," she hesitated the fraction of a second, "I thought I heard a car backfire once."

"Well, that wasn't a car. It was a gun shot. Or shots."

"Has anything happened? What's wrong?"

"Red Gilpin," Asey told her, "got killed."

Judy gripped the back of the bench. "When? Where?"

Asey pointed. "No—don't go there, Miss Dunham."

"But who did it?" Her voice was as taut as a violin string. "Who did it? Why don't you do something instead of just sitting and watching the waves?"

"What is there to do?" Asey asked gently. "I've sent for the p'lice. They'll bring the medical examiner with 'em. There's nothin' more to do till they get here. But there'll be enough then," he promised grimly. "You wait an' see. I venture to say you'll look back on this little piece of quiet with a lot of yearnin'."

"You mean—of course! I never thought of all that! Vic, there'll be detectives everywhere and an inquest, too, I suppose?"

"Got thirty days for that in this state," Asey said.

"And the papers! Oh, Vic, you'll never get any rest. And the Lord knows what'll get raked up!"

Asey shot a quick look at her as she stood there, her hands still gripping the back of the bench. He seemed in that instant to have taken her in from the top of her brown bobbed hair to the tip of her new black and white sport shoes.

"D'you have this front window open in the livin' room last night?" he asked—and I felt somehow that it was not the question he had originally intended to ask.

"It stuck," Judy told him, "so I left it closed. I opened the back windows instead. They were all hard to get open."

"Gilpin a stranger to you?"

"Yes."

Asey was silent. "Tell you what," he said, "Miss Dunham, you take Mrs. Ballard indoors an' make her drink some coffee an' eat somethin'. Then you tell the others. Tell 'em to stay put till the p'lice come an' not to be trailin' out this way. I'll only run 'em in again. Oh, yes. Might's well let 'em get some breakfast before you tell 'em if you can manage it that way. Odds is that they might not want it otherwise."

Judy nodded. "Have you called the local police, or who?"

"Local lawr," Asey's eyes twinkled, "is aged sixty-nine an' in Washin'ton at the moment. He's been a mournin' dem'crat for twelve years an' now he's rejoicin' in a trip to Washin'ton. Feels the city's his. An' he's all the lawr there is. Weesit's only got eight hundred folks in it with maybe a few hundred more in summers. So I called the county fellers."

"What are you going to do?" I asked as I turned away.

"Just set an' think. All I can do."

On the way back to the house I told Judy about Asey Mayo. "He's rather a remarkable person, you know. The Porters and the Whitsbys and Stephen Crump all swear by him."

"But just who is he? What does he do?"

"He used to take care of Bill Porter's houses in Wellfleet and he worked for old Captain Porter before that, I think. But he's no hired man. He's been a sailor in all sorts of boats. He's been everywhere. He was the captain of Porter's yacht. He's a sort of jack of all trades. Then he's solved two murders. That's why I asked him to help us here."

"Did you know him before now?"

"I'd seen him once. Even so," I said as I went indoors, "I have perfect confidence in him." It was on the tip of my tongue to answer her subtle rebuke by saying that I hadn't known her very long, either.

Edie and Hat Allen were sitting in the living room.

"Such a grand sleep," Edie said blithely. "Who's that out on the bench, Mrs. Ballard? He looks exactly the way I've always expected Cape Codders to look."

"He even talks the way you expect them to," I informed her. "No g's and t's at the end of his words. And a lovely flat 'a'. They're all like the 'a' in Miss Allen's nickname. Say 'car' with the 'a' like the one in 'Hat' and you'll see what I mean."

Rose called us to breakfast then and the Allens rejected my suggestion to invite the men. I'm afraid that Judy and I paid scant attention to the meal or to our guests. I was surprised to find myself as outwardly calm as I was. But I remembered what

Adin had once said after describing a train wreck from which he'd miraculously escaped death.

"There I was, Vic," he said, "with Jim West dead at my feet and Mallinson crushed and bleeding in what was left of the compartment. And there was I, adjusting my necktie and hooking my watch chain into my vest! Just as though I'd heard the luncheon gong and was taking a last primp before I went downstairs at home. I was so stunned that I couldn't do anything but be mechanically natural."

That was rather the way I was during that meal. Mechanically natural. It's only when you're immeasurably startled out of yourself that you can really be calm. You're too afraid to be otherwise. You know that if you do one unnatural, excited thing, you'll go stark, raving crazy.

Dan Allen and Punch appeared just as I began my second cup of coffee.

"Red here?" Punch inquired casually, "or has he charged off on one of his solitary walks? I'm getting sick of this new tendency of his to disappear for a nice long jaunt by himself. Dan and I decided this morning that we wouldn't save him any breakfast. He can jolly well get his own when he makes up his mind to return to the fold."

The look Judy gave me was too awful to attempt to describe.

I swallowed the last of my coffee and set the cup back in its saucer. I nodded to Judy to bring in Rose, and then with as little beating about the bush as there could be on such an occasion, I told them what had happened to Red Gilpin, how I had found him and all about Asey.

Rose immediately howled and burst into tears.

"I said we'd all be shot!" she wailed. "Ooohah! Murder!"

I don't think the others really comprehended what the situation was until they heard the word murder, which I'd purposely refrained from using.

"Why didn't you let us know about it the instant you found him?" Dan Allen demanded with his eyes blazing. "That's what I'd like to know! What have you done about notifying people? Who is this Mayo? Who is he?"

He was working himself into a fine fury when his wife got up, perched on the arm of his chair and gently placed her hand across his mouth.

"Dan! Mr. Mayo's a friend of Mrs. Ballard's. And what could you have done even if she'd called you?"

"But who could have killed him?" Punch asked dazedly. "Red was such a swell lad. He hadn't an enemy in the world. Certainly we'd have known if there had been anyone who wanted to kill him. You can't knock about with a fellow six months without knowing pretty well all there is to know about him."

"Maybe we didn't know as much as we thought," Hat Allen said quietly. "Punch, has he any family or relatives you could notify?"

"No. He was an only child and his family died years ago. His uncle who brought him up died just after Red got through Tech."

"Who'll take charge? Country cops?" Edie asked.

"Asey called the county officials. And I've asked Asey himself to help us."

"That's good," Dan said. "We'll be under a cloud to begin with because we're show people, and—"

"But Dan!" Punch began.

"You don't think we'll be dragged in? Punch, where are your wits? If you have any deep dark secrets, prepare to hide 'em. Yes, we'll be number one. If Mayo's on our side, it may help. Mrs.

Ballard, I'm sorry we ever came here. You've been so decent and now you'll get the backwash of this. Lord, it's like an old-fashioned third-rate movie, the sort of thing you can't imagine happening. I haven't got it straight yet. I feel—well, I'm all mixed up. It doesn't seem real about Red. And somehow, I feel frightened. I always felt sorry for innocent bystanders, but I never realized how easy it was to get tossed into the part. I—"

He stopped as Asey walked into the room. I introduced him and noticed that more interest was taken in him than he showed for the rest. He didn't look much like a detective or a policeman as he sat in the big blue arm chair and balanced his Stetson on his knee.

"Syl's come back in the car an' I left him out there," Asey said. "Now, 'fore we get down to brass tacks, how come you people happened to land in this godforsaken spot last night?"

"Why," Dan replied, "last Saturday when we were in Hyannis, I got a letter from a man who said he'd seen our show somewhere in the western part of the state, last season. He said he was on the Cape and wanted us all to entertain some guests of his after dinner Tuesday evening. Said he'd seen our posters—we do a lot of poster advertising in advance—and he'd noticed that we had Tuesday night free between the Orleans and the Wellfleet programs Monday and Wednesday. Asked if we'd come if we didn't have other plans. I wrote and told him we'd be there. He'd offered us twenty-five dollars and gave directions how to get to his place in his letter. But it was foggy last night and somehow we must have taken the wrong turn. That's the story on that. After we got out here the van got a flat and the truck's lights gave out."

Asey nodded. "Whyn't you try to find him even then?"

"No phone, Mrs. Ballard didn't know the man, the van tire took nearly two hours to fix. It was the inside tire, right rear. By the time we'd finished with that, it was too late to set out even if we'd known where Guild was."

"What was the name of this phil'nthropic gent?"

"Guild. Maynard Guild."

Asey whistled softly. "Sure?"

"Of course I'm sure," Dan said with some asperity. "Why? What's the matter?"

"Mr. Allen, I know Weesit's well as I know my own town of Wellfleet. An' I been spendin' these last few days with my cousin Syl Mayo helpin' him open up cottages hereabouts. He owns some himself an' he takes care of a lot of others. An' I been helpin' Bangs take likely tenants around. I know all the summer folks's names even if I don't know 'em personally. I'd be sure to know or of heard about anyone that had enough company to have shows for. Weesit ain't big, you know. Y'see, Mr. Allen, the whole point's just this. There ain't no one in Weesit named Maynard Guild."

"But there must be," Dan insisted. "There must! He wrote me that letter and gave me explicit directions—"

"Got the letter here?" Asey asked eagerly. "Let's see it."

Dan Allen's eyebrows rose in a perfectly straight line. His face grew red.

"Got the letter with you?" Asey repeated.

"Well," Dan said lamely, "the fact is—well, I'm sorry, but I threw the letter away."

It was Asey's turn to raise *his* eyebrows.

3

Just as Asey started to speak, a short little man with a drooping moustache ran into the living room.

"S'matter, Syl?" Asey asked, throwing in an explanatory, "My cousin, Syl Mayo."

"They've come, Asey! The whole caboodle. Parker himself. An' Doc Hart, the medical examiner. An' a couple of strangers. An' who else d'you s'pose? Hamilton Kemp."

"Who's he?"

"Who's he? Why, Asey, his great-grandmother an' yours was sisters!" Syl said seriously.

Asey grinned. "Rel'tive, huh? You know," he got up from his chair, "best thing about bein' a Cape Codder is the number of rel'tives that crops up. I found a great-uncle I'd never seen before once in Tahiti. Be right back."

He returned a few minutes later. "Got a room in the house the doc could use?"

"Why—Judy—show them my bedroom."

"They'll be careful," Asey said. "We got a piece of luck here. When Syl phoned Parker he said it was a gun-murder, an' Parker remembered a friend of his had a gun expert spendin' the week.

Bullied him into comin' along. Named Bernsdorf. Big shot in the gun world."

Very little was said during the half hour we waited there in the living room. Personally I watched Dan Allen smoke one cigarette after another and wondered about this letter from the mysterious Mr. Guild.

Had there really been such a letter? It seemed absurd to think otherwise; Dan Allen would have been a fool to lie, knowing that in a small place like Weesit everyone knew everyone else. He couldn't have escaped being found out.

But if there had been a letter, who had sent it? What had been his purpose in giving directions to my cottage? Probably no one knew that Mr. Bangs had let the place. Even at that, it was thoroughly stupid. Why entice five people to an unoccupied cottage? Once they discovered that it was empty, they'd only have turned around and gone away. Perhaps it was just a foolish practical joke. If that were the case, it certainly had been perpetrated at a bad time. Nothing on earth could save the joker from being labelled the murderer of Red Gilpin. Maybe he really was.

Finally Asey came in with the four men. It wasn't hard to pick out which was which in spite of the fact that little had been said about them.

Usually there is something about a doctor that marks him, even if he doesn't carry the inevitable black bag, or smell of disinfectants, or have a speck of unravelled gauze bandage adhering to his person. The plump bespectacled man had both a bag and bandage specks.

The one with the bullet head and the pompadour could only be Bernsdorf; I could imagine him easily as a Prussian guard with a spiked helmet.

Of the two remaining men I chose the younger, with the air of authority, as Parker, and the one with the sunburned face as Kemp. It pleased me no end to find that I had been right when Asey mentioned their names.

"What have you found out?" Dan Allen demanded.

"Shot four times," said the doctor briskly. "At fairly close range. Powder marks. First shot probably got him square between the eyes. Killed him instantly. Other shots pumped into him as and after he fell. Because a man shot between the eyes from in front falls over backwards from natural reflex action aside from the force of the bullet, and Gilpin was lying on his back. Other bullets in his side, abdomen, chest. Wouldn't have knocked him down that way if they'd hit him first. Angles. Position of the body. All that."

He spoke about as feelingly as a housewife ordering two pounds of chops and a bunch of celery, please, from the corner grocer.

"Couldn't even consider suicide. Killed instantly. That's all."

"When did it all happen?" Dan asked.

"Am I a wizard?"

"Well, you've just examined him, haven't you?"

"Yes. But I've not performed any autopsy."

"But can't you tell what time he was killed?" Dan persisted. "What time the shots were fired?"

"Certainly not. I suppose you want me to look wise, young man, and say, 'That boy was killed at six minutes and thirty-two and one-half seconds past one, or two or three.' Well, let me tell you something. I've been in the medical profession thirty-five years and I've been a medical examiner fifteen of 'em. And I can't do any such thing. Person dies quickly, nine times out of ten rigor mortis sets in quickly and leaves quickly. Tenth time, maybe not." He stopped to light a cigar. "Person dies from, say, consumption, and rigor mortis sets in slowly and goes slowly. Maybe so. Maybe not. Probably Gilpin was killed between one and two. Maybe so, maybe not. Tell you better later. When did he eat last night?"

"Dinner around six," Dan said. "Sandwiches and coffee around eleven."

"And a drink a little later," Punch added.

"That's all I want to know. I'll be setting off, Parker, and take him along with me. Coming, any of you?"

Bernsdorf nodded. "I think I've given you everything you'll need, Mr. Mayo," he spoke to Asey, which rather surprised me. "If you find a gun, let me know. Or fire a cartridge into a pail of cotton batting, if you have a couple in the gun. You can tell pretty much by what I've shown you if it's the gun you're after. Or send for me and I'll see what I can do. Don't hesitate to call on me."

"Thank you kindly," Asey said. "You've saved us a lot of time an' told us a lot. You goin' too, Mr. Parker? I wonder—you'll do all I asked?"

"I will. Everything. I've got it all down. Kemp will stay. I'll be back tonight."

As the three departed I saw Syl Mayo and a state policeman carry out a long grey blanketed stretcher from my room.

"What about the bullets?" Punch asked.

"Fired from an old style single action Army Colt revolver," Asey said. "An old .45. Old fashioned black powder cartridge."

"How could he tell all that?"

"Well," Asey said, "that feller Bernsdorf's spent the best part of forty years firin' off guns. Spent five years just at the Colt place. He can look at a little blob of lead an' give you a two hour lecture on it. One bullet was near perfect. Had a little hollow in the end an' there was still a smut of black powder on it. N'en Bernsdorf smiled at it like it was an old friend an' told us the story."

"All the bullets from one gun? D'you suppose you'll find it? Are there any clues?" Punch shot question after question.

"Seemin'ly all from one gun. We ain't really b'gun to hunt yet. An' you can't leave a lot of clues in beach grass. An' when you set out to kill someone, you don't usually strew things around all over the lot, even if stories say so. Now, let's go back to that letter an' you, Mr. Allen."

"See here," Dan blustered, "by what right do you carry on this investigation? Why don't you let Mr. Kemp do something? He's the boss, isn't he?"

"No," Kemp said quietly. "Asey is. Officially I am, but actually I'm not. Asey's worked under Stoughton Parker before this and he knows a lot more about this sort of thing than I do. Asey's a—"

"Pro-tem cop," Asey finished.

"But I understood from Mrs. Ballard," Dan's voice was querulous, "that she'd already hired you—"

"You understood nothing of the sort," I interrupted angrily. "I said that Asey had consented to help!"

"Yes, but I got the idea that he was on our side. Now—"

"Listen, Mr. Allen," Asey said gravely, "I want you to get one thing right at the start. There ain't no sides to this p'ticular game an' the sooner you understand that, the better! I don't b'lieve Mrs. Ballard had any of this side business in mind. I know she didn't. But get this: this investigation can be as pleasant as any of the sort can be—none of 'em's very pleasant, either. Or it can be just as nasty. It's up to you."

"Are you threatening us?"

"No. Tellin' you. I don't want to stand here an' dig things out any more'n you want 'em dug. But bein' as how I'm here an' on deck, you'll answer my questions an' tell the truth an' do what I say. No need for any of you to try to lie. Things'll come out sooner or later. They always do. Now, what about it?"

"You're perfectly right, Mr. Mayo." Edie Allen spoke up. "I'm sorry Dan's been this way. He's upset about Red and he doesn't realize what he's saying. Dan, apologize."

And Dan did. I was beginning to see how completely he was under his wife's thumb. It wasn't the henpecked husband sort of thing, but rather more as though he understood that she knew what was best.

"I've got a foul temper," Dan added, "and I get to wrangling when I don't mean to at all. Carry on about the letter."

"Why'd you throw it away?"

"I was mad. Last night just before I went to bed I found it in my pocket and read it over. The thought of those twenty-five lost dollars just rose up and hit me on the chin. I tore the letter up and threw it away. That's all."

"Anyone else see it?"

"Red did. I managed the business end of the crowd. Punch used to help me, but after Red came he eased out. I showed the letter to Red and he advised accepting. I intended to anyway. Then when I read the letter over last night I got to wondering how we'd missed the place. You see, we stayed behind at a garage in Orleans to get gas, and Punch came straight here. Got the directions I wrote for you, Punch?"

"Nope. Threw 'em away after I got here."

"Well," Dan continued, "I gave him directions right from the letter and sent him on ahead. We were late in starting because we'd had trouble with the truck in the afternoon. I thought Punch could go ahead and reassure the Guilds that we were coming. Red drove us, and I told him the turns. It was foggy, so we went slowly and made the turns very carefully. And both Punch and the rest of us in the van turned up here."

"Notice the postmark on the letter? Handwriting at all familiar?"

"I never gave any thought to the postmark. The letter itself was typed. If you're so sure there isn't any Maynard Guild, why don't you go to the Weesit post-office? You'll find my answer there."

"Providin' Guild ain't collected it already. Kemp, will you go? But even if the letter's there, Mr. Allen, that don't mean a lot. Just because you wrote an answer ain't no reason why there should be a letter *to* answer."

Dan started to splutter again, but he caught his wife's eye and refrained. "You think I'm lying? That I wrote the letter to lure Red here? Or just lied about the letter and lured him anyway? Why, even if I'd wanted to kill Red Gilpin—and God knows that the thought never entered my head—don't you think I'd plenty of opportunities without wandering off to a forsaken spot like this? It's not sensible."

"May not be sensible," Asey said, "but it works the other way around."

"What d'you mean?"

"That—this is just pos'ble, you know—that you wrote, or had someone else write, a letter to lure him an' all the rest of you here, because it would seem afterwards that it wouldn't be reasonable for you to do any such thing."

"God!" Dan looked admiringly at Asey. "What a brain! It wouldn't occur to me to be so elaborate. If I wanted to kill anyone I wouldn't take pains like that. I wouldn't make fancy plans. I couldn't. I'm not built that way. I suppose if I'd ever got angry enough at Red to want to kill him, I'd probably have picked up the first thing that came to my hand and fired it at him. That is," he amended, "unless Edie was there to stop me. I'll admit I once threw a telephone at another fellow. You see, I'm taking you at your word and holding nothing back. I'll throw things, yes. I've hurled a lot of objects about. But, by God, I don't go pumping four bullets into one of my best friends! That's that!"

Asey nodded. "Where'd Gilpin sleep last night?"

"In the truck. Punch slept with me in the van. That's not usual. Edie and Hat and I bunk in the van as a rule, with Punch and Red in the truck. But Red snores. Snored." He corrected his tense. "Punch said he wanted a peaceful night for a change, so he took Hat's bunk."

"What happened after you left here last night?"

"We left here about twelve. I got some night things—no, I'd got those for the girls before. Well, Punch and Red and I had a nightcap in the truck. Then Punch and I came back to the van and went to bed."

"Either of you get up during the night?"

"I didn't stir," Dan said. "Punch can swear to that."

"That's right," Punch backed him up. "I didn't get up either. Dan would have known because I'd have had to crawl out over him."

"Heard no noises? No shots?"

"No."

"How about the rest of you?" Asey turned to Edie Allen.

"I didn't hear any noises. I just hit that bed and slept like a log. First time I'd slept in a bed for months."

"I went out," Hat Allen confessed. "Dan brought Edie her cold cream, but he forgot mine. I could have used hers, but it's awf'ly greasy stuff—"

"It's not," Edie retorted. "It's—"

"Don't let's bring that up again, Ede. The floor's mine now and I say it's greasy. So I went to bed uncold-creamed. Then I got to thinking of my dirty face. Sounds silly, doesn't it?"

"Nope," Asey replied serenely. "I knew a feller once that near went insane if he couldn't brush his teeth within ten minutes after finishin' a meal. Go on."

"The more I thought about it, the more I wanted my cold cream. I'd put on a lot of make-up in preparation for the Guilds, and frankly, I had a feeling that the brown powder would ruin Mrs. Ballard's sheets. So I slipped on my coat and went out and got the cold cream."

"Where were the men?"

"In the truck with Red. Having a nightcap. I started to join you, Dan, but I was cold and I knew you'd laugh at me for coming out just for cold cream. I slipped in the van and got it and then went back indoors. I cleaned my dirty face in the bathroom and then went back to bed, feeling a better girl for it. But I didn't hear any noises later. Like Ede, I just slept like a log."

"I never even heard you go out," Edie commented.

"Nor I," Judy added. "Did you go out the front door?"

"I didn't know of any other. I just snuk out and snuk back."

"How about Rose?" Asey asked. "Will you send her in?"

Rose was distinctly nervous. At first I attributed it to her occupation. I've yet to see a maid who could not manage to look guilty even if she were not personally responsible for the broken platter of the moment. But as she continued to jitter about, I decided that there was more to it than met the eye. She was certainly trying to hide something—without even waiting for Asey's question in order to know just what *to* hide.

"Go out last night, Rose?"

"No. I didn't. I didn't! I went right to bed just as soon as I'd cleaned up!"

"We had some food just before we went to bed," I explained.

"Didn't get up again, Rose?"

"No, I didn't—I didn't. I mean, yes, I didn't."

Asey smiled and waved her away.

"Okay," he said. "That's all for the time bein'. Nobody heard any noises except Mrs. Ballard an' maybe Miss Dunham. No one went out except Miss Allen. That right? None of you knew anybody that wanted to kill Gilpin?"

"No!" It was a chorus.

"Scatter, then, while I talk with Mrs. Ballard. You can't run away because Parker left some cops about, an' Syl'll keep an eye on you elsewhere."

Obligingly the group dispersed except Dan.

"What'll we do about the show? Our schedule—"

"I'll notify people you're unavoidably detained. This is just one of those places where the show ain't goin' on."

"Well," I asked, "what do you think?"

"I don't think. I wonder. What's your maid lyin' about? She go gallivantin' off last night?"

"She's not had time to find a gallivanter. Except for the ice man—"

"Pickrin' Nickerson or his boy Toby?"

"Toby."

"Then she was off with him. I know that boy. By the time fall comes he's just a shadow, what with totin' ice all day an' carryin' on with all the servant girls all night. Well, we can fix that easy. I'll wangle the story out of Toby. I ain't worryin' much about Rose anyway. She don't look like the sort that'd fire four bullets out of a .45 into a stranger just for what you might call a whim."

"Aren't you going to hunt for the gun?"

"Syl's huntin'. No point in searchin' the van or the truck or the house just yet. You aren't apt to leave guns around casual like after you kill someone, not unless you're pretty sure the gun can't be traced back to you, or sure it can be traced to someone you never thought much of anyways. Sure's fate, if we do find it, no one in this bunch'll have ever set eyes on it before. That feller Punch is a nice appearin' feller. Reminds me of Bill Porter."

"He is pleasant."

"So little to do with all this on the outside that he might of been in Siam. Allen seems a pep'ry sort, but you know what the whole trouble is in dealin' with these people, Mrs. Ballard? They're show folks, whether they're real show folks or just depression ones. An' bein' that they're all on the stage, they're all the time on the stage, if you catch what I'm drivin' at. They know how to face an audience and put on a face that goes with the words they're sayin'. That's why I didn't bother to come in an' see how they took this. You can usually spot when most folks begin to make up lines, but these folks is used to it. Take Allen's wife. Looks like a princess out of a fairy story. See the way she orders Dan around with a dip of her eyebrow. An' that sister's smooth. Nobody did nothin', nobody heard nothin', nobody seen nothin'. Bunch of model deaf mutes, the whole caboodle. How long you had this girl Judy?"

"Since day before yesterday." I told him of Elizabeth Houghton's note.

"Oho! I thought she'd been with you for some time. Puts a dif'rent light on things, don't it? Guess I'll have to ask you for that woman's address. Parker's goin' to check up on all these people an' I'll have him look into her. Already got people goin' about Gilpin. Wasn't much in his pockets to go by."

"Asey, what about the papers?"

"Newspapers? Well, I'm hopin' Parker'll keep this out of 'em till tomorrow. He seems to think he can do it."

"And I've forgotten all about George!" I said. "I should send a telegram to him. I'll say I stood the journey well, which is by way of being the truth. He'll lose his temper when he hears of this—probably say it's my fault. He thinks I'm altogether too casual in my choice of acquaintances and of course, if I'd followed his original plans and brought Cousin Mercy and my housekeeper Mrs. Tavish along, this probably wouldn't have happened. That is, they'd never have allowed me to keep the Allens and the rest here. Well, I'll just tell him I'm all right. How can I send the message?"

"Write it out," Asey said, "an' I'll relay it to one of the cops. Yup, a lot can happen in twenty-four hours an' I want some breathin' space, so's when the reporters begin to howl about hayseed detectin', they'll get a little seed up their noses. Lots of good cold truth in sayin' that it's good business to go slow when you're in a hurry. Funny how them copy book lines get truer an' truer as you get older, ain't it? But the more you fiddle around with somethin', the more chance you got to look at it from all angles, so to speak. Now you take this, f'r instance." From his pocket he produced a small piece of twisted wire.

"What's that odd looking object?"

"It's a paper clip. That is to say, it was a paper clip once. Someone's yanked both ends of the coil apart an' twisted 'em around. Sort of thing you might do if you was nervous an' there was a paper clip handy. I found it out front an' Syl's found a couple more."

"A clue!" I said enthusiastically. Somehow, insignificant as it looked, it relieved me a lot that a clue had been found. To my simple mind it indicated progress.

"I dunno," Asey replied. "Someone might of left it last night. Twisted it to quiet his nerves same way you'd smoke a cigarette. Only a cigarette would of left a glowin' tip for someone to notice. An' if he, or she, had thrown butts down on the ground, we'd of had the what-d'you-call-it—the classic butt clue. N'en them scientific fellers now can take the end of a butt an' find out from it whether the feller that smoked it was black or white or spotted or class A or B or something. Read about it last week. But, on the other hand, this clip might of been left here two nights ago. Or a month. This place is real pop'lar among the younger set at night. Anyway, it's nice to rum'nate about."

He slipped it back into the pocket of his shirt.

"If we could find someone in this party," he went on, "that made a habit of bendin' paper clips, an' had some to bend, an' bent 'em just like this, that might be dif'rent. On the other hand, someone might of planted it."

"You look at all sides," I remarked.

Asey chuckled. "My father used to say that if a man bought a hoss an' just looked at it from the dealer's side, he was a fool. If he looked at it from a buyin' angle *an'* the dealer's side, he was a reas'nbly sensible feller. But if he could see the whole durn business from the point of view of the hoss as well, then he was a genius pure'n simple."

I laughed appreciatively. Prue and Denny and Stephen had not overstated Asey one bit.

"So," Asey continued, "you can follow the paths of genius, Mrs. Ballard, an' even if you don't get there, you can at least smell of success, as the feller said. Wonder where Kemp—h'lo. What kept you so long, Ham?"

"I went over to Wellfleet," Kemp replied, "just to make sure this letter hadn't been sent there instead of to Weesit. It hadn't. You see, Asey, there wasn't any letter waiting for any Maynard Guild in Weesit. And both the postmasters said they'd have known if anyone had taken it from either office, too."

4

"That," Asey remarked, "is int'restin'. Very. Let's see Dan Allen some more."

Dan Allen came in, followed by his wife. Smilingly Asey motioned to her to stay outside.

"Got the letter?" Dan demanded.

"Nope."

"Why not?"

"Wasn't no letter at Weesit."

"Look," Dan said, "I've been thinking about that. D'you suppose I might have sent it to Wellfleet? It would have been a perfectly natural mistake for me to make because I was sending posters ahead to Wellfleet that same day. The names are a lot alike."

"But Kemp went to Wellfleet too, just for fun. There wasn't any letter there either."

Dan was obviously crestfallen. "I can't understand this at all. It's beyond me. I sent that letter off Saturday afternoon from Hyannis and I'd swear to it on every Bible in New England. Look, maybe this Guild got the letter—?"

"He didn't. Postmasters in these small towns know a terrible lot. They'd have remembered any stranger with a name like that. If Guild had come for his letter, don't think they wouldn't have remembered it. Post the letter yourself?"

"Yes." Dan answered positively. "Yes. I—no, wait a minute. I've got to think this all out. I sent that Saturday afternoon before we gave our show at the hotel. I walked down to the post office from there. Um. Punch was with me. Come to think of it, I didn't mail it myself. I remember it all now. I brushed against some fresh white paint and went into a drugstore to get something to clean it off. Punch walked on alone because we didn't have a lot of time. He mailed all the letters and then came back to me at the drugstore. That's the way it went."

"Okay," Asey said, "let's have Punch."

Punch was sure that he had mailed the letter.

"I had six letters and two packages and I mailed them all. I counted 'em all when Dan gave them to me and then I counted 'em again at the post office. I always do."

"Tell me," Asey said, "what about Dan and his wife? They get along together all right?"

Punch hesitated. "Why, yes. Yes, they do."

"Except what?"

He hesitated again. "I hate to say this right now. It sounds as though I were trying to throw suspicion on Dan and it's the farthest thought I have in my mind. But Dan's very jealous of Edie. And Red, well, he was a good-looking fellow, and," Punch added with a little envy in his tone, "Red certainly had a way about him."

"Women liked him, huh?"

"Yes. All women, from babes in arms to great-grandmothers."

I remembered my first reactions to John Gilpin and felt my-

self blush. It didn't help any to have Asey turn and ask me gravely if I thought that were true.

"He charmed me at once," I admitted.

"So women fell for this lad, huh?"

"Yes, but don't get the wrong slant on this," Punch said earnestly. "Red wasn't any Don Juan or anything like that. He just—
well, he just naturally charmed every woman he met. He didn't
set out with that in mind. I've heard him wonder any number of
times why women didn't let him alone. He had piles of letters
every place we stopped and most of 'em were from women."

"Sort of an It man," Asey commented.

"In a way. But he never answered more than one or two. Usually he chucked 'em away without even reading 'em."

"Hm," Asey said. "So he answered some particular letters,
huh? Know who she was?"

"No. Red never mentioned names. He wasn't that sort. He
never bragged about his—his, I guess you'd call them conquests."

"Don't remember postmarks?"

Punch shook his head. "You see, Asey, it was sort of like this.
Red loved good-looking women. Or else he attracted 'em. I don't
know which. But sure as shooting, the best looking women in
any audience always seemed to gravitate toward Red after the
show. He just liked 'em because they were ornamental. That was
all there was to it so far as he was concerned. But the women had
a tendency to—"

"Pursue?" Asey suggested. "Was that the trouble with Dan
Allen and Edie?"

"In a way. Edie's good-looking and you can't get away from it.
But I'd swear that Red never made love to her. Of course, once
in a while he'd say something about her hair. That it was spun-

gold or like bales of moonshine. You know," Punch waved his hand in an embarrassed little gesture. "All that sort of thing. That was just as much as he ever meant, too. But Dan would get purple around the gills and flare up and grit his teeth and all. Now I come to think of it, though, Red never made any effort to see Edie alone. Usually Red and I drove together in the truck and we slept together in it at night. I'd have known if he'd been running around with Edie. He never did, though. He just admired her hair and her beauty. That was all there was to it but it used to make Dan furious."

"What about Edie? She like Red?"

"Yes, but no more than she likes me. She's terribly in love with Dan, only he just doesn't have the sense to realize it. If he saw me making love to her, he'd probably indulge in a little temper and throw the van at me."

"What about last night? Oh, h'lo, Rose. What's wrong?"

"I've got lunch for Mrs. Ballard and if she don't have it now, it'll get spoiled." Rose's voice was plaintive. "I've got it for the rest of you, too. Everyone else's had theirs in the kitchen."

The cottage boasted no dining room as such; we used part of the living room for that purpose.

"You've fed the whole crowd?"

"Yes, Mrs. Ballard. Miss Judy and the others helped me."

"I never expected you to cook for an army," I said. "I'm really sorry for all this extra work."

"We've not got groceries for an army, either," she reminded me.

"I'm sorry. I'll raise your wages for as long as this keeps up, Rose, but I'm sure I don't know what we can do about food."

"Ain't no reason why you should feed all hands," Asey remonstrated.

"Well," I returned, "you told the others not to stir away from this place and naturally they can't get provisions. I don't in the least mind feeding them. I'm worrying about Rose."

Asey thumped the table with his fist. "Syl's wife! That's it! Rose, you an' Mrs. Ballard make out a list of what you need an' I'll have Syl tell one of those cops to go up an' get it an' bring Jennie back. She's an a-number-one cook an' she'll be handy to have around. That all right with you, Mrs. Ballard?"

"Yes, but there's no room for her to stay here."

"She don't have to. The women'll have to go back to the van tonight an' Kemp'll stay out in the truck, an' I'll take the couch. Just in case. Well, that's settled."

So, after lunch, Kemp and one of the men departed for food and Mrs. Mayo, and Asey resumed his questioning of Punch.

"How 'bout last night? All s'rene?"

"Honestly," Punch said, "I wish you hadn't asked me that. I hate to go on. It makes me feel that I'm a squealer. There was a little squabble last night while we were having our drink. But it wasn't over Edie exactly. That is, it didn't begin that way. Dan laughingly said that Red had been eyeing Judy Dunham, and Red got mad. He doesn't lose his temper very often, but we were all pretty much on edge last night. As I told Mrs. Ballard, we'd had a foul week. Torrents of rain and car trouble and all that. The flat and the short circuit and losing the Guild twenty-five dollars were the last straws, plus. None of us was exactly chipper. Anyway, Red flared up and said he didn't make eyes at every girl he met for the first time, and Dan said he thought it wasn't the first time Red had met Judy by a long shot.

"Red wanted to know why.

"'Because,' Dan said, 'she automatically put five lumps of sugar in your coffee.'

"Well, Red just hit the ceiling. He said that she'd asked him and he'd told her, and that one of these days Dan was going to get a large fist—do I have to go on? I hate to."

Asey nodded.

"A large fist between those beetling brows. That made Dan madder, as Red knew it would. Dan's very sensitive about those eyebrows of his. Then Dan said if Red didn't have the sense to cut out running after Edie, he'd get something more than a fist between the eyes."

"That," Asey said, "sounds almost too good to be true."

"It's true, Asey, but can't you see that it didn't mean a thing, actually? We were all so cold and tired and mad and discouraged. I know Dan didn't have anything to do with killing Red. Even if all that sounds incriminating, I know it's not."

"What happened then?" Asey wanted to know.

"I told 'em to shut up, gave 'em another drink and told Red I was going to sleep in the van because I was sick of hearing him snore. I really wasn't, because it never bothers me. But I thought that Red was dog-tired and fed up with things. He'd spent most of his spare time lately repairing cars. I thought he had a right to a bit of privacy for a change. The snoring business took their minds off their squabble. I had a fear that they might really fight and I didn't want to rouse Mrs. Ballard with any brawl. It wasn't that they were violent or anything like that. But you know yourself how it is when things go wrong. You get edgy and find yourself saying things and doing things that you'd never dream of otherwise."

"Parted friends, did they?"

"Oh, yes. Slapped each other on the back. All that."

"Folksy. Well, what about Red and the other Allen, sister Hat?"

"They're just good friends. Hat's a decent, capable, dependable sort. She's rather reserved, too. Dan said she and Edie never hit it off together till Hat joined the show. I don't know why. They get along well enough now. But Hat's quiet and Edie's the kind who burbles a lot. Tells everyone about herself and expects to know everything in return. Hat's not like that at all. She rarely speaks about herself. Red liked her and admired her brain. He said she had a man's brain."

"It's funny," Asey remarked with a twinkle in his eye, "how whenever a man wants to praise a woman, he always says she has a man's brain. Never heard a woman praise a man by sayin' he had fem'nine intuition. So you don't think that Hat an' Red was any more'n good friends?"

"I'm sure of it. He thought Hat was clever and intelligent, but Hat's not really beautiful, you know. Just very striking looking. I wonder if I can't make you understand what I mean about Red. Yes, I think I can. A while back, around the first of May, we were in Nashua, New Hampshire. We'd played around Springfield and at Northampton and worked up to South Hadley, then we went to Manchester and then Nashua. I had a friend there who wanted us to perform for a club of his. We got on so well that we stayed four days and gave two shows a day in a hall. Usually we don't go in for cities, but we did a good business there. Well, the second day—maybe it was the first—Red met this girl. I remember her name. It was Aristene Satterlee. Some local matron barged up and introduced her to the whole bunch."

"Sort of name you might remember anyway," Asey said with a grin. "Aristene! New one on me."

"Well, Aristene was about eighteen. She was rangy and sallow and her hair was stringy. Dressed as though someone stood at a distance and flung her some clothes and she let 'em stay the way they landed. But she had the most beautiful hands I've ever seen in all my life. Red noticed 'em, too, and he spent all the rest of his time while we were in Nashua taking that girl to restaurants and feeding her, just so he could watch her hands move. Then just before our last show, the rest of Aristene suddenly burst upon his consciousness. He dropped her like a hot cake. As a matter of cold fact, he left her sitting in a little tea room. Just left her sitting there. He told me about it later. I think it was the only affair he ever spoke about. Believe me, I was darn glad to leave that city, for I think Squire Satterlee sort of had the notion that Red was hooked. I don't think men had trampled each other to death in the race for Aristene. But that's not the point. Point is, d'you see what I mean about Red now?"

"I do. You've helped a lot."

Punch got up. "I'll run along then, if there's nothing else. Only I wanted to tell you this. I grew up in Wyoming and I was a pretty good shot till I came East to Boston and fell out of the habit of shooting and acquired a broad 'a'. But even with the broad 'a' I'm still pretty good. I've got a gun out in the truck, too. But it's a thirty-eight Colt, detective special."

"I like that feller," Asey said after Punch left. "Take back all those harsh little thoughts I had about him. Humpf. This is gettin' a little involved-like, ain't it? Dan gets mad at Red because of Edie. Jealousy. That's always a nice motive. Hat Allen's one of them still waters that runs deep. I'd figgered that. An' Red seems to of left a long line of pinin' hearts in his wake. That's food for thought. An' Judy knew enough to give him five lumps in his coffee. I wonder. What you—say, I plumb forgot you was an invalid. Ain't you gettin' tired? Don't you want to lie down or somethin'?"

"I'm inclined to think, Asey, that my principal trouble has

been too much lying down. It seems perfectly callous, but I haven't felt so well in weeks. I don't mean to insinuate that a murder was necessary to rouse me—"

"I know. You get stale, convalescin'. Got any ideas?"

"Not one. I think you'd best confide in someone else, Asey. I'm no earthly good."

"I don't agree, Mrs. Ballard. Av'rage woman's apt to see details a man don't notice. B'sides, who else've I got? You're the only person I can honestly say's I think's in'cent. You ever fired a gun?"

"Never. I'm scared to death of them. Adin, my husband, liked to shoot. It used to make me nervous just to have his guns about the house. I've given them all to George."

"That bein' the case," Asey said, "I don't think it was you pumped Gilpin full of lead."

"I've just thought of something, Asey. What about rum-runners or smugglers? Couldn't Red have wandered out—Punch said he'd taken to long wandering walks—and run into some one of them?"

"They still land a lot of liquor here," Asey said, "even if it's on the ocean. They land in the inlet where the bar makes in. Right in the face of the coast guard, up beyond Syl's house, three miles or so up the beach. They know the place well enough to land even if there was a little fog. But I don't think they'd of killed Gilpin. Take when Syl run into some of 'em last fall. They blindfolded him an' told him to set quiet like a nice boy, an' to stay quiet for half an hour after they left. He did, an' found they'd left a quart of good Jamaica rum settin' beside him. If they didn't kill Syl, why should they of killed Gilpin?"

There was no answer to that. "Except, perhaps, they were a different and more bloodthirsty crowd."

"But usually the same crowd lands in the same place, an' how's all that goin' to tie up with that letter? Bootleggers wouldn't be likely to invite a show here."

"No," I replied, "but they could have shot Red even if someone else sent that letter. The letter might have been a practical joke. There are some people who might think it hilariously funny to get a troupe out here expecting an evening's work to find only an empty cottage."

"Yup," Asey agreed, "only I sort of think the letter's got something to do with it. Now you take this as it stands. Here's Gilpin with four bullets in him. Seems to me that means one of two things. Either someone was terrible mad an' killed him on the spur of the moment-like,—just shot an' kept right on shootin',— or else it was someone that was cold an' deliberate an' methodical that wasn't going to take no chances about Gilpin's dyin' quick an' final."

"The first," I said, "would point to Dan."

"Yup, but it might be a woman, too. Ladies don't like guns much, but when they shoot they kind of lose all sense of time. Bill Porter made me read a book once about a girl named Lorelei Lee. You ever read it?"

"Yes." I laughed. "'Gentlemen Prefer Blondes.'"

"That was it. Well, there was one line out of that book I always remembered. It was so fem'nine. Went sort of like this: 'I had a case of hysterics an' when I came out it seems I had a revolver in my hand an' it seems the revolver had shot Mr. Jennings.'" Asey chuckled. "That's usually the way ladies are with guns. An' Edie's a blonde. Then, on the other hand, it might be a cold-blooded planner. If so, I'm favorin' Guild."

"The doctor didn't seem to know when Red was killed," I said.

"I've been thinking about those noises. Wouldn't it help if we knew which was the shot or shots?"

"Might both have been cars," Asey said. "Maybe you didn't hear the real shots at all. You say you're a heavy sleeper. Or maybe both sets of noises was shots. We'd better wait until we see the doc's report."

"How can he tell?"

"Food, stomach, all that." I remembered the doctor's question about when Red had eaten, and shuddered.

It was around three o'clock when the message from the doctor came.

"Says," Asey reported from the lengthy communication, "that he probably died between one an' half past. Goin' on that, chances are that the first noise you heard should have been the shots, Mrs. Ballard. We'll split the dif'rence an' call it around one-fifteen."

"Yet as I remember them, Asey, the second set of noises was much louder. The first noises were more of a rolling boom. Like a real backfire. The others were sharper and more distinct."

"Hm. I forgot to ask you one thing. D'you recall how those noises sounded? Was there any spacing? Were they quick an' all together, or what?"

I tried to think. "It's difficult for me to say," I told him finally. "It seems to me that the first noises were spaced. One, then a pause, then two-three-four. But I'm not sure. I probably wouldn't have thought of it if you hadn't mentioned it. I can't even remember how many noises there were later. I think those were perfectly even. I wouldn't want to swear to any of 'em in court, though. Why?"

"Just wondered." Asey got up and strolled to the front window. "Here comes Syl, runnin' for dear life."

"It seems to me," I remarked, "that I've not seen that little man today but what he's been dashing somewhere or dashing back from somewhere."

"Syl's a dasher when he gets started, an' I tell you, he's been waitin' all his life for a murder he could stick his finger in. He's a nice, calm, sensible feller. Ain't bloodthirsty one bit, not a bit. But he's crazy to detect. He's got three houses he should be openin' up, but he won't. Says he can always open houses. He's opened 'em for twenty years an' prob'ly will for twenty more, but this is the only murder that'll ever come into his life. Or words to that effect. What's up, Syl?" he asked as Sylvanus burst into the room.

"Hey—Asey—look!" he panted. "Look—what I got—found it—on the bankin'—"

He held out a large revolver.

5

ASEY REACHED out his hand.

"Good boy, Syl! Just what the doctor ordered! Old style single action Army Colt .45. Like my own I got to home. Four shots fired an' two bullets left. Where'd you find it, Syl?"

"Well," Sylvanus pulled proudly at his moustache. "Well, it was half way up the bankin', Asey. Right on the brink of a skunk hole, too. Wouldn't of taken more'n a little nudge for it to of gone square in."

"Lucky it didn't. We'd never of got it then."

"Oh," Syl replied casually, "I've been in four skunk holes so far today. It wouldn't of made any dif'rence. Not to me."

"Might of," Asey said, "might of. If you'd met up with an aggravated skunk, Syl, I'd of buried you in a hole for thirty days myself. How come you looked on the bankin'?"

"Well, if it was tossed down on the beach, Asey, chances are t'would of been under ten feet of sand, now, what with that undertow, or else half way to Chatham. An' say, you remember that story of the feller that lost a hoss an' they couldn't find it? An' everyone hunted for it an' finally they all give up, an' then another feller come along an' asked what the matter was, an' went out an' brought the hoss back?"

"Any more to it?"

"Yup. They asked this last feller how he knew where to hunt for the hoss an' he said, 'I thought if I was a hoss where I'd go an' I went there an' it had.' Well, that was how I found the gun," Syl concluded gravely.

Our merriment didn't disturb him in the least.

"I stood up there near where Gilpin was shot," he continued, "an' then I figgered out that the feller that shot him stood kind of facin' sou'-east b'sou'. So I faced sou'-east b'sou' an' figgered what I'd do if I'd just shot Gilpin. Decided I'd throw the gun away. Now, bein' as how I'm right-handed, chances are it would fall—"

"Sou'-sou'-east or sou' by east," Asey interrupted with a perfectly straight face.

"Just so, just so. On t'other hand, it mightn't. He might of thrown it into the pines, but that'd be silly when you had the whole Atlantic Ocean staring you right square in the face. But anyways, I took a monkey wrench an' tossed it, an' then worked in a line where it fell. I started at high water mark an' worked up the bankin'. It was about half way up, not ten feet to the left of that bench. You must of come pretty near it when you come down the bankin' this mornin', Asey."

"Lot of poison ivy there," Asey said.

"I cut a lot away while I was huntin'. Now, what I don't see is this. My wrench went way down on the beach. If this feller'd thrown half way hard, the gun'd gone down on the beach an' got washed away. He couldn't of pitched it hard at all. S'pose it might of been a woman? They can't never pitch anything."

"Either that," Asey said, "or else he wanted it to be found. Syl, thank you very kindly. But when I told you you could have a look around for that gun, I didn't mean for you to risk your life clamberin' over clay banks, exposin' yourself to skunks an' poison ivy. Syl, you had anything to eat today?"

"Don't that beat all!" There was utter astonishment in Syl's voice. "I forgot all about eatin'. First time I ever forgot my dinner in all my life!"

"Well, Jennie's either here or on her way, an' I want you two to help around. Now, you go get some dinner!"

"I will. Say, Asey, did you notice that trigger? It's tied back to the trigger guard with a little piece of adhesive tape. Why for?"

"I noticed that first off, Syl. Feller fanned the gun."

"Why'd he tie the trigger back? He didn't have to. He could of held the gun in his right hand an' held the trigger back with his finger an' fanned with his left hand just as easy."

"Guess he didn't want to take no chances. He stuck the trigger back an' give full attention to shootin'."

"I see." Syl departed.

"What on earth are you talking about?" I demanded. "What d'you mean, fanning? How can you fan a gun? Why should you? Because it's warm or something?"

Asey chuckled as he extracted the bullets from the cylinder.

"I'll show you. It takes time to pull the trigger an' then pull the hammer back so's the cylinder'll revolve. But if you have the trigger tied back this way, see, then you can hold the gun in your right hand, take the heel of your left an' with it either jerk or snap the hammer back till the cylinder revolves. So. Then you let the hammer snap back again, see?"

"I get the theory. You eliminate the trigger and do everything by snapping the hammer. But what's the use?"

"An expert at fannin' could fire six shots in a couple of seconds. Bernsdorf said so this mornin' an' I—er—know a feller that can. I once—well, this all goes to tie up with what I asked you about the spacin' of them shots last night, too. See, this feller's waitin' with his gun for Gilpin. Fires once; see, holdin' the gun in his right hand with his thumb crooked over the trigger, he threw down. Then after that shot there'd have had to be a pause while he sets himself to fan for the other shots. Those'll come quick. So the reports sound one, space, two-three-four."

"Then that clinches the time, doesn't it? The first noises I heard were the shots. He was killed a few minutes after one."

"Guess that's right. An' everyone but Hat Allen claims they didn't go out. Huh," he looked at the cartridges, "these is old-timers. Prob'ly reduced charges an' that's what made the noises seem rollin'. Prob'ly why they didn't sound up so much."

"What about finger prints on the gun?"

"Like as not we'd get a skunk's toe print if we got anything. B'sides, the gun's all covered with salt spray. Don't think we'd find much. Clever man'd wear gloves anyway."

There was a knock on the door and Punch walked in, looking very red and uncomfortable.

"Say, Asey, I've got an apology to make. Here's the letter. The one to Maynard Guild. I found it in the pocket of my polo coat. There's a hole a mile wide in it and the letter slipped into the lining. I got to thinking about what might have happened and remembered that cavern."

Asey took the letter and read it through.

"Seems all right. Told Dan?"

"Yes. He was hopping mad. Still thinks there is a Maynard Guild and that if I'd posted this everything would have been fine."

"Ever see this before?" Asey pointed to the Colt.

"No." Punch surveyed it with interest. "Haven't seen a Colt

like that since I left Wyoming. My father used to swear by that model. Good old Peacemaker. Fanned it, did he?"

"Yup. You know how?"

"Dad taught me all the tricks. I can slip shoot better, though. Using a thumb instead of the heel of your hand. I could shoot looking into a mirror, too. All the fancy bits."

"Honest feller," Asey said as Punch left. "Somehow it seems to me that under these here given circumstances I don't know's I'd admit that I was an expert shot. Think I'd maintain what Steve Crump'd call a discreet an' in'cent silence on the subject. I'll admit I asked 'em all to be honest, but there ain't no need of bein' as honest as Punch is. Don't the chump realize that not mailin' that letter ain't a lot in his favor? Why, for all we know, Punch may be Maynard Guild himself." He turned around as Syl entered. "Syl, what you gone an' found now? Thought I told you to eat!"

"I did. I had a ham sandwich." Syl was beaming so widely that he almost had to turn sideways to get through the door. "I ate it an' then I got to thinkin', s'pose that feller had extry cartridges?"

"S'pose you'd need more'n six bullets to kill anyone?"

"No, but I'd take spares. Well, 'sumin' that this feller did take spares, what'd he do with 'em after? I figgered he'd throw 'em away after the gun. So—"

"I know." Asey grinned. "You thought where you'd go if you was a bullet an' you went there an' it was."

"Laugh all you want, but all the samey I found 'em."

From the pocket of his clay-daubed coat he took a small pasteboard box around which was a broad elastic band.

"Fourteen of 'em," Syl continued. "Box of twenty. Six bullets in his gun, four in Gilpin, two left, an' here's the rest. That's simple 'rithmetic. An' that ain't all."

"What else, Syl?"

"There's a name stamped on the bottom of the box with a rubber stamp."

Asey turned the box over. A peculiar expression crossed his face. Then he grinned.

"Seems," he said as he passed the box over for my inspection, "that one of Gilpin's pinin' loves has come home to roost."

On the box in small blue letters was the name, "Oscar P. Satterlee." Underneath, "Hardware, Paints, Varnish, Gen. Mdse., Nashua, New Hampshire."

"Satterlee! Why that's the name of the girl with the beautiful hands! The one Punch told us about. Oh, Asey, that's wonderful, isn't it? Squire Satterlee, as Punch called him, thought Red had compromised his daughter Aristene and then went gunning for Red. Don't you think that's it?"

"Maybe, but—"

"And," I ran on, "probably father Satterlee sent that letter. Dan said they had handbills and posters and he could have found out the date of their future shows from those. Oh, rhyme!" Asey smiled. "Or he could have phoned about the troupe and followed them that way, by long distance, from place to place. Don't you think that's it?"

"It would be sort of nice to have it turn out that way," Asey agreed. "Sort of wash out the folks here in one mighty fell swoop. Only it's almost too fell. Y'see, if Satterlee did write that Guild letter an' go to all the fuss of killin' Gilpin, what'd he go leave his cartridges with his name on 'em behind for? Might's well of left a callin' card or his address an' phone number. Where'd you find these, Syl? Near the gun?"

"Just b'low where the gun was. 'Mong some baybries. I'd seen that buff color of the cardboard box before, but I didn't pay no attention to it while I was huntin' for the gun."

Asey opened the box. "Yup. Same old cartridges. Old black powder. Wonder where they'd be picked up these days. Syl, got your car here? I'm goin' up an' do a little New Hampshire phonin'. Come along, Mrs. Ballard. Do you good to get out in the fresh air an' you ought to get it. After all, it's what you come for. You come too, Syl. First I'm goin' over to Wellfleet an' git my own car an' I'll want you to drive your car back. Kemp out there?"

"Yup."

"Tell him I'd like to see him." Asey assisted me on with my coat. "Oh, Ham. If you can get into the van an' the truck without causin' a lot of trouble, I wish you would. See if you can find any papers clipped together. Don't care what they are so long's they're clipped."

"I can do it right now," Kemp said. "They're all down on the beach."

"You don't really need your car," I remarked as we set off in Syl's Ford.

"I know you got a nice Buick, but I like my own car. Also, I want a gun an' some clean shirts."

At the first crossroad two motorcycle cops jumped up from the side of the road.

Asey slowed down. "Goin' to be r'lieved soon?"

"Five-thirty."

"When you go back, have someone find out about last night, will you? I want a list of all arrests. Everything there is on the blotter an' what anyone remembers as bein' funny besides. Any numbers you took, any out-of-state cars, any speeders. Any accidents. Bumps. Everything. Bring me the list as soon as you can."

"Why did you ask that?" I wanted to know, feeling like a why-man in a vaudeville skit.

"If some person did pop up to the Hendersons' last night, there's a chance he might of been in a hurry to get away. Might of got pinched or spoken to severe by a cop. Might of had an accident. Might of been a New Hampshire car about. If anything funny did happen, it'd be smart to try an' tie it up. Long shot, but you can't tell what you might hit. Arrow into the air. All that, as Punch says."

"You make me feel stupid," I said. "That never would have occurred to me."

"Don't know why I thought of it, either, 'cept I've been thinkin' of coincidences. Y'know, there's a lot of things that happen to jibe in this world. Seem queer an' strange, but they ain't at all when you come to think it out. Wonder to me there ain't more funny peculiar things instead of less."

"What d'you mean?"

"Ever stop to think, just for example, how many folks you know? An' how many of 'em turned out to know other folks you knew, or had heard of from still other folks? You get on board a ship or a train an' dollars to doughnuts you'll find someone you know, or someone who's heard of you through so-an'-so or maybe so-an'-so's friend. Well, when you stop to figger out this spiderwebby arrangement, with all the people you know meetin' new people, an' so on an' so forth an' so forth an' so on far into the night, it don't seem to be so funny about the Satterlees' goin's on, an' Red, an' that box turnin' up."

"Wait, now. Let me catch up. You mean that human relationships are so involved that any combination of events is not only possible, but probable? When and after, of course, you've traced the threads?"

"Somethin' like that. Just think. Maybe Satterlee is a rel'tive of yours. Or mine. Maybe he's visitin' people in the next town. Maybe he died the day after the Allens left Nashua. Maybe he ate a bad oyster. Nope, no R, is there? Well, maybe he's gettin' over pneumonia or solvin' a murder. See what I mean? When you think of all the things that could happen, it's funnier that they don't all happen instead of just some of 'em. Anythin's possible. When you begin to think of all the loose an' strayin' ends that could get hitched up, the wonder is that they don't. I guess all that long-winded c'njecturin' led me to ask those cops that."

More and more I began to see the truth of what Prudence Whitsby had said about Asey:

"Vic, that man's got an imagination which runs half way between that of Baron Munchausen and Ananias and Scheherazade. And the funny part of it is, he's so utterly logical. Touch of Euclid mixed up in him somewhere."

In Wellfleet Asey got his gun and packed a suitcase, and then transferred me to a long sixteen-cylindered roadster which all but took my breath away. He announced casually that Bill Porter had given it to him.

"Porter fac'try outcast. Bill calls it the Monster. I used to fiddle around the fac'try myself an' I like good engines. Had this feller apart last month an' put it together again just to keep my hand in. Bill laughs because I don't know all the names an' call parts whang-doodles an' what-cha-ma-call-its, but, by gum, it runs better now than it did!"

We floated back to Weesit and left Syl to bump home by himself.

On the outskirts of the town we drew up in front of a small Cape Cod house which broke all the rules by being yellow with black blinds.

In front of it Toby Nickerson was listlessly weeding a flower bed. He showed no sign of visible pain at leaving his work when Asey called to him. His greeting to Asey was cheerful enough, but the glance he directed at me was nothing short of suspicious. Whether it was the car, or my presence with Asey, or that he had really been cavorting around with Rose, I couldn't guess.

"Tobe, you go out last night with Mrs. Ballard's maid?"

"'Twasn't," Toby grinned, "that I didn't spend half the day tryin' to make a date with her."

"An' didn't?"

"An' didn't."

"Anyone else take her out?"

"Not that I've heard of. Guess if I failed, the others didn't get far."

Asey nodded. "Okay. Humpf," he muttered as we drove away, "that kind of surprised me. I thought for sure she'd been out with Tobe, an' I know he wouldn't be a one to lie about it. No reason why he should, not knowin' about Gilpin. Well, we'll go see Lonny Bangs."

We found Mr. Bangs just preparing to leave his office for the night.

"Well, well, everythin' goin' all right, Mrs. Ballard?" His genial greeting shocked me until I remembered that Mr. Bangs, like Toby, had yet to know what had gone on at the Henderson house.

"Fine," I said hoarsely. "Fine!"

"What Mrs. Ballard wants to know," Asey said, "is did you ever hear of a feller named Maynard Guild lookin' for a house here or in Wellfleet? He's a friend of hers an' she thought he said he was comin' down this way—"

"Never heard of him here or in Wellfleet. I got a couple of pretty good houses left, Mrs. Ballard—"

"Another thing," Asey interrupted, "did you show the Henderson place to many people before you rented it to Mrs. Ballard?"

"Why?" Mr. Bangs was a perfect New Englander. He answered one question by asking another.

"Woman come over there this afternoon," Asey lied fluently, "an' said she'd been shown it an' was intendin' to rent it. Mad to find folks there."

"She lied," Mr. Bangs said angrily. "I didn't show that house to a soul. Why, the Hendersons only wired me to rent it the day I got Mrs. Ballard's son's letter askin' for a place."

"We thought she just wanted to see the inside of the house," Asey answered knowingly. "Thanks, Lon. Be seein' you."

"What you doin' over here now?" Bangs demanded. "Askin' ques—"

"I'm subbin' as a chauffeur. Miss Dunham's sick. They told Syl an' he told me an' I offered to sub." Asey started the car. "Bye."

"D'you think," I asked after we'd gone some distance, "that he believed that?"

"Dunno, Mrs. Ballard. Dunno. Hope so. If I'd told him the truth, the whole Cape'd know in ten minutes. Gossip ain't all confined to women—hey!—look out!"

I never knew whether he intended that as a warning to me or a comment to a sedan that swerved out of a side road on the right. But I gripped the side of the roadster and started to yell as the car met ours with a good round crash.

"Okay? Good."

Asey hopped out and I slid over and followed him as fast as

I could. Aside from the front right mudguard, which was crumpled like one of Rose's frilled caps, the roadster seemed undamaged. But the black sedan was in a bad state. The left running board was twisted half off where it had been caught on our bumper. The rear mudguard was wholly crushed and the wheel wobbled drunkenly.

The two occupants of the sedan, a stout apoplectic man and a tall girl, reached the scene of the general wreckage as I did.

"I had the right of way," the apoplectic man told Asey belligerently, "I was on your right!"

"Yeah," Asey said scornfully. "You was! Comin' out of a blind side road at forty-five miles an—don't interrupt me—hour! Onto a main travelled highway without slowin' up! Keep quiet! An' there's a blinker an' three signs tellin' you it's a dangerous intersection. If I—shut up! If I hadn't just been crawlin' along, with my foot on the brakes because I know this spot, you'd be in Kingdom Come, Mister." Asey was bellowing now in what might best be described as a quarter-deck voice. "Shut up! I'm doin' the talkin' here. Stranger in town, I s'pose, an' think you can be just as careless as you like. Huh!"

The stout man, now thoroughly quelled, maintained an abashed silence as Asey walked around to the rear of the car. I felt for him. If Asey had spoken to me in that voice, I should have been down on my knees grovelling for mercy.

"Don't they have drivin' lawrs where you come from?" Asey continued. He surveyed the license plate. "New Hampshire, huh? What's your name, Mister?"

"Satterlee," said the man in a small voice. "Oscar P. Satterlee."

Asey looked at me in blank and utter amazement. I watched his jaw drop till it could drop no further. Words froze to the roof of my own mouth. They were all formed and ready to be spoken, but they stuck.

"Not," Asey said, "not Oscar P. Satterlee, hardware, paints, varnish an' gen. mdse.? Nashua? The Squire?"

"That's what they call me, Squire Satterlee. But how did you know?"

Asey turned to me.

"When I was gabblin' about funny coinc'dences," he announced with a faint grin, "I hadn't no idea they was goin' to coincide so soon. Age of miracles ain't passed, has it? Satterlee. Satterlee! God A'mighty!"

6

"How DID you know who I was?" Satterlee demanded.

"Fame," Asey said, "travels quick. In this case it sort of got here before you. This your daughter?"

"Yes." Satterlee was bewildered and looked it. "My daughter Aristene. But what's all this about? I don't intend to stay here all day and answer personal questions. What I want to know is, who's going to pay for my car? How am I going to get to Orleans?"

"Guess your insurance company'll have to pay for your car. I shan't. Prob'ly in due course of time you'll get back to Orleans. Why Orleans? Stayin' there?"

"I am. With my cousin Nate Hopkins, if you really want to know."

Asey turned to me.

"Nate," he said in an aside, "is my third cousin. Will you laugh that off? Don't things beat hell?"

I agreed that they did.

"How long you been on the Cape, Mr. Satterlee?"

"Since Monday night." The Squire sounded exasperated. "We drove from Nashua and stopped in Boston, then came on here. At exactly seven o'clock in the evening."

"Just in time for Amos 'n' Andy," Asey remarked cheerfully. "Well, well—"

"Your car's all right," Satterlee interrupted. "Won't you go get us a garageman?"

"Not just yet. I feel more like askin' you questions. An' a state cop ought to be ramblin' along here any minute."

"I don't want to make a police affair out of this," Satteerlee protested plaintively. "I only want a garageman to fix my car up so that I can get along. You've got my name and number. What more do you want?"

"Want to set," Asey perched on the roadster's bumper, "an' ask you things. Lots I want to know about you an' your daughter—"

"Is this man crazy?" Satterlee appealed to me. "What's the matter with him?"

"Nothin'. Oho!"

One of the state troopers who had been at the house earlier in the day drew up beside the machine.

"What's been going on?" he demanded. Then, as he saw Asey, his tone changed. "Fellow run into you, Asey?"

"I had the right of way," the Squire said feebly.

The officer ignored him.

"What happened?"

"Just a little bump," Asey explained. "But we raked him consid'rable. When you go up the line, ask Randall to stop along here with his wrecker, pronto, will you?"

"Sure." The officer scribbled things in his notebook. "What about these people?"

"They're coming with us," Asey informed him. "I'm takin' 'em to Henderson's. Need 'em in my business."

"Officer!" Satterlee tugged at the trooper's sleeve. "Officer, who is this man? He's done nothing but ask me questions and now he says he's going to take me home with him! I think he's crazy! Yes, sir, I think he's a dangerous lunatic!"

"If he wants to ask you questions," the officer returned, "I'd advise you to answer 'em. He's my boss for the time being."

"Boss?"

"Yes, even if I don't look it," Asey said. "Now, Carey, you run along to Randall an' don't forget that list I wanted."

"You don't look like an officer," Aristene spoke for the first time.

Asey's eyes twinkled. "I know I don't, but I am. Listen, you folks, my name's Asey Mayo. I'm sorry if I've been awful fresh, but meetin' you two here sort of scattered my wits. It was a pleasure, but kind of unexpected, as the starvin' man said when someone threw the soup at him. I'm kind of a cousin of Nate's, too, so that makes us some kind of cousins. Right now I'm busy on somethin' I think you might be able to help me out on. Ever hear of a feller named Gilpin?"

Aristene's face grew crimson and her father became apoplectic again.

"I guess I have heard of that rascal! I guess I have! By George!" He couldn't go on.

I thought, irrelevantly enough, of the men I knew who said "By George!" when they became angry. Without exception they were stout and red-faced and tried hard to be pompous.

"Take it you don't like Gilpin," Asey suggested.

"I should say I don't! Faugh!" Satterlee snorted. "Do I understand you're of the police? Has Gilpin done anything?"

"Er—not exactly. It's what someone did to him. But he's involved in this case I'm on."

"Let me tell you," the Squire said earnestly, "whatever anyone did to him, he deserved it! I tell you he—"

"Please, father!"

"Don't try to stop me, Teen. I'm going to have my say. You can excuse the man all you like. You can think he's an angel with wings on if you want to, but I'm going to have my say. I say horse-whipping's too good for him. Yes, hanging's too good. It wouldn't surprise me to see someone kill that man one of these fine days. I'd like to myself."

"Seems he's struck other people the same way," Asey said ironically, "already. Look, Mr. Satterlee, would you help me out in the matter of Gilpin? Would you come back to Weesit with me an' tell me what you know about him? Here's Randall with the wrecker. I'll see you get in touch with Nate, an' he'll vouch for me, an' I'll get you back to him safe an' sound."

"Mr. Mayo, if I can help you get that man into trouble, I'd be glad to. Keep still, Teen. I'm your father. Now, I'll admit I didn't think much of you at first, Mr. Mayo, but you should have told me sooner what you wanted me for and why you asked me questions. No hard feelings about the bump, I hope? Good. By the way, how did you know who I was? How did you get my name?"

Asey hesitated for the fraction of a second.

"Details is sort of complicated," he said slowly.

I knew then that he intended to keep the Satterlees in ignorance of Red's murder as long as he possibly could do it. It seemed sensible to me. The Squire was clearly an impressionable sort and he would without doubt volunteer more information about Red, not to speak of information about himself and Aristene, if he did not know what had happened.

"Very complicated," Asey went on, "but I got your name sort of by chance an' someone suggested you knew Gilpin. I was just on the point of callin' you up on the phone when we met. That's what made this seem so amazin'."

"Were you really? Well, it's a small world, isn't it? Looks like the Lord's work. He intervenes when He sees there's justice to be done," Satterlee said piously.

He seemed perfectly content with Asey's explanation but I noticed that his daughter was looking suspicious. Incidentally Punch's description of her had been apt. She was lank and stringy and thrown together. I found myself wishing she would take her gloves off. I wanted to see the hands which had captivated Red Gilpin.

Asey conferred with the garageman, who, after much guessing and reckoning and calculating, decided finally that he could fix up the Satterlees' car "good enough to go" by ten o'clock that night. Just as Asey was unlocking the Monster's rumble seat, we heard a great rattling. It was Syl in the Ford.

"Thank goodness," Asey spoke to me in a low voice, "I thought he was dead or somethin'!"

"You've been waiting for him?"

"Sure thing, Mrs. Ballard. I want him to go ahead an' see there ain't no signs of habitation at the house. I want to keep them show folks out of sight till after I've got all I can out of these two. No mention of the murder, either!"

"Stage manager," I whispered as Syl got out of the car.

"Oh, I love to stage manage. Often thought if I'd been on deck when God set the scenery for this footstool drayma of his, I could of given him a lot of good likely hints."

He walked over to Syl and spoke briefly to him. Syl nodded, got into the car and drove it away at a speed of which I, personally, should have thought it thoroughly incapable.

"But we'll be home before him," I said.

"We would if we went straight an' fast. Only we're takin' the long road an' he's taking the short road an' he'll be to Weesit before us."

He bundled the Satterlees into the rumble and we set off.

"Goin' to take this slow an' easy," he called back to them, "I don't want to take chances on that jar upsettin' her any, p'ticularly now it's dark. Randall said she was all right, but I'm goin' careful."

The three-odd miles home, by Asey's long road, turned into exactly nine. We stopped for Satterlee to phone his cousin and then we crawled at a snail's pace from one back road to another. It all seemed perfectly reasonable to the Satterlees. Their faces, as reflected in the rear view mirror, were perfectly complacent. I suspected that Nate Hopkins's reassurance of Asey's worth had allayed whatever suspicions they might have felt.

As we drove along the road to the house, I was surprised to see no traces of the van or the truck. They were nowhere to be seen in the growing dusk.

"Moved," Asey whispered as he turned into the garage. "Moved up the road there a piece. I don't know where Syl's put the people, but he's done a good job, ain't he?"

He certainly had. Except for Judy and Rose, the house was bare.

"What's going on?" Judy whispered as she helped me off with my coat.

"Clues and suspects," I told her. "No mention of what's happened."

She nodded in a puzzled fashion. Asey put the Satterlees at their ease, arranged them comfortably before the fire and looked for a moment at the dining table, set for three.

"I'll tell Rose to add some plates," he said.

"Oh," Satterlee began, "we wouldn't think of troubling you—" But Asey stopped him.

"No trouble attall," he said hospitably and disappeared into the kitchen. Rose appeared at once and laid the extra places. She was in a much better humor than I had anticipated.

When Asey did not return, my curiosity got the better of me, and I too went out into the kitchen.

Asey was busily talking with Syl and Kemp and a woman whom I'd not seen before but judged to be Syl's wife. Jennie Mayo was one of those six-foot Amazons, and she towered over her husband by a good ten inches.

"Mrs. Ballard, it don't seem right for me to be in your kitchen without even what you might call knowin' you, don't it? But I'm real glad Asey had sense enough to send for me. Think of all this happenin' to you, an' you just bein' over sick an' all!" She clucked her tongue. "It's a pity, that's what it is, an' everyone here just as nice as you could wish. Them two women from the show, they helped us make pies an' were just as handy people around a kitchen as you could find anywhere. Weren't they, Rose? Said they'd been dying to get into a real kitchen for months. Think of it, havin' to get all your meals over an alcohol stove or a camp fire! It's a pity, a real pity!"

"It's awfully good of you to help," I said. "And where have you hidden the others?"

"We didn't know just what to do with 'em at first. Finally we put 'em in Miss Judy's bedroom upstairs, an' put their supper up with 'em so that they'd be able to eat an' stay there as long as they had to."

"An' Parker's come an' gone," Asey said to me. "He's comin' back later. Bernsdorf's comin' back too, 'cause Kemp told him about findin' the gun. Let's go in an' charm the Satterlees."

"What are you after?"

"Well, I'm fishin' for cod," Asey returned, "but I wouldn't turn my nose up at a flounder."

We ate our dinner without haste, and Asey regaled his guests with Cape Cod stories. I wondered what the four prisoners upstairs must be thinking of the gales of laughter which floated up to them. Most of the time I watched Aristene Satterlee's hands.

They really were beautiful. Very white, and very long slender fingers with curiously pointed tips. The sort of hands, I thought, which practically every woman wishes she possessed and which seldom exist outside the imagination of artists who draw designs for nail polish advertisements.

After dinner Asey supplied Satterlee with a fat black cigar, settled him in the biggest, bulgiest chair the Hendersons owned, and began.

"About this Gilpin now," he said, as though the subject had been left off two seconds before. "Last month he was in New Hampshire, wasn't he? Around the first of the month?"

"First to the fourth," Satterlee returned promptly. "Now, Mr. Mayo, suppose I just tell you my story of that scoundrel. If Teen wants to amend it, she can later, but understand, Teen, I don't want any interruptions. Well, it's like this."

He leaned back in his chair and stretched his toes out toward the fire.

"On May first a friend of mine asked Teen and me to go to this show at a club of his. Turned out to be this troupe. Husky fellow with eyebrows—he sang pretty well; blonde that danced and sang what they call those torch songs; girl that gave sort of monologues. She was good, that girl was. Then there was a Punch and Judy show. Well, after that there was this magician. By George, he was good, too. I've seen 'em all, Thurston, Blackstone and all the rest, and while he wasn't in their class, still he was good. I'll never forget the expression on Harold Anselm's face when this fellow pulled that rabbit out of his vest pocket! Well, that was all there was to the show.

"I went home early and left Teen for the dancing that was coming afterwards. Teen didn't get home till three. She said this magician had met her and he'd taken her home. Well, sir, next day and the next and the next up till about six, this red-headed magician was under my feet like a rug at the house, that is, when he wasn't giving one of his shows or out with Teen somewhere. Seemed to take right to her, and she thought he was wonderful."

"I still do, father. I think—"

"I told you not to interrupt me. About the third day, I decided I ought to find out something about the man. He was nice looking, real pleasant, seemed all right from the outside. But as I said to Teen, you can't be too sure of these travelling troupers. I asked him about himself and he was sort of non-committal. As well as I could, I asked him just what his intentions were. You know what I mean—as one man to another and all that. He just laughed. Laughed right in my face, mind you! And I tell you, I was furious!"

"I bet you were," Asey agreed.

Aristene looked at him sharply.

"I gave him a piece of my mind," Satterlee went on. "I told him what I thought of a man that toyed with the affections of a young girl and then laughed in her father's face when he asked his intentions. Gilpin just laughed again and said he was afraid that I'd made a mistake.

"'No, by George,' I said. 'I haven't made any mistake. I know you for what you are!'

"'Listen,' says Gilpin, 'I'm not in love with your daughter. I never said I was.'

"'Then why've you spent all your time with her?'"

Satterlee puffed at his cigar. "That's just what I asked him. What'd he spent all his time with her for? What were his intentions anyway? Well, sir, I tell you he sobered up when he saw I was in earnest. He said he was very sorry, and that he'd not see Teen any more. Said he couldn't explain why he'd taken her about so much and made so many dates with her."

I could see where Red's explanation of the beautiful hands would have no effect, or considerable effect, depending on how you chose to look at it, on Squire Satterlee.

"Well, sir," Satterlee shook the ash off his cigar, "I gave him another piece of my mind and he left. But Teen, she met him as he was going and she made him keep his engagement to have dinner with her. And what do you suppose? That red-headed scoundrel left her in the restaurant. It wouldn't have been so bad, but a lot of people in the place knew Teen. Well, that was bad enough for her, but stories got going around about her and this Gilpin. There was another boy in Nashua who liked Teen a lot, and since those stories got around, he hasn't been to see Teen once. Now, Gilpin made my daughter a laughing stock and drove away a good likely husband. That's the kind of a man that magician was, Mr. Mayo."

"I see," Asey said thoughtfully. "I see. Huh."

Aristene said nothing. She sat there, her hands folded in her lap, and looked down at the designs on the rug.

"Want to add anything to what your father said?"

"Only this, Mr. Mayo. Father had and still has some crazy notion that Red was, well," she smiled, "he says Red's intentions weren't honorable. That covers his meaning, I guess. But it wasn't so. I liked Red. I still do. I think he's the nicest man I ever met. Of course the finale wasn't so hot. Or what's been said about me later. It was tough that so many people I knew should have seen him leave me cold. But, well, I'm not sorry."

"Utterly shameless," her father announced.

"My say, father. You've had yours. I don't know why Red dated me up so much. There were plenty of good-looking women who'd have jumped at the chance to go with him. I don't know why he left me that night. Somehow I don't think it was because of what father said. Red didn't take that seriously. He wouldn't have. That's all there is, there isn't any more."

She tried to say it lightly, but I could see that even now she couldn't treat the affair as a joke. I began to realize the other side of Red Gilpin's affairs, the side that Punch had never seen or dreamed of. How many other girls like Aristene had been rushed off their feet only to have Red walk out in the middle of a meal, or turn to another good-looking woman, or someone with beautiful eyes or beautiful hair? And Red, I knew from my slight acquaintance with him, would never understand the hurts he inflicted. Nor would it ever occur to him to explain.

I wondered how many other men were feeling the same way Squire Satterlee felt. Probably any number of indignant fathers and brothers and jealous husbands had entertained harsh thoughts about Red. Hundreds, probably. I decided that whoever killed Red undeniably did it because of some woman. Unless what Punch and Satterlee told us was absolutely false, the old war cry of "Seek the Woman" was in order.

"I see how it went," Asey repeated. "Miss Judy, you met Gilpin the other night for the first time, didn't you?"

Before she could answer Aristene spoke up.

"Is Red here? Was he here? I didn't—"

"He was here." Asey accented the "was" ever so slightly. "What did you think of him, Miss Judy?"

"I thought he was charming," Judy said quietly. "I agree with Miss Satterlee that he seemed one of the nicest men I'd ever met. But I had a feeling that he might be ruthless without in the least meaning to. About women, that is. I've met men like him. They take you around and rush you here and there till you find yourself thinking that the sun rises and sets in them. Then suddenly it's all over. Without any explanation at all. Or," she added with a touch of bitterness, "the explanation usually hurts your pride so much that you almost wish they hadn't bothered."

Asey nodded again. As he started to speak, Syl came in with a letter.

"Your list with last night's goin's on from the cops," he explained.

Asey tore open the envelope and read through three long pages. Then he put the pages back in order and read them all over again. At last, rather deliberately, he folded the sheets and replaced them in the envelope.

"What's your car number again?"

Satterlee gave it.

"What were you doin' speedin' off this road, off the main road along here, last night around half-past-one?"

7

SATTERLEE SIGHED.

"There," he said plaintively, "I knew that would happen if you let the cops come into that little accident of ours today! I told you right then and there that I didn't want to be involved with the police of this region any more. Maybe I didn't say it just like that, but that was what I meant. Good Lord! I should think, Mayo, that if you're in the police, you ought to be able to get that speeding business quashed. After all, I've done my best to try and help you!"

"Yes—yes. I'll say this much," Asey promised, "you'll get let off the speedin' charge if you can explain to me, with all the frills, just why in blazes you should be gaddin' about this region last night at that time. Alone, was you?"

"Yes, I was alone. You see, it's very easily explained. Nate's beer gave out last night and I volunteered to get some more for him. He had a cold," Satterlee explained ingenuously.

Asey smiled. "Go on."

"He said there wasn't any place I could get beer that time, and anyway, he liked best the beer of this man in Eastham some-where. He said I couldn't ever find it and I said I could. He had such a bad cough that he didn't want to go out, but he wrote me directions to find the place and I took my car and set out. That was a little after ten. I got to the place all right. It wasn't a store. It was a house. Portygee Someone—"

"Portygee Pete. He's still bootleggin'."

"That's right. Then, with the fog, I must have missed a turn somewhere, getting from his place to the main road. I landed up beside a pond."

"Easy enough to do that there. Ponds enough in that part of the Cape to float the British Navy."

"You said it," Satterlee told him. "There certainly are. Well, sir, I turned around and went back, and then I landed beside another pond. In fact, I either went back to that one pond four times, or I went to four different ponds. I've never seen so many ponds in all my life. I've never seen so many roads that landed up at ponds, either. You'd think all the people in that village spent all their spare time making roads to ponds. At last I got off on a small tarred road and came to a house. The man there gave me very careful directions, but I got lost again. I landed in a cranberry bog once, and near the ocean another time. It sounded like the ocean, so I went back on my tracks. Then I found the main road and later I turned the spot on a sign that said 'To Weesit' on it and I knew I was all right. I just naturally plumped my foot down on the gas and hustled. That was when the cop stopped me for speeding and having only one headlight."

Asey chuckled. "That r'minds me of the time two fellers come to the Porter house one foggy August night. Asked if it was the Chatham Bars Inn. So happened they was twenty-odd miles away. Instead of turnin' one way in Orleans, they'd turned another an' their directions went perfect for down the Cape as well as up. It's easy. But can you prove where you was a little after one?"

"I might have been in Jericho. I don't know. I reached home about quarter to two or two o'clock and found that the beer had all slopped out of the can onto the back seat. Nate'd gone to bed. I tell you, I was a pretty disgusted man."

"Ever hear of a feller named Maynard Guild?" Asey shot out the question with his eyes boring through Satterlee.

I watched to see if there were any reaction to the name, but not a muscle of the Squire's face moved.

"Guild?" he shifted his cigar from one corner of his mouth to the other without using his hands, an operation which has never ceased to fascinate me. "I know a Bob Guild who's vice-president of Acme Saw and Tool, and he's got a cousin named Morton Guild. Would that be the one you mean?"

Asey sighed. "No. Sell guns at your store?"

"'Everything for the Sportsman.' Do much duck-shooting down here, Mayo? I've got the finest double-barrelled—"

"Sold a .45 Colt, single action, old style, lately? Or wouldn't you know?"

"Let me see. Yes, yes, I did. I remember that old gun well. It'd been in the store at least ten years. Man gave it to me in part payment of a bill he couldn't meet. He was—"

"Now," Asey interrupted him briskly, "just what are the lawrs in your state about sellin' guns? In this one you get your picture took an' go through a long rigamarole an' then the gun number is registered along with your identification in the State House. As I r'call, you don't do it that way in your state."

"No. The purchaser signs a form and the number of the gun is taken. I keep my blanks filed away in a loose leaf notebook in my safe. We don't make duplicates, though, or send them anywhere."

"Then if you wanted to find the number of a gun bought

in New Hampshire, together with the name of the feller that bought it, you'd have to hunt around from place to place?"

"Unless you published the number in the papers or something like that. Blanks aren't collected in one place."

"Nice state to buy a gun in if you was contemplatin' murder."

"I suppose so. You know, speaking of that old Colt, I sold that gun to a member of the troupe that Gilpin was in. The afternoon of the fourth of May. Just before they left. Now I don't know why I remember that," he went on, quite unconscious of the news he was divulging or of the effect it was having on Asey and me. "No, I don't. It's funny how you'll remember something like that and then entirely forget very important things. Just last week I put the keys to my safe deposit box away somewhere, and I'll be jiggered if I've been able to find them since, or even remember approximately where I hid them. Think of it! I forget things like that and then I remember customers I'll probably never see again! Well, this man, he was the fellow who sang. Remember his eyebrows. What was his name? Something like—"

"It was—" Aristene began, but her father waved her to be silent.

"Don't tell me! Don't tell me! I'll get it in a minute. It's right on the tip of my tongue this instant. Something like Dalton. No, Galton. Dalton. Dall—"

I was reminded of the time Adin had addressed Angela Coffin as Mrs. Corpse.

"Ah, I have it. Allen. That was it. Allen. Fellow that sang. Stocky man, with eyebrows that met."

"Sold him a gun?" Asey was perfectly casual.

"Yes. That old Colt." Satterlee laughed heartily. "Yes, sir, I remember that. I'd bought a lot of stuff from Bannerman's once.

You know, old Army overstock. Well, among the stuff were some old fashioned black powder cartridges for a .45. Reduced charges, twenty-eight grains of powder instead of forty. Old government cartridges made at the old Frankfort Arsenal, years ago. Eighteen seventy or eighty or around then. Well, sir, when Allen bought this gun, I remembered that I had just one box of those cartridges left. Didn't have anything in the store they'd fit except that old Colt, so I brought them out and offered to sell them to him cheap. First off I thought I'd throw them in with the gun, and then I decided not to."

"Didn't know much, to take 'em, did he?"

"No, I don't think he knew much about guns," Satterlee admitted. "He bought the Colt because he said it looked like a cowboy's gun. Ha-ha! That's what he said. Of course, those cartridges might have been bum, but as I told him, they'd be all right for him to pot around with. Might sound weak, but otherwise they'd ought to be all right unless they exploded." He laughed. "But I'd shot some of 'em myself once before. Even if they were a little weak, they had a penetration of three inches or more in pine."

"How they come packed? Boxes of twenty?"

"Yes. Say, hadn't we better be getting along? We mustn't stay here all night."

"No hurry," Asey said. "Randall told you the car'd be ready for you at ten, but you want to allow him an hour's leeway, easy. Maybe more. Randall's like that. Do much shootin', yourself?"

"I was in the National Guard for fifteen years," the Squire said, pulling out a pipe and a tobacco pouch. "Quite a shot, I was. Always liked the old Colt," he added reminiscently. "Always carry one."

Asey gulped. "Got one with you now?"

"Yes, indeed. Always take one in the car. I slipped it into my pocket when we left the sedan."

Calmly he got up and fished it out of an overcoat pocket. "Nice gun."

"Yes," Asey said weakly, "nice gun."

Aristene had been staring at Asey for some time. Now she spoke up. "Mr. Mayo, what's all this about? What's been going on? What are you trying to dig out of us?"

"Dig out of you?" Asey picked up Satterlee's gun and casually unloaded it. "Well—"

A commotion upstairs interrupted him. It sounded to me like a machine gun and I jumped from my chair as though I had been shot. I felt a little foolish, but after the shooting that had gone on, not to speak of all this talk about guns, I felt that anything was liable to happen.

"What's all that?" Satterlee asked. "You got other people staying with you? What's wrong?"

"Wait a sec." Asey got up as the din continued. Opening the door into the tiny front hall, he shouted for Punch, who promptly clattered downstairs. He stuck his face, grinning from ear to ear, just inside the door.

"Terribly sorry, Asey. Awfully sorry. It was all my fault. We found a long closet back of the eaves and we explored it. Found a lot of kid's games there. We've been playing tiddly-winks. Then I found this net bag of golf balls. Must have been rotten, the webbing, because it burst when I picked it up. The balls just bounced around. Really, I'm sorry, but it scared us just as much as it scared you." He opened the door and walked into the living room. "May I come in and get warm? It's chilly upstairs. Oh. Oh!" he looked at Aristene. "Oh! How d'you do, Miss Satterlee?"

She nodded, but said nothing.

"Call Dan," Asey ordered.

Punch bolted upstairs. I watched Dan as he came into the room. The effect of Aristene on him was even greater than it had been on Punch.

"Why," the Squire remarked in some surprise, "that's the man I was telling you about, Mayo. That's Allen, who bought that gun. How'd the cartridges go, Mr. Allen?"

Dan stared at him. "What cartridges?"

"Why, that old Colt I sold you when you were in Nashua. And the old cartridges from Bannerman's. Don't you remember? You bought the gun because you said," Satterlee laughed uproariously, "you said it looked like a cowboy's gun!"

"Is he crazy?" Dan demanded. "What's he talking about? I never saw him before in all my life!"

"You never what?" Satterlee snorted. "Well, sir, you certainly did. I could pick you out of a crowd as the man I sold that gun and those cartridges to. Why, you even signed your name on the form. Daniel Allen. Yes, sir! You may have forgotten me, but I haven't forgotten you."

"I haven't got a gun." Dan was getting angry. "I never bought a gun in all my life. Never owned one. Never bought any of your old Banner bullets, or whatever they are. You're crazy."

"Do you mean to stand there," the Squire spluttered, "stand there and tell me I'm a liar? I tell you I sold you a .45 Colt and cartridges to go with it. On the fourth of May. You don't deny that you were in Nashua on the fourth of May, do you?"

Dan thought a moment. "No, I was there. But I never bought your—"

"Liar!" Satterlee stormed. "Scoundrel! Rascal! Teen, you see what I told you. I was right. All that troupe was a bunch of lying rascals. I thought that Gilpin was the worst, but I guess this man's just as bad as he was. Of all the bare-faced liars, of all the rotten dirty blackguards, you, Allen, and that Gilpin—you—"

"See here," Dan said, "you can say what you like about me. I don't know you from Adam unless you're the father of Miss Satterlee here. But you leave Red Gilpin out of it! At least under the circumstances you might have the common decency to speak respectfully of the dead even if you are crazy!"

"What—what d'you mean, speak—of the dead?" Aristene asked with a little catch in her voice.

"Why, Red Gilpin was murdered here last night! That's what I mean. And whoever you are, you can take back what you said about Red, or I'll paste your fat person into jelly!"

"Dead?" Aristene repeated. "Murdered?"

"Shot," Asey added, "with a .45 Colt."

Aristene turned to her father.

"So that's what you were doing last night? I thought that pond and fog business sounded hollow." Her voice was perfectly steady for all the white heat behind her words. "You said you'd kill Red if you ever saw him again. That's why you came to the Cape, is it? You followed him up. I thought it was queer that you should suddenly want to see things like sand dunes and long lost cousins again! Well, now you've gone and killed him and let this Mayo sew you into a sack. You went right into it with your eyes open. I knew he was trying to trick you. He didn't pull the wool over my eyes. He didn't fool me. He's got you. And I'm glad. D'you hear that? I'm glad!"

Her hands, still folded in her lap, did not move although the knuckles were white and tense. I wondered how anyone could be as furious as her words sounded and still be so outwardly calm.

Her accusation cut Satterlee as though she had stabbed him with a knife.

"But Teeny! I didn't kill this man. I didn't! That's all true about last night. I did get lost. I never knew Gilpin was within a thousand miles of here when I decided to come and see Nate. You can rest assured that I'd never come if I'd known it, too! All I wanted was to get you out of Nashua. That was all I really came for. I hoped a little trip might take your mind off—off everything. I'd intended first to take you abroad, but business was too shaky to leave. I took you just as far as I could afford. It wasn't much." His voice broke. "But it was as good as I could do."

"I don't believe you."

"It's true, Teen. It is." He got up from his chair and went over to her. "Teen, I know I said I'd kill Gilpin if I ever set eyes on him again. I know I said I wanted to kill him. But I didn't mean it. I wouldn't have and you know it. I—well, I know that I splutter a lot. But you know that your father wouldn't have killed that man!"

She waved him away. "I don't believe you."

Helplessly, Satterlee shrugged his shoulders.

"Mayo," he said to Asey, "you believe me, don't you?"

Silently Asey went to the peg where his coat hung and from a pocket removed the box of cartridges and the Colt which had killed John Gilpin.

"This the box you sold Allen?"

"He did not—" Dan began.

"Keep still a minute, Dan. This the box, Satterlee?"

He took the box and examined it. "It's the same box. It would have to be."

"Why?"

"I got a new stamp last April. This is it. And that box was the last I had of those cartridges. This box has the new stamp. So it must be. Where'd you get it? And the gun? Yes, it's the same gun. See that nick in the handle? Allen said I ought to take something off for the nick. Where'd you get it? Where did these come from?"

"They was the gun and bullets someone threw over the bankin' after they killed Red."

Satterlee's face was a study.

"Dan, you say you didn't buy these from Satterlee in Nashua?"

"I certainly do! I never bought them."

"Wait." Asey warned Satterlee as he was about to protest. "What time of day did you sell that gun?"

"Just before the store closed. Say, half-past-five to six."

"Okay. Now, Dan, s'pose there's any way of provin' where you was from half-past-five to six on May fourth?"

Dan thought. "Let me see. Gee, Asey, I don't know! That's over a month ago and we've moved about so much since. We move around so much anyway that a few minutes of one afternoon are hard to account for. Five-thirty to six. Well, the show would have been over. In Nashua we left the van out of town near the house of Punch's friends. Went into the city and back in the truck. Red and Punch had to transfer their stuff from the truck into the hall. Couldn't I ask Edie? She might be a one to know."

"Think a bit more first," Asey urged.

"It doesn't seem likely that I'd be alone. We don't wander off alone much even if we have the time. Except Red, and he didn't a lot. Probably we'd all have bundled off somewhere together for dinner."

Asey called the rest downstairs.

"Mrs. Allen, I want you to do some tall rememberin'. May

fourth. Nashua. After your afternoon show. Where was you? Where was Dan? More p'ticular, where was you all between five-thirty an' six?"

Edie closed her eyes. "Lord, I don't know. I can't remember. It seems to me that we all had dinner together. Red came in late. He—" she stopped short, opened her eyes and looked at Aristene. "Red was late. I can't think just what we did directly after the matinee. Can you, Hat?"

"Indeed I do remember. You and I went shopping for some new stockings and most of the stores were closed. We wandered around for years before we found a little shop that was open. I remember it vividly," Hat smiled wryly, "because I had a corn. I was nearly exhausted before we met the rest for dinner. Punch was mending Judy—"

Asey looked surprised, then laughed. "Oh, for his show. That right, Punch?"

"Yes, Judy was acting up that week."

"And Dan," Hat continued, "went off with Red. You were going to get a gadget for the van."

"Hat," Dan said fervently, "you're a peach! It all comes back to me now. Punch, you remember that the van needed a new radiator top? We'd bought new washers till we were sick of it. And we needed a new baggage carrier. Red and I went to half a dozen stores. Yes, that's where I was, Asey. With Red. He left after we got the things and I met Punch and the girls at a restaurant. He came in later."

"Let me get this straight," Asey said. "You think you was with Red from five-thirty to six?"

"Sure."

"When," Asey asked Satterlee, "did you have your set-to with Red?"

"After I got back from the store. Just after six, I'd say."

"An' then you, Miss Satterlee, went out with Red after that?"

"Yes."

"Humpf." Asey wrinkled his forehead.

"But it all proves I couldn't have bought those things," Dan argued, "doesn't it?"

"Don't forget," Asey reminded him, "that we can't exactly check up on that. Just like you say you showed Red the letter from Guild. You say you did, but we can't prove that either."

Dan sat down suddenly on the couch.

"Look, Asey. There's one straw I see to catch at. He says I signed my name on something. I'll give you my signature and you can have it compared with that one, can't you? I know he's wrong and I'll stake my life on it. You can take my signature and you'll find the other's a forgery."

"I was goin' to anyway. I'll see what can be done about gettin' a photostat copy or somethin'. Satterlee, you'll have to get in touch with someone an' give p'mission to have someone get into your store tonight. Got a clerk?"

"Four." The Squire cleared his throat.

"Well, we'll go do some phonin', then. The form's in your safe, ain't it?"

"But—but—you can't," Satterlee stammered.

"Can't what?"

"Get a copy of that signature. Or the form, either."

"An' I," Asey said firmly, "would like to know why in time I can't."

"Because I put it in my safe deposit box at the bank with a lot of other papers. I did it by accident. I didn't—"

"Got your keys, ain't you? We can get into a box as easy as a safe."

"No. No, you see, it's just as I said when I was trying to remember Allen's name. I said I couldn't remember where I put the keys to the box. They're lost. Both of 'em. The one I use and the duplicate."

"Kept 'em together?" Asey asked disgustedly.

"Of course."

"Huh. Well, even at that, the bank'll most prob'ly have another duplicate tucked away somewhere out of sight."

Satterlee shook his head.

"I'm afraid they haven't. You see, I just got a newer—a bigger box. They warned me then that they had just those two keys. Used to have another but the man who had the box before me lost it."

8

Once in a little park on the outskirts of Paris, just after the war, Adin and I got on a Ferris wheel. Something went wrong with the machinery, and for one solid hour we rose and fell in wide wobbling circles. The more they fiddled with the thing, the faster it went. When we finally reached ground, I was so dizzy and sick that my knees gave way and down I sat, hard and unintentionally, on the very good earth. I continued to sit there for some minutes while all Paris—all France and all the universe, for that matter—listed and swayed about me. Sympathetic gendarmes, excited soldiers, jabbering shopgirls and joyful children all wavered and bumped into each other and became one blurred mass of faces and figures in the general upheaval.

When I pulled myself together, I knew that I had attained the ultimate in confused states. I knew that it would be impossible for me ever really to be confused again. In fact, ever since I have bragged to my friends that after that Ferris wheel experience, nothing could upset me. It secured for me a certain placid frame of mind. Nothing could rumple my equilibrium. Nothing could bewilder me.

It shocked me to realize as I went to my room Wednesday

night that I had been wrong all those years. Compared to that day's madness, the Ferris wheel was a bagatelle.

After I got myself ready for bed—I had one slipper off—I decided to see if I could make order out of the chaos. I slipped my mule back on, girt my dressing gown about me, and went to the little writing desk in the corner. I have to see things down before me in black and white before I can get them straight.

I'd not opened the desk before. Now I found it stocked with writing paper: single sheets, double sheets, grey paper, white paper—all neatly engraved with a long name in small type along the upper right corner. Apparently, I thought as I put on my reading glasses, the Hendersons were grim correspondents. Apparently, I decided as I read the small type, they had a grim sense of humor, too.

They had chosen to name their house "The Peaceful Place Where Nothing Ever Happens."

Mentally I made a note to write them after all this was over and done with and suggest a more fitting label. At that moment my choice for a revision was "Out Damned Spot."

I picked out one of the largest sheets, scratched out the name and divided the paper into sections. I like orderly memoranda. I'm one of the few women I have ever encountered who fills out the stubs of her check book before writing a check. Adin always said I had a tabulating mind.

First I set down the facts from which there was no escape:

Gilpin was killed with a .45 Colt—(and how I was beginning to loathe the sound of Samuel Colt's name!)—a little after one o'clock Tuesday night. The troupe was lured to the Peaceful Place by a letter, if there *was* a letter, written by one Maynard Guild, if there *was* a Maynard Guild.

Under LETTER there were many details:

—Assuming that Maynard Guild was an entirely fictitious person, who wrote the letter? Dan could have. Except for his say-so, we would not have known of its existence. But Punch might have written it. So might Satterlee. After all, why eliminate the women? Why assume that Guild was a man? Hat Allen had a man's brain. Edie was nobody's fool. Aristene, for all her youth and stringy hair, had infinite self-control.

I remembered my father's dictum: "Beware the person who can control himself. He can control anything."

Rose and Judy I eliminated. Neither knew she was going to Weesit until Monday afternoon, and Dan said he had received the letter Saturday.

The section GUN filled up its space and ran onto another page.

Squire Satterlee (I wrote) says Dan bought it. Dan says he didn't. Without doubt the women are exempt from the buying end. But Punch's time on the fourth is not really accounted for. If Dan didn't buy the gun, who did? It would not be difficult to make up one's eyebrows to resemble Dan's. When Satterlee recalled Dan first of all, he mentioned the eyebrows that met. Punch probably knew all about make-up. He could have pretended to be Dan Allen.

On the other hand, Satterlee's story might not be true at all. He could have taken the gun himself, and written Dan's name on the form. His entire story of Dan's coming there and buying the gun might be a lie.

And even if the women could not have bought the gun themselves, Hat or Edie could have filched it from either Punch or Dan.

The section headed MOTIVE was reasonably brief. I was getting tired:—

Satterlee: revenge for Red's treatment of his daughter.

Dan: jealousy because of Edie, and Red's attentions and compliments.

Punch: the Lord only knew.

Aristene: "Hell hath no fury, etc." She was scorned.

Edie: She loves Dan, but Red might, in spite of Punch's assertion to the contrary, have annoyed her with his attentions.

Hat: "Still waters—"

Rose and Judy: none, so far as I knew.

I was yawning deeply when I began to fill in the last section, OPPORTUNITY TO KILL RED.

Satterlee, it seemed, might have wandered out to the Peaceful Place. Even if his story about the beer and the Portuguese bootlegger were true, he still could have hit our road.

Dan and Punch said they had not got up during the night. But they admitted to a tiring week and a tiring day. Either might have been sleeping heavily when the other went out.

We had assumed that Aristene had not gone out, but as Asey said, anything was possible. Hat had gone out and admitted it. But Edie had not heard her. Why, on the other hand, should Hat have heard Edie *if* Edie had gone out? The chances were that she wouldn't have. Moreover, if not one of us had heard Hat go out, it was highly possible that Rose or Judy might have gone out too.

The pen nearly slipped from my tired fingers by the time I reached CONCLUSIONS.

It seems to me, I wrote, to hinge on the form. If the signature turns out to be Dan's, if he bought the gun, if it was true that he quarreled with Red that night—then, knowing that he had a motive, a quick temper, a gun and the opportunity, it is logical to assume that he killed Red. On the other hand, if the signature is a forgery, then Satterlee or Punch—

In some disgust I put the cap back on my fountain pen. Thrusting the papers into the desk, I tumbled into bed.

I admitted cheerfully that I was no detective.

As I fell asleep the horrible thought smote me that while the Ferris wheel experience lasted at the longest an hour and a half, this confusion might go on indefinitely. There stretched before me visions of days and days spent filling up The Peaceful Place's engraved stationery with garbled maunderings headed "Order From Chaos."

It seemed to me that I had scarcely touched my head to the pillow before Jennie Mayo woke me.

"It's seven, Mrs. Ballard, an' a perfectly beautiful day. I've got your breakfast right here on the tray an' don't talk loud because Asey don't want anyone to get waked up yet."

I yawned. "What on earth did he do with the Satterlees? I was too sleepy to think about them last night. Did he fit them in the house after I went to bed, or did he send 'em to their cousin Nate?"

"He gave the girl the other bed in Miss Judy's room an' the man's still sleepin' on the couch in the livin' room."

"What became of Asey?"

"Oh, he slept on the floor," Jennie said casually. "It don't matter to him where he sleeps. Tuesday night he stayed all night out in the woodshed with our dog. He's just like a piece of elastic, he is. Now, you eat your breakfast. Don't hurry any, but Asey says if you want to get caught up, you'd better come out soon's your breakfast's finished. He's out front. Says he wishes this house had more privacy."

I devoured my breakfast as speedily as I could, and even

though Jennie had brought enough food for an army, I found myself wishing she had brought more. The Cape air was getting in its deadly work. I hadn't been so hungry in months.

I found Asey sitting out on the rustic bench, gazing moodily at the ocean. He got up and greeted me cheerfully.

"What's this?" I asked, "the Early-Bird Club?"

He laughed. "I was thinkin' only the other day how the rest of the birds must of hated the first robin that thought up that early risin' stunt. Sorry to get you up, but I wanted to chat with you alone. I been watchin' the breakers here for half an hour. It ain't true that every seventh wave's bigger than the other six. I always wanted to have time to prove that, but somehow I never got around to it till just now. Real restful, countin' waves."

"What happened after I went to bed?"

"Oh, I tried to separate everyone with a friendly hand shake, as old Parson Howes used to say. Parker an' Bernsdorf come back after midnight. Parker had a lot of dope on these show folks. Nothin' much more'n we already know. Seems to me cops don't know a lot about people in their own home town. I could of gotten a lot more from a furnace man. Anyway, they don't know a lot about Gilpin. He had an automobile agency way out on Commonwealth Avenue an' he bought it eight years ago from money an uncle left him. In January he had to give it up. Note he couldn't pay an' a mortgage on the prop'ty an' so forth an' so on. This firm he owed just sort of eased him out. Wasn't no need, p'ticularly, but they done it anyway. Then 'twas that Red took to pullin' rabbits out of silk hats. He don't have no p'lice record except for speedin' once an' once for disturbin' the peace when he was in college, after some rah-rah riot. That's all. They don't give what you might call any juicy details about the ladies in his life."

"Did you find out anything else about Judy?"

"By gum!" Asey slapped his thigh. "I knew I'd forgotten something. That was it. I forgot all about askin' Parker to look her up. Wait till I see Syl an' have him get into action on that."

"What," I asked when he returned, "about that safe deposit business?"

"Easy. Made Satterlee let us have permission to open the box anyway."

"How, if the keys are gone?"

"Drill, acetylene torch. Owner's s'posed to sit an' watch 'em while they work, but Parker's takin' care of that. We took Dan's signature an' sent it to Boston an' when they get the box open, they're to send the forms to Boston for some handwritin' sleuth to get at. Just for good measure, I had all the rest of the bunch write 'Daniel Allen' on a piece of paper. Bernsdorf's taken both guns, the one Sylly found and the Squire's, an' he'll check up on those. Kind of restful, havin' experts around. Only one trouble. When you take a case to court that's got a lot of experts in it, then the other side begins to get experts too, an' then the fun begins."

"But if they're experts, why don't they agree?"

"Why? I dunno. Just ain't the custom. Remember Mister Dooley? You do? That feller's still some of my fav'rite readin' matter. Well, once he wrote somethin' about expert test'mony that always pleased me a lot. Y'see, Mister Dooley'd been goin' on about how the more money you had, the more experts you hauled into court an' the smoother you got out of court your-self. Hennessy asks the dif'rence between expert test'mony an' perjury, if that's the case, an' Dooley says the dif'rence between expert test'mony an' perjury is a question of you pay your money an' you takes your choice. Sometimes that's about the size of it."

"What about other things?" I asked. "The papers you asked Kemp to get?"

"Clipped papers? Only two. Dif'rent sort of clips from the ones I found. Those had little ridges on 'em. That was all I want-ed 'em for."

"And the rest of the state police's list?"

Asey sighed. "Them fellers took me at my word. There's forty odd items on that list. Right now with this gun an' handwritin' business brewin' I ain't got the patience to sit down with such stuff as 'Roadster passin' on hill' an' all. 'Course, we can trace such numbers as they is, one by one, an' then go after the people an' try to find out more about 'em, but that's a long hard pull. It's a sort of come to me, too, that if I'd killed Gilpin an' had to get away in a car, I'd probably have blotted out a number or two on my license plates an' driven with a consid'rable care an' caution. Wouldn't of taken no chances."

"What about the newspapers?"

"All out in the wash today."

"Late editions, I hope?"

"Yup."

"I must telegraph George," I remarked. "If I don't, he'll come bouncing down here in a fury. Probably he'll set me to work drinking buttermilk again, too, and take away all my cigarettes. And I must wire Janet, too. They'll both feel it their duty to come here and we've certainly no place for them. You know, Asey, I wish I hadn't come here. I wish, rather, that I hadn't come when I did. I feel terribly about Red. I'm still filled with horror at the whole affair, but I find I'm thinking more about myself and all the rest of us now, than about him. I'm thinking of the papers, and what will follow being mixed up in this. It seems callous, but—"

"But it ain't," Asey interrupted. "It ain't, Mrs. Ballard. You forget that self-pres'vation's the first lawr folks obey. Sometimes it's the only one they do. A murder's a lot dif'rent from a death. You feel the same way in the beginnin', but in a murder you get a feelin' creepin' into your grief that says, 'S'pose they pick on me an' say I'm the killer?'"

"But just the same," I said, "I'm feeling ashamed of myself for the way we've all acted. We haven't—"

"Why should you? Mrs. Ballard, I've done a lot of work with Parker an' I got mixed up in a lot of funny cases like this here'n there in the world. In these things people feel just as bad as they do when anyone dies. Worse. Only the scare they get thinkin' someone might clamp handcuffs on 'em's stronger than their grief for whoever's got killed. It's just human nature to feel that way. There's more to a murder than that gone feelin' you get when death takes someone you know an' like. More'n just the feelin' about what's been an' what's happened to someone else. There's the feelin'— What's comin' to me?'"

I nodded. "Yesterday I thought Dan and Punch and the rest were, well—"

"I know. But let me tell you they're feelin' a lot sadder'n they seem. Kemp said Punch cried like a baby last night out in the truck. You look at 'em when you think they ain't lookin'. You'll see how they really feel. But as I said to you yesterday, they're actors. They're doin' their best to cover their feelin's but it's all just coverin'. You wait'n see the sort that turns up after the papers come out. Then you'll see how callous some folks can be. That's why I got them cops out by the cross roads. To keep 'em off."

"You mean reporters?"

"Partly. I hate r'porters on princ'ple. But mostly I mean tourists. What Bill Porter calls 'hoy-ploy.' Tourists may make a lot of money for the Cape, but I'd like to chloroform the whole bunch. Sun visors an' im'tation silk shirts an' sunburn! Strewin' papers in nice clean pine groves an' road hoggin' an' throwin' tin cans an' beer bottles on bathin' beaches! You wait till the tourist trade turns up here an' starts in. You can forgive the folks mixed up in a murder for worryin' about themselves, but you can't forgive the folks that ain't got nothin' to do with it actin' like it was a picnic, or a real estate outin' with free hot dogs an' vod'vil acts. An' they do. I seen 'em before this."

"You make me feel better," I said. "Asey, tell me. What are your ideas about all this really?"

"What're yours, Mrs. Ballard?" he countered.

I told him about my maunderings.

"That's sort of where I am," he said. "Right now I'm feelin' awful sorry for that Aristene girl. That day in Hyannis when I saw Red, the cashier of the garage was hangin' onto her cage by her eyelashes tryin' to get a good look at him. I thought he was an appealin' sort, but it seems to work two ways. Funny, you often hear of women that play around with men an' then ditch 'em, but you don't often hear or run into the comb'nation Gilpin was. One thing's sure. Whoever killed him was a pinin' female or a jealous male, an' that's something. Least we know they wasn't after his money."

Judy strolled out then and announced that breakfast was ready. She was pale, but the lines of hunger that had been in her face Monday were beginning to iron themselves out.

"I've eaten," I said as I rose, "but I rather think I shall eat again. Pig, that's what I am."

"You're getting better, Vic. There's color in your cheeks and your skin is losing that parchment tinge."

I had my second breakfast and then wandered down on the

beach. It was quiet there except for the roar of the breakers and the swish of the beach grass as it moved with the wind. I found that Asey had been right again. There was something restful about counting waves. At the three hundred and tenth, I fell asleep and woke only when Punch called me for luncheon.

We were quiet at lunch, and behind the forced cheerfulness I sensed a general feeling of uneasiness. Everyone knew about the safe deposit box and knew that, no matter what the verdict was when it came, someone would, as Punch expressed it, get theirs. In a calm-before-the-storm-ish mood I played bridge after lunch. Around half-past-two Sylly Mayo panted in.

"Stuff from Parker." He passed over a letter and a bundle wrapped in brown paper.

Such is human curiosity that every one of us stared at the bundle instead of watching Asey's reactions to the note. And everyone seemed intensely disappointed when he made no attempt to open the package.

"You can all rest easy for a while longer," Asey announced. "They run into some snag with the box. May not know till late tonight if they got it open, even. Then they'll have to send the stuff to Boston. Satterlee, if it'll make you feel better, it was the gun Syl found an' not yours that killed Red. Miss Judy, will you an' Mrs. Ballard come out with me?"

He picked up the bundle and Judy and I trailed after him to the bench.

"I had the p'lice check up on you, Judy, but they didn't find anything. Mind tellin' me about yourself?"

"Of course not. I left college sophomore year and went to business school. My family died and I had to go to work. No money left. I got a couple of little jobs and then found a really good one with Silverman and Harris, advertising, in Boston. I thought it was permanent, but they blew up a year ago. Since then I've lived in one hall bedroom after another until the rent came due. I couldn't get a thing to work at except some temporary stuff once in a great while. There's nothing I can sum up for you. I've got Silverman's references. Would you like to see them?"

"No matter."

"Look, Vic," Judy went on, "it's getting chilly. Can't I get your coat or a blanket or something? And that reminds me, what's become of that steamer rug we brought down? I wanted it yesterday for the beach, and I couldn't find it anywhere."

"I took it from the living room Tuesday night. It's in my closet and you're welcome to it. Personally I'd as soon sleep under a layer of concrete."

"Tuesday night? I didn't hear you," Judy remarked thoughtfully.

"It was quarter after three or so. You were sound asleep under your white blanket."

"White blanket? I haven't any white blanket."

"Well, you had one that night," I said positively. "I was sleepy, but I noticed it. Meant to ask you where you found it. It isn't on our inventory."

"Really, Vic, I didn't have any white blanket. It must have been the fire light and the reflection."

"Or," Asey added, "a sheet."

"Sheet, fiddlesticks! She wouldn't be sleeping with a sheet on top of her that cold night, Asey!"

Judy looked at him queerly.

"I didn't mean that," Asey explained casually. "I meant that she'd drawn the covers back over the foot of the couch."

"But that's even sillier," I protested. "You know yourself it was cold enough for half a dozen blankets that night."

"What Asey's getting at," Judy said, "is that he thinks I wasn't in bed at all, Vic."

"Wasn't either, was you, Judy?"

She shook her head. "No."

"What were you up for?" I demanded. Even though Red had been killed at one, Judy's absence after three o'clock might have been protracted from that time. Or even before.

"That's something," Judy said briefly, "that I don't think I want to tell you about."

"You mean," Asey corrected her, "it's something you *won't* tell about?"

She hesitated. "Well, yes. Yes. If you want to put it that way, Asey, it's something I *won't* tell about."

9

ASEY'S NEXT question startled me as much as it startled Judy.

"You got a fuzzy bathrobe?"

"A what?"

"You know. A fuzzy bathrobe. Camel's hair or one of those woolly ones. Something that's got a fuzz on it?"

"No." Judy shook her head. "My dressing gown is a long coat-like thing with wide sleeves. It's cotton pongee."

"Got a light coat? A polo coat?"

"Yes."

"New?"

Judy flushed. "All my clothes are new. Mrs. Ballard had to clothe me when she hired me."

"Mind bringing it out here?"

"Certainly not." Judy got up and went into the house.

"Just what streak of fancy," I asked wonderingly, "compels you to prowl around with fuzzy bathrobes and polo coats?"

"Why not? No funnier than paper clips an' the Satterlees, are they?"

I kept quiet.

Judy brought back her coat, a perfectly ordinary light tan coat with raglan sleeves and large brown leather buttons.

Asey took it and fingered the cloth. "Easy shedder, ain't it?"

"Easy what?"

"It's fuzzy. Rubs off easy. Anyone in the house got on a blue serge coat?"

"Punch has."

"Then bring him out, will you?"

Judy trotted off.

"Asey Mayo," I said in exasperation, "what is this all about? Of course you're having a lot of fun, but you might let me in on it. After all," I added pointedly, "I'm not in the Satterlee class."

"Nothin' to tell, yet. I'm just findin'. Okay, Punch. Now, Judy, will you slip into this coat of yours? Thanks. Now, please just lean enough against Punch's coat so's your coat touches, will you? Thanks again. Now, Punch, you can take your coat off an' go back. Don't ask any questions. Hop along."

I noticed that on the arm of his coat there was a little fuzz. It wasn't really thick enough to be called fuzz. Rather, I decided, it was down.

Asey was busy opening the brown paper bundle which he had brought out with him. From it he produced another blue serge coat, very much like Punch's except that it was double breasted. He looked at it a moment and then passed it over to me.

On both the shoulders between the lapel points and the sleeve seam, were similar patches of down.

"Yup, easy shedder," Asey remarked. "Huh. I saw those bits on Gilpin's coat—this is his coat, y'see—but I didn't think much about 'em. Just thought he wasn't careful about brushin' his clothes. But Parker got to broodin' about it an' sent it along. Glad he did. So you saw Gilpin Tuesday night, Judy?"

"What makes you think so? After all, Asey, mine isn't the only woolly polo coat in existence. There must be millions in the world."

"Yup, but there ain't more'n nine or so in this p'ticular portion of it."

"Punch wore one the night he came," Judy continued. "I've seen Hat Allen wearing one. Even Aristene Satterlee has one that's almost a duplicate of this one of mine. In fact, she picked up mine by mistake last night before she went up to bed."

Asey sighed and unwound his long legs. "Okay. I'll go roust 'em out. I'll get all the polo coats in the place an' see what can be done about 'em."

Judy sat down on the bench beside me.

"I s'pose, Vic, that at this point you're rueing the day you ever hired me, aren't you?"

"Why should I?"

"That's decent of you. It's the sort of thing you would say. I'd so hoped that I wouldn't be dragged into this. Word of honor, Vic, I had nothing to do with Red Gilpin's death. And if Asey—well, I hesitate to think of what your son will think of me then."

"I'm hesitating to think of George's reactions anyway. There's only one thing, Judy. Tell Asey the truth. He won't take the wrong side of things even if they sound bad."

"Uh-huh." My advice was not accepted with anything approaching enthusiasm.

Asey came back with three coats over his arm.

"Punch's worn so thin it wouldn't leave anything on fly paper. Hat's isn't much better."

Industriously he rubbed the sleeves against Punch's coat. "Nope, neither'll leave a speck behind. Now for Aristene's. It's the same color, but it's flannelly while yours is fuzzy. Nope, none of 'em works. Judy, you come here an' prove this for yourself. Rub them three coats against Punch's blue one, an' then rub yours."

"I'll take your word for it."

"Now, Judy," Asey said coaxingly, "you did go out an' see Red, didn't you? Rubbed against him?"

"I did *not* go out. Besides, Asey, Red was killed around one, wasn't he? And I was out of bed at three. There's that to consider."

"But you might of been out since one. Come on, Judy."

"On my word of honor, I didn't go out of the house."

"But you knew Gilpin well before you come here, now, didn't you?"

"What makes you think so?"

"Five lumps of sugar in his coffee, for one thing. An' what you said yesterday mornin', too. About no one knew what'd get raked up. Wouldn't of said that unless you had somethin' you didn't want exposed to the light of day."

"And," I said, feeling that the necessity for telling everything should be impressed on her, "when Punch first spoke of Red, you asked if his name were Kilpin. Not in exactly the same tone you'd use if you really wanted to be reassured. Rather as though you wanted to make certain that it was Red, and didn't want to ask directly."

Judy smiled. "You're sharp, Vic. I didn't think that you noticed that."

"Now, Judy," Asey said, "look at this sensibly. If you won't tell me the truth, you know durn well I'll only make your life mis'rable 'till you do. An' when it comes to p'sistency, I got the bloodhounds that tracked Eliza beaten miles. Look like a pack of nervous moskeeters when it comes to me."

"You win," Judy said quietly. "I should have told you when this first happened. Only, you see, I hadn't made any mention of knowing Red when he first came or when Punch spoke of him, and after yesterday morning, it seemed sort of asking for trouble to tell. I did know Red. I met him two years ago in Boston while I was working for Silverman and Harris."

"Don't want to be awful personal," Asey sounded as though he really meant it, "but just what was your relationship with Red? Good friend, or what?"

"'Or what.'" Judy lighted a cigarette skilfully in the wind. "I'm another Aristene."

"You—?"

"One of the discards. Not hands. I judge it must have been her hands that got Red. They're perfectly beautiful, aren't they? I was hair."

"Hair?" Asey repeated.

Both of us stared at her head as though we'd never before been conscious of the fact that she possessed one. Her hair was brown, naturally wavy, and evidently she'd had it cut Monday by an expert barber, for it lay close to her head and the neckline really was a bit of artistry. But it wasn't greatly different from the hair of a dozen girls I knew.

"You've a right to look surprised," Judy went on calmly. "You see, my hair was long then. Very long. Mother always loved long hair and I never had mine cut till last January. It was long and wavy and," she smiled, "if I do say so myself, it was rather nice. It didn't have that bulky look. I wound it round my head like—"

"Like a halo," Asey suggested, cocking his head to one side

and looking at her critically. "Yup, I see how 'twould be. Make you look dif'rent from other girls an' prob'ly more dignified. Not so much like a college girl all set for a frisky game of tennis."

"That was it, Asey. Thanks for helping me out. I got my job because of my hair. Harris, my boss, liked long hair and wouldn't employ girls who were bobbed. Aside from that little prejudice, he was rather a nice man. Well, I met Red at some amateur theatricals. He was giving his magician stunt and I was the sleeping beauty. We were doing 'Beauty and the Beast' for some children's hospital benefit. I had a lot of that goldy dust in my hair and he sort of fell for me. Even with the dust brushed out, my hair still got him. That's all. Only Red didn't walk out on me the way he did on Aristene. We parted in a friendly, but none the less firm, manner."

"When?"

"Last January. I might as well give you all the gory details. At the time I took it as hard as Aristene seems to be taking it now. But it wore off very soon. You see, we met just two years ago in June. From then till last January I saw a lot of Red. After a year I got to take him for granted; last fall I even had the idea that we were engaged. That's one of the reasons why I didn't feel so badly at first when I couldn't get work. Though nothing had ever been said definitely about the matter, I assumed that when I really ran out of money, I'd marry Red. I wondered why he didn't think of it when I lost my job."

She stopped to light another cigarette.

"In January Red's business came to grief. I was pretty near the end of my tether. I'd been out of work six months. It seemed time for a show-down, and so one night I asked him what we were going to do. He said he'd met up with a lad and he had some idea of taking to the road with a travelling show. He was going to make a living out of his sleight of hand work. Somehow he didn't even mention me at all. I said, 'What shall I do?'"

"He just rubbed his chin and said it was tough, wasn't it, and then I began to wonder if I'd made a mistake in thinking that he cared anything about me. What he said next neatly dispelled any remaining notions on the subject. He said that he'd been neglecting his business and that was why he'd failed, even though this company he owed money to had no real need to force him."

"Neglectin' his business? Why?"

"I'm coming to that. He said, oh, so very casually, that he'd met a woman he'd fallen in love with and that she'd taken up all the time he should have spent at the store. At that point I knew I'd been all wrong, because I knew darn well I'd not taken up much of his time."

"Who was the woman?"

"I don't know. I never knew. I never even asked her name and I don't think he would have told me anyway. I was, well, I was shocked. When you think a man's in love with you, and you're in love with him, and you fully expect to marry him, it's a—a little startling—"

"To have him up an' announce he'd let his business go to pot on account of bein' in love with someone else," Asey finished for her. "Huh, I can see that. An' me thinkin' Gilpin was such a nice feller!"

"Asey, he really was. You must remember, he'd never said a word about our being engaged or getting married either. I remembered that about that time. Of course I was angry clear through. But more because I'd made such a fool of myself than because of him. I said, keeping my voice as casual as I could, that I thought under the circumstances it might be well if we didn't see each other again. He couldn't see why at all. And really, he meant that. He didn't. He said we'd always been good friends and there was no reason why we shouldn't continue to be. But I insisted, and after a while, he agreed. He was very decent. Tried to get me a job with some friends of his. He'd always done his best to find work for me."

"Sweet of him." Asey kicked a stone over the banking and leaned forward to watch it bump down the cliff onto the beach. "Real sweet. Huh!"

"Don't be so grim, Asey. I realized then and there that it was all my fault for thinking he was in love with me when all the time he just admired my hair. Red liked good-looking women, always, but just to admire 'em. Well, anyway, after we'd said a friendly good-bye, Red said with some bitterness that the irony of the whole situation for him was that, after years of admiring women, the one he'd fallen in love with was married, and loyal to her husband."

"Served him right," Asey said.

"I asked him what he was going to do about it and he said he didn't know. He admitted that the woman liked him—"

"Followin' the fashion."

Judy laughed. "But I gathered that she just liked him. Nothing more. And it was a bit ironic, when you come to think it all out. Here women fell in love with Red, just right and left, and he just liked 'em. Then he went and fell in love, and for a change, the woman just liked him."

"Nem'sis," Asey remarked. "I'm glad of it, even if everyone seems to think that Gilpin meant right by all his Nells an' that it was all the Nells' fault anyhow. What'd he plan to do about it?"

"I asked him. He said he couldn't do anything. She'd said he could write to her, if he wanted to. So he was just going to write her every day."

"D'you mean to tell me," I said, "that he was going to waste the only passion of his life out on a lot of letters?"

"Sounds foolish, doesn't it, Vic? But that was it. From what he said, I gathered that he'd just gone romantic. Usually his kind does. All the old stuff—of wandering to the ends of the earth unless she needed him, giving up his life to her if she wanted it for a stair carpet. Always waiting and hoping and loving her. Practically troubadour. After he left I began to giggle a little. Next day I cut off my hair and promptly forgot all about him."

"An' you never knew the woman or even who she was?"

"Never."

"Does it occur to you, Asey," I said, "that it might be Edie?"

"Yup, only what price letters then? What d'you think, Judy?"

She shrugged. "I don't know. All I'm sure of is that she's beautiful and loyal to her husband. Red didn't seem at all annoyed about the husband. Didn't know him and didn't want to. Just discounted him entirely, as though he were a statue. Said he didn't want anyone to think it a triangle, because his was not that sort of love."

"Humpf." Asey wrinkled his nose. "How 'bout Aristene? Why'd he run after her if he had this great passion?"

"Admiring Aristene's hands wouldn't have been Red's idea of infidelity to his ideal. He probably thought of her hands in terms of the Great Unknown. Wouldn't doubt it at all."

"When Bill Porter was a kid," Asey said thoughtfully, "he busted the last real windmill on this end of the Cape pretendin' he was some Spaniard. Don Somebody."

"Don Quixote?"

"Yup. Red must of had the same ideas. So you ain't seen Gilpin since all that happened, Judy?"

"Not till Tuesday."

"Why didn't he recognize you?" I asked.

"Because I'd made up my mind not to recognize him. I didn't. Red was no fool. When I didn't fall all over him, he grasped the idea. I don't think he particularly wanted me to be known to his friends, either, for that matter. Maybe because of Edie, or Hat. I don't know. Anyway, as he left, he whispered to me that he wanted to see me later. I said no. Seeing him after all those months, I realized how little I'd really cared for him. I'd just been in love with that infectious buoyant spirit of his. Red was rather like a small child. He'd never really got to be an adult, and I'm inclined to think that most of his charm lay in that. Anyway, I said no. But just before I slipped into bed, I heard someone at the kitchen door. There he stood."

"So you told us the truth about not goin' out. He come in, huh?"

"That's it, Asey. I didn't want to let him in, but neither did I want him to set up a din."

"What did he have to say?"

"He didn't have a chance to say anything. I told him what I'd been through lately. Said Vic had taken me in without question and that I didn't want to bring up the past. Most certainly he was not to wake her up or make her think I was carrying on. Told him I wanted the sleeping dogs left on the hearth and to run off. He did."

"How'd the fuzz get on his shoulder?"

"Oh, he kissed me," Judy said coolly. "He stood on the kitchen step. Just like a couple of servants. My arms were on his shoulders. I'd put on my coat because it was next to the couch and my dressing gown'd proved too light weight for the weather."

"You say you didn't love him," Asey mused, "an' then you kissed him. That's just one of them fem'nine reactions, I s'pose?"

Judy chuckled. "Asey, you're swell. It was just the easiest way to get rid of him, and he did so look like a naughty child when I'd sent him off."

"Went right back to bed? What was the time?"

"About quarter after twelve or so. I'm not sure. I went back to bed and stayed there till after three. But that getting up had nothing to do with the murder. I'll swear to that."

"Won't tell more?"

Judy shook her head. "It didn't have anything to do with this. It would only mean involving some perfectly innocent people."

"Wouldn't be involvin' 'em if they was in'cent," Asey remarked.

"True. But I've told all, Asey."

"Have anything to do with any of the troupe?"

"Don't try to make me play twenty questions with you, you old sleuth! I've given you my word that all I've told you is the truth. It is. And it's all I know about Red and what happened."

"Okay," Asey said after a pause. "We'll save the rest till later. Run along an' take the coats back."

"D'you believe her?" I asked, after she had gone.

"I do. I knew yesterday mornin' that she knew Gilpin. It was all over her face in big red letters. But I don't think anybody would have been able to act the way she looked when I told her he was killed. I b'lieve her. Besides, she didn't know she was comin' here. Even if she met Red an' felt dif'rent from what she's told us, she wouldn't of killed him. She's too much of a lady. That sounds queer. But—"

"I know what you mean," I said. "She's capable of getting furious, but she wouldn't have killed Red in a fury. She's too reasonable and she sees too many sides. Her explanation of cutting her hair off and promptly feeling better, for example, proves that. I think she's temperamentally unable to sustain anger. She could be mad just so long and then her sense of humor would come to the rescue and get the better of her. At all events, it seems to have got the better of her long before Tuesday night. Besides, how could she have bought the gun, or stolen it from anyone in the troupe, assuming, of course, that someone in the troupe had the gun? And you can't connect her with the Guild letter."

Asey nodded. "Yup. Well, we'll be gettin' back. Little more of the jigsaw puzzle in place, but I can't say as I see outlines. Just a lot of sky. Say, I wonder about Aristene."

"So do I."

"We just took it for granted that she was at Nate's on Tuesday night. I think we'll run up an' make a call on Nate Hopkins. Lord, look at Jennie! Syl's got her so she's dashin' too. By gum, watch her sprint out here!"

Jennie was sprinting so fast that Asey had to grab at her to keep her from going over the banking.

Her face, usually red, was ashy white.

"S'matter? My God, Jennie, what's wrong?"

"Asey—come quick—come quick! The—cellar! Someone's groanin'. It's awful. Oh, come quick, come quick!"

10

ASEY PULLED a whistle from his pocket and blew a shrill blast as he started for the house on a dead run. Kemp came running from somewhere near the van, and Syl's head appeared over the top of the bluff like a jack in the box. His small legs pumped along behind Asey's long ones.

Leaving Jennie to recover her lost breath, I squared my shoulders and joined in the marathon.

The cellar, I knew, although I'd never been in it, was under the kitchen. You reached it from a trap door in the kitchen floor, or from a bulkhead to the left of the back door.

I wasn't much behind the three men as they scrambled down the bulkhead steps.

In the middle of the tiny square cellar stood Rose, gripping a clam hoe. Her screams would have put the proverbial stricken panther to shame.

Asey snapped on the cellar light with one hand, and pulled a gun from his belt with the other. Rose yelped a little louder at the sight of the gun.

"What's the matter?" Asey roared at her in his quarter-deck bellow.

She whimpered and brandished the clam hoe.

"What's the matter? Who's groaning? Who is it? What's wrong?"

Rose pointed a trembling finger toward the small coal bin which stood between the water tank and the engine which pumped our water supply.

"Coal bin? Who's groaning in the coal bin?" Asey demanded. "Can't you say anything? Jennie, what in blazes is wrong?"

Jennie lumbered down the steps.

"We was gettin' coal for the stove, Asey. I come down with her to get some kindlin'. She took a shovel full of coal an' then we heard that groan! It was awful! It didn't sound human! It come an' then it went!"

"Where'd it come from?"

"In here somewhere. I thought first, after it stopped, that it was someone outside bein' funny. When Rose begun to shovel, it happened all over again. Oh, it was awful, Asey! Awful!"

Asey passed his gun to Kemp and picked up the coal shovel. He dug into the coal and poured the shovelful into the half empty kitchen hod.

Instantly the most unearthly sound I've ever heard in all my life filled the room. It wasn't, as Jennie said, anything human at all. It wasn't exactly a groan or a moan or a wail. It was a combination of all three. Suddenly it ceased as quickly and mysteriously as it had begun.

"By gum!" Asey said.

Determinedly he took another shovelful.

As he heaved it into the hod the noise commenced again. Without waiting for it to stop he continued his digging.

"D'you s'pose it's another killin'?" Jennie yelled hopefully in my ear. She had to yell, because above the noise of Asey's scraping shovel and the strange groaning sound, resounded Rose's yelps, as regularly as an alarm clock and a hundred times as shrill.

"S'pose it's another?" Jennie repeated, clutching my shoulder.

"Wouldn't groan if he were dead," I yelled back. "That's one comfort if you want to cling to it."

All at once Asey stopped shovelling and the weird noise ceased, too.

I caught my breath as he bent over, and Rose mercifully ceased her shrieks.

The stillness was broken by Asey's chuckles. He picked up something and held it out.

Dirty, with one leg missing, but with a jaunty red ribbon around its neck, was an unmistakable toy lamb.

The relieved laughter that followed was fully as loud as the screaming confusion before.

"Kid's woolly lamb," Asey said with something bordering on relief in his tone.

He squeezed it, and again the strange sound filled the cellar.

"Prob'ly one of the Henderson kids left it in the bin last year an' then when they put the coal in, they didn't notice it an' covered it up. Then after some of the coal got used, it shifted. An' every time you took a shovelful, he bleated."

Kemp put Asey's revolver in his pocket. Almost shamefacedly he wiped off the great beads of perspiration which stood out on his forehead.

"Gee!" was his only contribution.

Sylly swallowed twice and Jennie drew a long breath.

"Well," she said spiritedly, "I'm glad none of you can't laugh at me for bein' scared, or at Rose either. It'll be a great thing to remember that the rest of you was just as wrought up an' tremblin' as we was. More, I think."

"Jennie," Asey said, gravely passing the disheveled lamb over to her, "you're right. If Syl should ever kid you—I know durn well that *I* never will—you just let me know, an' I'll fix him. His hands was shakin' most as bad as mine. Oh—by—by—gum! I never heard anything like that noise in all my born days. Never! Jennie, this an'mal,"—the light caught one of its beady eyes and it seemed almost to wink,—"this is all yours. Trophy of the chase. By gum! I want to get out of here!"

He picked up the full coal hod and took it up to the kitchen.

"Never," he announced to me as we went into the living room, "never was so scared. Honest! Not even when that big Swede on the 'Betsey B.' went crazy an' run around hackin' people with an axe. You can dodge a feller like that, but there's no dodgin' a sound. I sort of expected to find someone half dead under that coal pile. Or else someone quartered an' cut into little pieces. I know how the feller felt now when the kid yelled 'Wolf!' an' there wasn't none. Say—will you gape at those fellers?"

Dan, Punch, Edie and Aristene were at the bridge table. Satterlee—he'd hardly opened his mouth all day long except to remove or replace his pipe—sat over a backgammon board with Hat Allen. Judy seemed, as the saying goes, to be kibitzing.

"Of all the calm, cool, collected people," I said disgustedly. "Didn't you hear the excitement?"

Judy looked up. "Anything wrong?"

"Wrong!" I spluttered. "Wrong!"

"What's the matter, Vic? You see, Hat's getting licked on a nice thirty-two game and Dan's just bid and made a grand slam. I thought I heard a little yelling, but we weren't exactly silent over Dan. I thought of going out, but I simply couldn't tear myself away. What happened?"

Asey looked at me and I looked at Asey.

"I'll be switched," he said with infinite control, "if I tell you. Go an' play your games, you cold-blooded gamblers!"

He walked over to the bridge table. It was Dan's deal and Edie, his partner, was shuffling. She had that little trick of flipping the cards back into place, and I watched her enviously. It's simply a matter of finger control, that flip-back, but I've spent years littering a room with cards trying to learn how to do it.

But Asey's eyes were not on Edie's intricate shuffling. He was watching Dan closely as he dealt, and for the life of me I couldn't imagine why.

"Always deal that way?" he asked when Dan started to pick up his cards.

"What way?"

"Holding the pack in your right hand an' dealin' with your left?"

"Why, no. Sometimes I hold the pack in my left and deal with my right."

"Amb'dextrous, huh?"

"Yes. My father lost the use of his right hand when he was thirty. Accident." Dan arranged his cards. "He had to learn to lumber along with his left. Had a terrible time. Got to be a crank on the subject. Two spades, Edie. Hear me, Edie? Two spades. Anyway, dad made Hat and me both learn to use our left hand. Hat's terribly right-handed now in spite of it, but the training made more impression on me. I still use my left a lot.—Two spades, Punch. Asleep?—Always for tennis. Used to play the violin left-handed. I still play better golf with left-handed clubs."

"Write with your left?"

Dan nodded. "Hurry, Punch. Two spades."

"But," Asey landed sharply on his point, "but when you wrote that signature last night for me to send to Boston, you used your right."

"So I did. You see," Dan was not at all disconcerted, "my official signature at the bank is my right-handed one. The two writings are a lot different. You passing, Punch? Took your time. I said two spades, Edie."

Edie Allen put down her cards and smiled slowly at Asey.

"Dan," she said softly, "you nit-wit! Don't you realize—oh, I should have remembered it. But I didn't."

"For Pete's sakes, Ede, two spades! Realize what?"

"Realize what you're saying, you idiot! Don't you see, Asey's trying to get your signature compared with the one on this form sheet, and here you hold out on him the fact that you can write with your left! Not only can, but do. You knew you're as likely to sign letters with your left as not. It's so beautifully sprawly and illegible and business-like!"

"I never thought of that angle," Dan said honestly. "Got a pen?"

Asey passed over a fountain pen and Dan, pulling a clean leaf off the score pad, proceeded to write his name, three times with his right and three times with his left hand.

"There. Both at once. Lot more papers out in my chest in the van that you're welcome to if you want to compare 'em with my regular every-day writing. I'm sorry, Asey. This left-handed business never entered my head."

"I don't think," Satterlee spoke up, "that Mr. Allen or," he amended hastily, "whoever bought that gun, used his left hand when he signed. I usually notice left-handed people."

"That's something," Dan said gratefully. "I almost expected you to say that this guy was a southpaw. That would have made me feel just a little worse than I do, if I could feel worse."

Asey took the paper and started out of the room.

"I'll give this to Syl and have it relayed to Parker an' he can send it to Boston."

"Two spades," Dan announced patiently, "two spades, Ede, and Punch passed."

"Tell me," Satterlee asked when Asey returned, "what's holding up the work on the deposit box?"

"Seem's if they'd run into the rock of Gibraltar," Asey said with a grin. "Anyway, they smashed their drill, an' it's all muddled up. Take it that it's a top row box."

"Top row in the corner."

"Uh-huh. Well, they've hit snags in either direction an' can't seem to do much. They've messed the lock up, too. Grand mess all around."

"Lovely," Dan remarked, "but there's an element of suspense that makes me not quite so cheery about it. Mr. Satterlee, are you sure you don't know where those keys are?"

"Sure," Satterlee said regretfully.

"Even if he did get a brain wave an' remember," Asey pointed out, "it'd prob'ly not make any dif'rence now. Not if the lock's smashed. Oh, Miss Satterlee, I wonder if I could see you a minute?"

"Sure." She got up from the bridge table and beckoned to Judy. "Take my place."

We walked out doors to the back of the house. Someone—I suspected Sylly—had brought out some wicker chairs and a hammock from the loft of the garage, and the space between the house and the garage was, as Asey said, all very Country Club. There was even a striped umbrella, faded and a bit inclined to tumble down, which lent a festive touch.

"About Monday," Asey said. "You got here when?"

"Seven o'clock," Aristene replied. "We started early in the morning and stopped in Boston for lunch. Father had to see some men there and we didn't start out again till half-past-three."

"What did you do that night?"

"I'd driven most of the way and I was frightfully tired. I took a bath and went up to bed almost right after supper."

"And Tuesday?"

"Father went fishing with Cousin Nate. At some pond. Uncle Thoph's, could it be? Anyway, they went off at eight in the morning and didn't come home till six. It took them all that time to catch two perfectly minute pickerel. They wanted Cousin May to cook them for supper, and she just laughed at 'em. She said that after they were cleaned there wouldn't be a mouthful for the cat."

"What did you do all day long?"

"Oh, I helped Cousin May put up orange marmalade in the morning. That is, I poured paraffin and made out labels. In the afternoon we took her car and drove around. She showed me the scene of the first encounter with the British in 1812, or maybe it was 1777 or '78. Then we looked at something she said was an Indian grave and then we went to Provincetown and saw the Monument and where the Pilgrims did their laundry."

"Hm. Historical pilgr'mage." Asey thought a moment. "I wonder if you didn't notice any of the signs that advertised the troupe's show."

"No. Were there any?"

"I saw a lot yesterday on the Wellfleet road," Asey said. "On phone poles an' fences an' such. Placards a couple of foot square."

"Why, Asey," I said, "I never saw them!"

Aristene looked grateful.

"Sure enough? They was there, Mrs. Ballard. I often wondered when all these comp'nies go litterin' up otherwise good landscapes with a lot of billboards an' handbills an' such, if they ever stop to figger out that not one person in a thousand ever pays much attention to 'em? You see the things, yes. But they don't exactly enter into your soul. Guess the troupe's signs are just about the same. So you honestly didn't know that Red Gilpin was here?"

"I didn't know he was in this exact spot," Aristene said hesitantly. "He'd told me their plans in a general way and I knew that they were coming to the Cape sooner or later."

"What you do Tuesday night?"

"Sat home and read the 'Saturday Post.' Cousin May went to a club—"

"Women's Tuesday Club?"

"Yes. They were playing bridge and she urged me to come. But it's deadly dull not to play if others are playing and I gathered that there were even tables. So I stayed at home."

"An' still the troupe played Orleans Monday night," Asey said. "Didn't anyone mention it to you?"

"Nate did say that there was a show in town Monday, but I was too tired to think of going and so was father. Both of us took it for granted that he meant the movies anyway."

"Were you serious last night when you 'cused your father of killin' Red?"

Aristene dug the toe of her brown pump into the sandy soil as though she had no other interest in life. She was sitting well forward on the foot rest of a deck chair, her shoulders hunched and her hands tucked away in her pockets.

It occurred to me as I watched her that her principal liability was her clothes. She dressed rather in the manner of a middle-aged matron. Her shoes were sensible arch-preserver things with cuban heels and her stockings were cast iron service weight. Compared to Judy and Edie and Hat, she was quite dowdy. With decent clothes, she'd have been able to compete with any of them. Decent clothes and a decent haircut, I amended.

"Were you serious?" Asey repeated.

"Yes, I guess I was, then. But I know now that I was all wrong. Father couldn't have done such a thing."

"What changed your mind?"

"You said it wasn't father's gun that killed Red."

"Yup. But we don't know yet if your father sold that gun to Allen or to someone resemblin' Allen or if he took it himself an' just made up the rest. An' you was pretty sure last night."

"Don't forget I was pretty excited, too. Father's a dear, but he's not always the easiest man to get along with, and he and I don't always agree, like in this business of Red. I couldn't see why he had to pull the heavy father act. I couldn't see why he dragged me off to the Cape. I understand now, though, that he was just thinking about me in both cases."

She began to cover the little hole in the ground with her other toe. Her hands were moving restlessly inside her pockets.

"I never realized until last night," she continued, "that father was like that. I'd never heard him talk like that until after I—let loose. He meant all he said. He wasn't acting."

"I see. Then you didn't know Gilpin was here, an' you don't think your father killed him. An' you didn't leave the house Tuesday night?"

"No."

"Who d'you think killed Red?"

"Dan Allen," Aristene said promptly. "Red told me Dan was jealous of him. And father doesn't lie. I think Dan did buy the gun and left things behind to drag in father."

"But why should he pick on your father? Why him?"

"Why not? Red probably told him about—about everything," her voice wavered. "It probably made a good story. Take the way Dan plays bridge. He's so cool and so shrewd. He's the sort who throws away an honor to get the lead somewhere else six tricks ahead. And suppose they say that this signature on the form sheet is a forgery. That still doesn't mean he couldn't have had someone else buy the gun for him."

Asey brought out a villainous looking corn cob pipe, filled it and puffed for a minute or two in silence.

"Only one fly in all that liniment. Punch don't think Dan could of got out of the van Tuesday night without him knowing. Sure, it's pos'ble he did. Well, thank you. If you want to run along to your bridge, you can, though I'd be a one to think it wouldn't be much fun playin' with someone I thought was a murd'rer."

Aristene smiled. "You asked me who I thought killed Red and I told you what I thought, that is, the way the thing worked itself out in my mind. But I know Dan didn't, really."

Asey chuckled. "Okay. Run along."

Aristene got up quickly. She was evidently glad to get away. She knotted a square silk kerchief about her neck, but as she started for the house, Asey stopped her.

"Just a sec." He rose, leaned over and picked up something from the ground. "Didn't you drop this just then?"

It was a twisted piece of wire, another mutilated paper clip like the one Asey had shown me the day before.

"Oh, that? Yes, I did. It's no matter, really. Just a twisted paper clip. There were a couple in my pocket and I've been playing with them. Silly habit, isn't it? Father does it too."

11

"I TWIST pipe cleaners," Asey said cheerfully.

"Same idea. Okay. Thought it might be a pin or something."

It surprised me that he let her go into the house without further questioning, and after she was out of earshot, I asked why.

"Because if I'd got her suspicious, she'd of lied about it anyway. For her sake or her pa's. That grandstand play of his about doin' his best for little Teen made a big impression on her. I don't know now if she thinks he's guilty an' feels she ought to stick up for him out of sheer sent'ment, or if she thinks he's not guilty at all. She's just one of them—them ado—somethings—"

"Adolescents?"

"That's the word. Them ado-what-they-are's that changes their minds like they was a necktie or a string of beads. Get 'em excited on one side an' they hop to one c'nclusion. Pull 'em another way an' they're there before you are. I wish," he ended up critically, "that she wasn't so untidy."

"What are you going to do now?"

"What I ought to have done before, Mrs. Ballard. Go call on Nate Hopkins an' see what he knows about these here long-lost rel'tives of his, an' what they done on Tuesday night. But havin' let it go this far," he added as Jennie whanged the dinner gong, "I s'pose it won't do such a lot of harm to wait till after we had somethin' to eat. Like the time they tried to get Eldad Atwood at his store when his father took sick sudden an' they thought he was dyin'. He, Eldad, was sellin' stores to one of the schooner cap'ns an' he went right on barterin' an' bargainin'. Someone says, 'Eldad,' they says, 'your pa's dyin'. Whyn't you hurry?' An' Eldad just looked at 'em an' says real drawly, 'He won't die no quicker if I sell this flour first. An' he'll die a durn sight happier if I *do!*' Same idea, exactly."

After dinner we climbed into the low slung roadster and rolled off to town.

One of the state troopers stopped us at the crossroads, where a group of eight battered cars were parked.

As we drew up, six women, nine men and a dozen children grouped themselves about the car. Asey's prediction about tourists had been all too accurate; for some remote reasons of their own, they decided that Asey and I were deaf. Their audible comments about us, the roadster, the whole business of the murder and their own thoughts on it, made me writhe.

The trooper, prying two children off the bumper, addressed Asey wearily. "Damn curiosity seekers," he said. From his tone I couldn't quite gather whether his comment was general or specific. "We've chased droves away, but these are all-day suckers. Got the news from the radio, I guess. Papers won't be down till the night bus. Say, Asey, shall we let Toby Nickerson through? He says you need ice. Said he'd come back later."

"Let him come. An' for Pete's sakes get things fixed so's this mob won't filter through tonight. Tell 'em about the skunks. Also that we shoot any prowlers on sight. Anyway, keep 'em out."

"Right." Peremptorily the officer waved the spectators to one side and we sped along.

"What about groceries?" I asked. "Has anyone thought of them? I know I haven't. I'm not being the perfect hostess one bit."

"Syl got a lot of grub this mornin'," Asey informed me casually. "I had the others pay for it."

"What?"

"Yup. I explained to 'em that even if you could afford it, it wasn't exactly your duty to pour the horn of plenty over a lot of unasked boarders. Satterlee, he said I was right, an' as long as I said he had to stick around, he wanted his meat three times a day an' he couldn't ask for it if he was a guest. Edie Allen an' Hat said they was glad enough not to have to cook over a camp stove an' so, everybody agreein', I took up a c'lection."

"But you shouldn't have, Asey!"

"Why not? Now they're all gettin' what they want an' takin' a personal int'rest in their food. Might as well give 'em all the pleasure they can get."

We drove through Weesit to Orleans, made numerous turns on narrow tarred roads, and finally pulled up before a shingled brown house that looked as though it had been ordered by number from a "Build Your Own" catalogue.

"Ugly place." Asey echoed my thoughts. "Cousin Nate used to have a real pretty house here that b'longed to his great-grandfather, but it burned down an' they put this thing up. Them colored glass pieces in the door r'minds me of the old Meth'dist Chapel when I was a kid. Y'know, Nate's great-grandfather was quite a feller. Had a big farm here an' used to have three hired men. Drove 'em within an inch of their lives, too. Monday mornin's he'd go out to the barn an' ring the bell for 'em. They bunked in the barn loft. 'Monday mornin',' he'd yell. 'Monday mornin'. T'morrer's Tuesday, next day's Wednesday. Week's half over an' none of you lazy critters up yet!'"

"Everyone seems related down here," I said with a chuckle. "You and Syl, and Mr. Kemp, and now this man."

"Only people on earth that's got more rel'tives than Cape Codders," Asey stated, "is Scotchmen. Same clanny feelin'."

I accompanied him to the back door, where a tall lean man in blue dungarees and a blue shirt answered Asey's loud knock.

"H'lo," he said amiably, and nodded as Asey introduced me. "Come right in an' set down."

Turning his head toward the next room, he shouted for his wife.

"Hey! May! Comp'ny!"

"I'm comin'." Mrs. Hopkins, plump and bustling, charged into the kitchen.

She smiled at me and turned promptly to Asey.

"What's all this I hear about a murder over to Henderson's? I got something about it over the radio this noon, but only the fag end. I didn't really understand till Mary Peters called me up. They just announced it again now. What's Oscar an' Aristene got to do with it?"

Asey picked up the tiger cat who was sleeping peacefully on the kitchen rocker and calmly usurped his place before the stove. Before he answered he soothed the cat's ruffled feelings and settled it comfortably on his knees.

"Here's the story." Briefly, his outline punctuated by loud purrs from the cat, he told what had gone on since the previous morning. "Now," he concluded, "Satterlee says he went out Tuesday night. What time did he get back?"

"Dunno." Nate shook his head. "He was kind of sheepish

about it next day. Said he got in around two. I stayed up's long's I could, an' then I went to bed. Sure this is murder, Asey?"

"Yup."

"Well," Nate filled his pipe carefully, "I want to say right now that I don't know much about this feller even if he is a cousin. His—"

"We don't hardly know him at all," his wife broke in.

"His mother married my father's oldest brother Caleb," Nate continued, paying no attention to May's interruption. "I don't remember Uncle Cale much. He used to be a cap'n for Eldridge and Eldredge. I ain't seen Oscar for twenty years. About ten days ago he wrote that he was comin' to the Cape an' May thought we ought to ask him to stay here with us, so—"

"You thought so just as much as I did, Nate Hopkins! I told you it'd be a lot of extra work, but you said blood was thicker than water and—"

"So," Nate went on, "we did an' they come. That's the story on them, Asey. Sure he was around Weesit way that night?"

"Cop got him for speedin' just beyond Henderson's."

"Did, hey? Well, if you get a chance, I wish you'd have it put in the papers, what I just said. About him bein' a cousin but a stranger just the same. Blood's thicker than water, but when it comes to a question of—"

"Spillin' it," Asey finished gravely, "that's a dif'rent thing. I see your point. Did the girl go out Tuesday night?"

"No," Mrs. Hopkins answered, "she didn't. I'm sure of that. You see, Asey, we had ham for supper an' 'twas kind of salty. Seems we don't get such good hams as we used to. Well, all evenin' long at the club I was thirsty, an' I had to get up twice durin' the night to get a drink of water. Well, I met Aristene gettin' a drink too, both times."

"Know just when it was?"

"I do, because I looked both times at my clock. First was one-fifteen, an' the next time around four. I always look at my clock when I wake up durin' the night. Nate didn't tell me when I come in that Oscar was out, an' it was just chance that I didn't lock the side door. I shouldn't of slept a wink that night if I'd known that door was open, with all my silver right there for anybody at all to take."

"Lucky," Asey said. "Say, Nate, Oscar say anythin' about his night ramblin'?"

"Said he got lost. But I knew before he started out that he'd get lost. I told him he would. But he wouldn't listen. There was a good fog when he left, but I don't see what kept him later on when the fog sheered off. I drew him a picture of how to get places, but I didn't bother to mark ever bayb'ry bush an' phone pole, an' I guess he counted some cow path as a road. That mixed him up, prob'ly."

"Don't you r'call anythin' he might of let slip that'd give us some idea of where he was, an' if he really did get lost an' didn't wander out to the Henderson place?"

"Well," Nate struck a match and lighted his pipe before he answered, "well, near's I can figure out, he got off the track around them Hatch cottages in Eastham. Then he wandered around the ponds there. 'Course, he might of wandered to Wellfleet an' got mixed up around the ponds there, for all I really know. Some woman finally told him how to get back to the main road, but Lord only knows where he was when he run into her. Might of been in Chatham."

"Woman? He never told us about any woman!"

"I r'call now that I asked him how in time he did get himself found at last. Not many sign posts on them back roads, you know, an' such as they are, they're too old to be much good. Why, Asey, you know you can go to Wellfleet from Orleans an' not hit the main road more'n once on that little stretch b'low where the North Eastham meetin' house was before it burned down. Go all the way to South Wellfleet. An' there ain't more'n two signs an' they ain't right. Anyways, I asked him, an' he said he thought he seen a light an' yelled out an' some woman yelled back from a bush or somethin'. He couldn't tell where she was—"

"Woman in a bush!" Mrs. Hopkins said with some heat. "Pretty likely, ain't it? What'd a woman be doin' in a bush in some wild back road the middle of a cold foggy night? He made that up, that's what, or else he was stark ravin' crazy! I never did take much stock in this Cousin Oscar of yours, Nate Hopkins! I said as much the night he come!"

Asey clucked his tongue. "Tch, tch! Lady in a bush, huh? I didn't give him credit for havin' that much imag'nation. You tell Oscar these show folks was in town?"

"Said there was a show if they wanted to see it," Nate returned. "I don't think I told 'em much about it because all they seemed to want was to go to bed just as quick as they could."

"I told Oscar about it myself after Aristene went upstairs to bed," Mrs. Hopkins announced. "I said he ought to go even if she didn't want to. I told him Mary Peters had seen it in Hyannis an' she'd said it was a good show."

"Tell him all about it?"

"I don't know, Asey. I really don't. I might of, because Mary thought that red-headed magician was wonderful. He was the one that got killed, wasn't he? Well, I'm almost sure I must of mentioned him because Mary said so much about him. She said he wasn't just a good magician. She said he was sort of vibrant."

"Vibrant!" her husband snorted. "Vibrant! Mary'd say a scarecrow was vibrant if it had pants on!"

"That's mean of you, Nate, to say things like that about Mary. She's a real good woman. She wasn't the only one that thought the red-headed magician was nice. Ella—oh, you got to go, Asey?"

Asey put the tiger cat back on its pillow and smiled.

"Yup. I got a lot to do. Thank you both. May, you cleared the girl of all this mess, because if you seen her at one-fifteen, she couldn't of been over to Weesit killin' Red Gilpin then. Taken her a half an hour either way, easy. I only wish you'd gone with Oscar, Nate. It'd of saved me a lot of work, by an' large. But there's one name to cross off my list, an' that's a help."

"I'm glad," Mrs. Hopkins said heartily. "She seemed a nice girl, only sort of lonesome an' wistful like. Her mother died when she was born, poor dear, an' I guess it's all that Oscar could do to be a father to her without bein' a mother too."

Nate carried the Satterlee family's suitcases out to the roadster, and we departed after Asey had cautioned them against repeating anything he had told them.

"Well," Asey remarked as we drove off, "Aristene's out. But the Squire, now, he's in a spot. Maybe he did know Gilpin was here, an' maybe not. Even at that, he wouldn't of known just where to find him unless he'd written that Guild letter. And this lady in a bush! He told us he asked directions at a house, but he never said nothin' about any bush-whackin' female."

"It is a little bizarre," I said. "Oscar in the car, lady in the bush. Sounds like a—er—like a game. I do trust that the Squire wasn't up to any mischief."

"Goin's on," Asey grinned. "Can't never tell, can you?"

He pulled up before a brilliantly lighted store.

"I near forgot to get Punch his cig'rettes. Fact is, I got four orders for four dif'rent brands. P'ticular, those fellers. Get any for you?"

"No. Up to the present I've been unable to tell the taste of one cheap cigarette from another, advertising to the contrary. But take my money for 'em. At least I can supply tobacco for my guests even if they buy their own food."

Asey laughed and shook his head. When he came out of the store he was all but knocked down by an impetuous young man who'd just jumped out of a car drawn up in front of the roadster.

"Huh," Asey said briefly. "Barradio! I wanted to see you. Wait."

"What for?" Barradio asked sullenly. "I ain't done nothin'."

"Who said you had, pink shirt?" Asey gripped his elbow and pushed him toward the roadster. "Don't care a rap for what you ain't done. Look here. Tuesday night's all night dancin' in that joint of yours, ain't it?"

"I got a permit—"

"All night dancin' Tuesdays?"

"Yeah."

"Toby Nickerson there this last Tuesday?"

Barradio's close set eyes glittered.

"Well, was he or wasn't he? Make up your mind quick if I want you to say yes or no an' say it quick!"

"What you want him for?"

"Heard about the murder Tuesday night over at Henderson's?"

"No! No, I ain't!"

"Well, you heard about it now. Want to get mixed up in it? Then tell me if Toby was at that dive of yours Tuesday. Might as well not lie because I can check up on you real easy."

"He was there."

"How long?"

"From half past twelve till half past two or so."

"Alone?"

"I think he had a girl with him."

"Think? You know, Barradio. Who was she?"

"Never seen her before, Asey. Honest. She was some new maid."

Briefly but accurately he described Rose, even to her best red dress with the red pumps that matched.

"Did they go out while they was there?"

"Might of, but I don't think so."

"All right. Beat it. Next time you knock anyone down, say you're sorry for it even if you ain't."

"He described Rose!" I exclaimed as Asey got into the car. "Toby *did* lie. But Rose! Nobody heard her come or go. And who's that man?"

"That feller I talked with? Ramon Barradio. He runs a cheap dance hall outside of Weesit. I don't like him. He's a slippery customer. I'd like real well to run him out of town, but he'll get run out sooner or later anyway. Well, we'll look into the Rose an' Toby business. I can't see why Toby lied to me when he didn't have no reason, not knowin' anythin' about Red. Toby's a good kid. Only trouble with him is he's seen too many cheap movies an' he's tryin' real hard to be what he thinks is a sport."

We stopped at the Nickerson home, but Toby had already gone out to the cottage.

We found him chatting with a trooper as we came to the crossroads.

"Carey's wandering around with a flashlight," the officer said, "and Williams's stationed further along. Between us we ought to keep that bunch off. Just after you spoke about skunks a big fat one walked along here, and did those tourists scatter!"

"Why you holdin' Toby?"

"Saw your lights and I thought I'd let you go together. Didn't want you to meet him when he came back. That road's not so good for head-on meetings."

That was true enough. Scrub pines and scrub oaks lined either side, and the ruts were barely wide enough for one car.

"Okay," Asey said. "If you find anyone prowlin', bring 'em up to the house no matter who it is or what he's doin'. Even Harmon Peters. An' if you hear my whistle or any good noises, just pop along. No one's got any business here, no matter how silver-tongued they are."

"Right."

Toby went to his truck. "Shall I go along first, Asey, or will you?"

"You. Then if Carey or anyone stops you, I'll be behind with expl'nations."

Obediently Toby swung his truck out and started up the lane. We swung in behind him.

We hadn't gone a hundred feet before Toby stopped, and a flashlight played on the truck.

"All right, Carey," Asey called out.

Apparently Toby had stalled the truck, for I heard the grinding of a starter.

Instantly the truck backfired, three times.

"That," I told Asey excitedly, "was what I heard after three fifteen Tuesday morning. The same identical noises!"

"I'm inclined to think you're likely to be prob'ly right," Asey agreed. "I've been kind of thinkin' that Toby was prob'ly noise number two. Ever since I talked with Barradio. Remembered then I'd heard that truck backfirin' when Toby was over to Syl's."

12

A SEY WAITED until Toby had filled our ice box before he brought up the question of Tuesday night. Rose sat at the kitchen table and pretended to be entirely engrossed in a confession magazine. Her attitude would have been more convincing had her head or her eyes moved. But she stared long enough at one paragraph to have it implanted on her brain for life.

"Guess," Toby said as he fitted in the last small chunk, "that'll last you till Saturday. Well, I must be gettin' on."

He was obviously disappointed at not being able to see Rose alone.

"Just a sec," Asey said quietly. "What'd you lie to me about Tuesday night for?"

"Lie to you? But I—"

"Tobe, don't try to stall. Just tell me the truth, quick an' exp'ditious. You come up here around twelve Tuesday night an' took Rose," the confession magazine dropped suddenly to the floor, "to Barradio's all night dance. Come home here after three. Truck backfired. Any additions or c'rections?"

Rose, characteristically, began to weep.

"You— you—"

"I didn't tell him," Toby said soothingly. "Someone else did."

Rose kept on wailing.

Asey waited until she had calmed herself.

"Now, let's get this all straightened out. Why'd you lie, Tobe?"

"I thought Mrs. Ballard'd found out how late we was gettin' home an' that she was mad. I didn't want Rose to get fired."

"Rose, why'd you lie?"

"W-wu-wouldn't you lie," Rose sobbed, "if you'd gone out when you hadn't asked to and hadn't tut-told and someone got killed that night? And—"

"I see." Asey turned to me. "But still I don't. Mrs. Ballard, you don't seem to me to be the sort who'd fire a girl because she come in late, even if she hadn't asked to go out."

"That's exactly what I was going to say," I commented. "I'd undoubtedly have given you permission to go out. Why didn't you ask?"

"I thought you might think I shouldn't go out with a man I'd just met." Rose sniffled and Asey thoughtfully passed her over an immense white handkerchief. She blew her nose stridently and her spirits revived somewhat.

"Even so," I continued, "what on earth made you think I'd fire you for coming in late?"

"Didn't Mrs. Tavish tell you?"

"Tell me what?"

"I came in late a couple of times and the last time she said she was going to tell you. I thought she did, because she said you said if I came in late once more, you were going to fire me. When I said I was coming with you down here, she said I'd better watch my step."

"She told me nothing about you at all."

"I thought she did."

"Besides, what business of hers is it to run my household?" I demanded hotly. "How'd she know you were late, anyway?"

"I tripped over her dough. Bread dough. But she'd left the pan sticking way off the table, and I'd been to a beer party, and—um—er—"

I began to see. Mrs. Tavish, the cook, is a particularly ardent member of the anti-saloon league and the W. C. T. U. Beery breaths would have roused her considerably.

"I see," Asey said, "I see a whole lot."

He got up and disappeared into the living room, to return shortly with Judy.

"Now," he said to her as he shut the door, "now, why'n't you tell us Rose was drunk when she come home Tuesday night?"

"She and Toby—or rather, Toby—asked me not to. He said she said she'd lose her job if anyone found out." Judy fell into Asey's trap despite Toby's frantic high signs. "And since I'd spent a lot of time hunting for jobs, I thought it was only decent not to tell."

"But you have!" Rose gurgled like water running out of a bath tub. "You have. You just did!"

"Oh. Oh, I see. Well, if you fire her, Vic, I'll go along too."

"Don't be silly," I said. "I've no intention of firing her and I've been trying to make that clear for hours and hours."

"Look, Mrs. Ballard." Toby spoke up. "Let me explain about all this. I came here before twelve an' left the truck down the road a bit and Rose slipped out the front door."

"I discovered that," Judy interrupted, "because I went into the hallway to make sure I'd put the chain across the door and I found the door unlatched."

"Hat must have gone out afterwards," I remarked.

"I guess so. I didn't go near the front door again, and I didn't hear her. You see, I'd shut the door from the living room into the hall."

"Go on, Tobe," Asey ordered.

"We went to Barradio's an' danced, an' then this Charley Smith that clerks over in Chatham came up an' sat at our table. He had a bottle of gin with him, but Rose an' I didn't have any even though he wanted us to. Well, he finished it an' got more from Barradio. When he came back he still wanted us to have some, but I said no. After I smashed up my car I decided not to drink any more when I had to drive. That's how I come to be usin' the truck that night. My own car's smashed. But Rose took a little—"

"And it was the worst stuff I ever tasted," Rose broke in. "When I finished it—I wouldn't have, only Toby'd gone off—and this feller made me. Well, when I finished—wheee!" Her gesture was expressive.

"I can b'lieve it," Asey assured me. "I seen the results of Barradio's likker before. Bill Porter got some once an' it took an inch of porcelain off our kitchen sink."

"When I come back an' found her like that," Toby continued, "I took her out an' walked her around an' give her black coffee an' all. Then I decided I'd better get her home. She'd been sick by then an' she was nearly asleep. Well, the back door was locked an' the front door was locked an' I would of opened a kitchen window only I couldn't."

"My own burglar-proof locks!" Rose said.

"I didn't dare try the other windows, so I knocked soft, an' Miss Dunham come an' let Rose in. I told her how the last thing

Rose said was not to let Mrs. Ballard know an' I told her the whole story then."

"So that's the explanation of what you were doing up after three?" I asked.

Judy nodded. "And did I have a time with that lass, too! She was half out and half asleep. I simply couldn't get her to move. There wasn't any chance of getting her upstairs to her room without waking you all, so I bedded her on the kitchen floor and stuck an alarm clock beside her, set for six o'clock. I'd intended to come out and make sure that she woke up, but I never opened an eye till I heard her setting the table for breakfast."

"Then I left," Toby said, "after Miss Dunham took charge of Rose. The truck backfired. I just skedaddled. I didn't have the courage to see if anyone had heard an' got up. The wind was blowin' a gale, though, an' the surf was noisy, so I guessed maybe no one heard anyway."

"See anyone when you left?"

"Nary a soul."

"Any cars?"

"I wasn't meetin' cars. I gave the ole ice wagon all she had. I had to get up at six. I thought I saw a light on the ice house cut-off, but I wouldn't be sure."

"Okay. If I send for you, Toby, you come runnin'. Rose, I'd advise you to lay off drinkin' with strangers or otherwise. It ain't nice for a young girl."

Rose nodded. "I'm right on the wagon. You don't need ever to worry about my drinking again, Mrs. Ballard, because I ain't going to. Not after the way I been feelin' since yesterday morning. Miss Judy, you was swell."

"Even though Asey tripped me up. You're a tricky sort, Sherlock. When you get to purring, you're dangerous. But I'm glad you've got it all cleared up. It's been weighing on my mind."

It had been bothering me, too, and I was glad to have the thing settled.

Before I went to bed, I added to my data. I started a brand new heading: OUT.

Aristene headed the list. Although she might have had a motive for killing Red, she was without any shadow of a doubt elsewhere when Red was killed.

Rose was out of the picture, too. Even if she had been in any condition to murder anyone, she'd been away from the place at one. So had Toby.

I put Judy down, too. Even though we could not prove that she might not have had a motive for shooting Red, and an opportunity as well, still there was the fact that she'd not known until Monday afternoon that she was coming to Weesit. She couldn't have written the letter signed by Maynard Guild. True, the gun could have come into her possession. Asey's "Anythin's Possible" theory always held. But that she might have got hold of that particular gun seemed altogether too remote. In addition to all that, I believed her story.

So there were four people, at least, about whom there was no further need to speculate. Somehow the appearance of some definite fact after two days of dithering possibilities made me feel better. At the rate of four exonerations a day, I felt, the mess would soon be over. I slept soundly Thursday night.

Not until we were settled out in the wicker chairs after breakfast Friday morning did Asey call out Satterlee and tackle him on the subject of the lady in the bush.

"Oh," he said pleasantly, "didn't I tell you about her, Asey? By George, I must have!"

"No," Asey said, "you left her in the bush an' she int'rests me a lot. Tell me more."

"Well, it was—why, I don't know the exact time. But it wasn't very long before that cop stopped me. You got that fixed yet?"

"The speedin' business? I'll try. Go on."

"Let's see. I was on this road. This side road. I thought I saw a light. I yelled out and said I'd been lost for hours and could anyone tell me how to reach the main road."

"What kind of a road was you on?"

"Just a road," Satterlee explained vaguely, picking at a button on his vest. "Just a road."

"I know, I know," Asey retorted with some show of impatience, "the sort of thing that stretches out like a ribbon an' you go on it. Road. But what kind? What'd it look like?"

"It was a lot like the one coming out to this cottage the other night, when you brought us here. I couldn't tell much in the dark. There were narrow sandy ruts, and grass grew in the middle of 'em and scrub pines on either side of the road. Just a common side road, Asey. I yelled out; you see, I didn't know what the light was, or anything, and I didn't want to scare anyone. On the other hand, I didn't want to stop and chat with any stranger at that time of night in a lonely place even though I had my gun with me. So I yelled out."

"What then?" Asey asked wearily.

"This woman's voice answered. She said to turn around and— by George, I've forgotten just what the directions were, now. Isn't that a pity? But they worked. I was on the main road in no time at all. Then I noticed this sign that said 'To Weesit' and you better believe I hustled. Just as I was hitting her up, that cop came along and asked me where was the fire."

"See the woman?"

"No."

"Well, where was she, just?"

"I don't know," the Squire said helplessly. "The voice just came from the bushes. It—it was a nice voice."

"That's good," Asey said heartily. "That's fine. I'm glad of that."

Satterlee looked at him with suspicion.

"Glad she had a *nice* voice," Asey explained. "I'd hate to think she had a nasty voice. Tch, tch!"

"You don't believe me!"

"Honest," Asey grinned widely, "would you if I was tellin' the tale?"

"Well," Satterlee admitted, "there is a—a—"

"A sort of murk about it. Foggy like the night."

"But it wasn't foggy then." The Squire passed over Asey's trap. "It was almost clear. And really, it may sound sort of funny, but it's true."

Asey sighed. "Yes, I s'pose it's just the crazy sort of thing that would be true. All right. That's all. What is it, Syl? Safe-breakers crashed through?"

"Telegrams for Mrs. Ballard. Sam Howes just brought 'em. Said he didn't stay at the station after train time last night an' he didn't get 'em all till this mornin' anyway. Tried phonin' me about 'em, but I guess that was b'fore Jennie an' me went home. They seem kind of hefty messages."

He delivered his burden and departed.

"These will be from my son George," I prophesied, looking

at the envelopes which had neatly been numbered one, two and three respectively by Mr. Howes.

And I was right. The first was from Chicago. It was dated Thursday evening at seven-ten.

"Flew to Chicago today on urgent business stop"

George, by the way, is one of the few people I've ever known who actually punctuates his telegrams with "stop."

"Glad to receive your assurance that you stood trip well stop address Athletic Club till Monday stop wire progress stop love George."

The next was dated Thursday at nine.

"Your wire regarding trouble at Weesit received stop what has happened stop do not understand stop wire all details at once stop was it an accident with automobile or what stop I told you that girl was no fit companion stop is the car hurt stop of course I shall come if you are injured stop let me know at once George."

That, apparently, was an answer to the telegram which I'd sent him at Boston, telling him to discount newspaper reports and not to come to Weesit. Probably it had been forwarded from his office. I'd been anticipating gory details from the press and it seemed I'd done just that and anticipated too much.

Asey whistled at the sight of number three.

"That ain't a telegram," he said as I unfolded four sheets. "That's a short story."

"And it's written on both sides of the paper in very small handwriting," I said. I glanced over it briefly and laughed. "It's not a short story, either. It's an essay on parents with a short appendix of rebukes for same. The murder has just burst on George's consciousness and these are his reactions. He now gets the point of my telegram. Oh, I've got to read this to you, Asey! For your benefit I'll eliminate the stops, though they make it much funnier. If George were here and saying this to me, I'd probably be impressed, but this way it just makes me laugh. Listen—

"*'Tuned in Boston station for New England news at eleven. Horrified to discover what you term trouble is murder at your cottage. Where did you pick these troupers up? It is high time you discovered the folly of chance acquaintances. I have no doubt but what that companion of yours or maid is mixed up with all this if not actually responsible. Had you taken Mrs. Tavish or Cousin Mercy or responsible people this would not have happened. Assume you also will be involved. Trust you are assured now of truth of my statements Monday regarding your ability to make plans. Have often tried to impress on you that only trouble would result from your habit of picking up every Tom, Dick and Harry and treating them as social equals in your informal and casual fashion.'*"

"Leetle mite hot around the collar, ain't he?" Asey asked with a chuckle.

"You've heard practically nothing yet. There's at least five dollars' worth more—

"*'Am arranging to conclude business tomorrow if possible and will fly to Boston at earliest opportunity. Will drive from there directly to Weesit. Report says you are actually aiding this hired man of Bill Porter's. Trust report is false. That you have not taken leave of all your senses. Think of horrible publicity.'*

I broke off. "What about the papers, Asey?"

"They done a pretty good job. I seen a bunch of 'em late last night that Syl got for me. Didn't show 'em to you or mention 'em because I didn't know how you'd take 'em. Run sort of like this: Cape Sherlock Aided by Society Woman. Vic Ballard, Famed as First Woman to Wear Hobble Skirt in Boston, Rises from Sick-bed to Play Watson. Adin Ballard's Widow was Pneumonia Convalescent."

"How amazing! How could they have remembered that hobble skirt affair?"

"Dunno. They did. How 'bout the rest of your message?"

"It's worthy of Patrick Henry. Oh, how mad George must have been! I'll wager he smashed electric light bulbs. He used to when he was really furious as a child—

"I have wired Stephen Crump to use all his power to stop slanderous stories. I have wired Janet under no conditions to leave Maine even though you may summon her. I shall come just as soon as I can. You absolutely must now realize futility of my letting you make your own plans.'"

Asey laughed. "He is sort of rhetor'cal like, ain't he? Kind of expected him to end up with askin' God to save the Com'nwealth of Mas'chusetts, like a Thanksgivin' Procl'mation. Somehow he don't seem the—well, he don't sound like you at all, Mrs. Ballard."

"He doesn't and he isn't," I said, and I was surprised to hear myself say so. "Our viewpoints are—well, George's family were friends of Adin's. His father was a minister. Very brilliant, but a little pompous. Adin always said he could see George perfectly as a ruling Puritan father, the sort who called the Indians heathen and tried to convert them. Or burning witches. But," I added hastily, "I'm tremendously proud of George, even if we don't see eye to eye on a lot of things. He really is a genius, Asey."

Asey nodded. "He was right in wirin' Stephen Crump. I know him, y'see. Stephen wired me right off, I got the message earlier. Said for me to do all I could for you an' for you to call on him yourself or through me, any time. Said he'd do what he could about the papers."

"That's good," I said. "That may calm George. I can tell that he's furious. In one sense he has a right to be. But he did annoy me dreadfully the other day, bursting in on me with all his plans about coming here, and I took things into my own hands just to annoy him and show him I wouldn't be bossed. It looks as though I'd have been better off if I'd let him manage things his own way. Asey, what'll we do with George when he comes? I know he'll be pretty angry."

"I'll cope with him," Asey promised. "He sounds a lot like Bill Porter's brother Jimmy. Blows off a lot of steam, but you—oh."

Sylly Mayo appeared around the corner of the house.

"Syl, you look like a satisfied cat," Asey said. "Don't tell me you went an' found somethin' else?"

Syl beamed and passed over a tube of toothpaste. It was unusual, so far as I could see, only in that whoever owned it had rolled it neatly from the bottom after they'd used it, instead of just punching the paste out from the plumpest part.

"How'd you find that? Oh," Asey answered himself without giving Syl a chance to open his mouth, "Oh, I just thought what I'd do if I was a tube of toothpaste. I know, Syl, I know. Where'd you find it an' what makes you think it's important?"

"Found it under the top step of the beach stairs. Not three

feet from where Gilpin was. Hadn't found it b'fore b'cause I'd never gone under the steps."

"Well," Asey scrutinized it, "what in time this's got to do with the murder is beyond what I laughin'ly call a brain. Syl, go in an' ask who uses this kind. I never seen this brand before. It don't even r'call a bad tenor. Can't see," he said as Syl dashed away, "why folks don't use tooth-powder. Cheaper an' a lot better for your teeth anyways. Your dentist," he smiled, "does."

In a few minutes Edie Allen appeared.

"Syl says you've found my toothpaste," she said cheerfully, "and I'm no end grateful. I've been using Dan's and it tastes like radiators smell in the fall. Banana oil and gilt paint. Yes, that's mine, all right. I always squeeze from the end of the tube and roll up. No one else in the bunch does. No one else uses that kind anyway. Where'd you find it?"

"When'd you lose it?" Asey countered.

"I haven't seen it since Tuesday night. At that point it disappeared from human ken. Where'd it turn up?"

"By where Gilpin was killed," Asey told her, his voice purring.

Edie Allen drew in her breath sharply. Her face was white as she sat down on one of the wicker chairs. Her poise, her self-possession, her bantering manner, all left her.

"How'd it get there?" she asked in a small scared voice.

"That," Asey told her firmly, "is what you're goin' to explain right now!"

13

"But I didn't go out Tuesday night!"

"Sure?" Asey fingered the tube. "Sure? You use this Tuesday night an' then it gets legs an' walks out an' lands itself underneath the top step of the beach stairs, an' stays there quiet an' comf'tble till the eagle-eyed Syl crawls under an' drags it out. Well," Asey's drawl was even drawlier than usual, "well, they claim a lot of these toothpastes is re-mark'ble, an' I'm beginnin' to b'lieve that maybe perhaps they must be almost right."

His manner annoyed Edie.

"But don't be absurd, Asey! Toothpaste doesn't just—"

"Just happen places. No."

"Oh, don't laugh! I mean, after all, someone must have left it or dropped it there—"

"Cur'ous," Asey agreed, "but that's just what I been thinkin' too. Let's see. Dan was the one who brought in your night stuff from the van?"

"Yes. He threw together some things of Hat's and mine when Mrs. Ballard asked us to spend the night. Put everything in a suitcase and brought it indoors."

"What you do with the paste after you used it?"

"Put it back into its place in the little rubberized case I carry that and my toothbrush in. I'm sure of that."

"Yet you ain't seen it since. Well, just ask Hat to come out, will you? You needn't tell her why."

Hat Allen strolled out, a cigarette held loosely between her long fingers. She wore a skirt of unbelievably vivid orange and a very severe white sweater with a high turtle neck. All in all, she seemed to me much more of a "show" person than did any of the others. Her invariably heavy make-up, dark tan powder and plum colored lipstick, added to that impression.

"I'm so glad you found Ede's toothpaste," she remarked. "She's groveled under the bed for it and even accused me of swiping it. You see, she left it behind her in the bathroom Tuesday night, and I took it back to the room and put it among her things. I'd completely forgotten about it in all—in all the confusion."

"But she said she'd put it in her case herself."

"She's wrong. She left it behind her. She's prone to be untidy and I loathe seeing stray toilet goods strewn around. She'd left it balanced precariously on that little glass shelf. Really, that's how it was. I didn't pay much attention to her complaints about having lost it. Seemed a little indecent to fuss about lost toothpaste. In fact, I didn't remember about picking it up till Syl brought it in. I didn't dare tell her at that point, having sworn I knew nothing about it. Where did it turn up?"

Asey told her.

"How could it have got there?" she demanded in some surprise.

"That's what we're trying to find out," Asey explained patiently. "Now, when you picked it up, what'd you do with it? Stick it in your pocket?"

"Probably. But I'm pretty sure I put it back among her things later. Of course, I might not have. I was frightfully tired that night, and when you're all worn out you do things more or less mechanically. Even if I'd left it in my pocket, I still don't see how it could have got underneath the steps. When I went out for my cold cream I just cut around the corner of the house and made for the van. I didn't wander out toward the bluff at all."

"Didn't happen to have a hole in your pocket, did you?"

Hat smiled. "Yes, I did. I mended it yesterday."

"Then," Asey said, "that problem seems to solve itself some. You picked up the tube an' stuck it in your pocket. An' there was a hole in the pocket of your dressing gown. Was it your dressing gown, by the way?"

"No. My polo coat. Dan didn't think of such things as dressing gowns."

Asey was silent. I knew that he was thinking of that down on Red Gilpin's blue serge coat.—Yet he'd already proved that her coat couldn't have rubbed off.

"An' you didn't go near the head of the bluff. Huh. That's where this gets mixed. How'd it get there if you didn't go there? Sure you didn't stroll to the head of the steps?"

"Positive. It was chilly and I was tired and cold. Practically all I wanted was to get back inside that soft bed and sleep. I did no wandering about the edge of the cliff."

"Pity we can't prove that."

Hat nodded as she stepped on her cigarette stub.

"Yes. You've nothing but my word for it all."

Dan came out of the kitchen door. "Asey, will she be back soon? It's her deal—"

"Run along," Asey said. "I should think you'd be sick an' tired of the sight of a pack of cards!"

"Don't forget," Hat told him, "that we haven't had time to play for months."

I noticed as Dan held the door open for her that both she and her brother had the same loping walk, and that both were very nearly the same height. While Dan was stocky and short for a man, Hat was tall for a woman.

I remarked as much to Asey. "There's a lot more family resemblance between those two," I concluded, "than I had noticed at first."

"I been toyin' with the idea of Hat, myself," Asey admitted. "She's more or less the same height. I take it she's the real actor in the bunch, too. Last night when I went into the livin' room to get Judy while I was checkin' up on Toby an' Rose, she was givin' a real classy p'formance for Oscar. She was bein' a mad mother whose kid'd got a failure in English, an' she couldn't see why, on account of the kid's always talkin' English since she was born. Sounds kind of dull when I tell it, but while she was doin' it, she had Satterlee in stitches. Like to bust, he was. Even the bridge table was stoppin' to listen, an' you might call that a major triumph."

I laughed.

"But the point is," Asey brought out his corn cob, "point is this. I'd sort of taken it for granted that whoever bought that gun was a man. But it might not of been."

"Hat was shopping with Edie," I reminded him.

"Said she was. But if you remember, Edie had to wait till Hat spoke about shoppin' for stockin's before she thought of it. Well, leave that for the time bein'. Here's Hat. Same height as Dan. Her eyebrows grow like his naturally, an' bein' a make-up artist it wouldn't be a lot of trouble for her to build eyebrows even if her own is shaved off. She's got a low husky voice, an' I heard her mimic Dan to perfection once or twice. She could of pretended to be Dan. She could of written the letter. She could of bought the gun. Admits she went out. An' here's this bloomin' toothpaste lyin' near where Red was. An' we can't prove how long she was out or that she didn't go near there."

"You've everything against her except a motive," I commented.

"She's a woman, ain't she? An' even Mary Peters," he chuckled, "even Mary said there was somethin' vibrant about Red. An' Hat was in more or less pretty constant 'sociation with him."

"But Punch didn't think—"

"Yup. Punch didn't think there was anythin' between 'em. Now, Punch's a nice boy, but he ain't the thinkin' kind. He knew Red admired Edie b'cause Red said so. But that don't mean that he never craved Hat, just b'cause he never told Punch about it."

"Even then," I argued, "she and Edie were shopping the afternoon during the time the gun was purchased."

Asey grinned.

"What does that foxy look mean?"

"Means," he laid down his pipe and rose, "I'm goin' to get Edie an' jolt her mem'ry."

He went into the house and brought her back.

"Now," he said, "Mrs. Ballard an' I was gettin' into an argument. Was Hat playin' bridge yest'day when we come up from the cellar?"

"Asey, did you tear me away from five hearts doubled to ask me that?"

"Uh-huh. Was she playin' bridge or backgammon?"

"Why, I don't know."

"Mrs. Ballard thought it was bridge."

"I guess she must have been, then. I don't know, even though it seems to me that Dan and I were playing Aristene and Punch. I'm probably wrong."

Asey smiled triumphantly at me. "See? As a matter of fact she was playin' backgammon with Satterlee. It was just when I saw Dan dealin' with his left hand."

"Of course!" Edie said. "What a goose I am! But I've the world's worst memory, Asey. I'm never really sure about things unless someone jogs me. Even then, if I think differently, I've never the spirit to say so for fear of being wrong."

"Then," Asey began to get to his point, "if you can't remember what happened yesterday with any sort of what you might call def'niteness, it's dollars to doughnuts you can't remember what happened over a month ago."

"It's a million to one. Don't tell me you're going to pick on April first or February sixth and ask me about it and tell me I've got to answer yes or no. I'd have to take a calendar and a ream of paper and just brood about it for ten days or so. I shouldn't be sure of being right even then."

"Okay. But I'm after May fourth again."

"That's easy," Edie said with relief, "Hat remembered that day. We bought stockings and she had a corn."

"Uh-huh. But in view of what you just said about not even darin' to say dif'rent even if you thought dif'rent, maybe you'd like to think again."

"D'you think Hat made a mistake?"

"Just so. Think about it again. Start from scratch an' forget this stockin' an' corn business."

Edie lighted a cigarette. "Hm. That's a tall order. What day of the week was May fourth? Saturday?"

"Let's see." Asey pulled a tiny memorandum book from his

pocket. "Let's see. April twenty-first. An'versary of the battle of San Jacinto. Huh. What sort of mis'laneous stuff they stick into these things! Here we are. May fourth. This don't give days. Just dates. But maybe I can figger out from what I done. Yup. It was a Saturday."

"How can you tell?"

"Note here says Bill Porter was due for the weekend an' to bake some beans for supper. That means," Asey smiled, "Saturday in this part of the country."

"Beans," Edie said. "Beans. Ah. I think I've got it. I remember wondering at the time if Hat was right about going shopping. She was right about Dan and Red getting things for the car, because we left Sunday and we had the things when we started. I'm sure it never would occur to any of us to have got 'em till the day before we left. And I recall that Punch had to mend Judy. She was coming apart or something."

"What about beans?"

"I'm coming to 'em. But I do think we got the stockings Friday. You see, some local matron asked Hat and me to tea on Saturday. I've forgotten what her name was, but Aristene would probably know it. Neither of us wanted to go, but she'd come to the show several times and Dan said she was good for a block of tickets Saturday night and that we'd better go. So we flipped a coin to see which would represent the troupe, and I lost. And I'd never in the world have been sure if you'd not spoken of beans, Asey."

"How come?"

"Well, the local matron asked me to stay for dinner, and murmured apologetically that her husband's father lived with them and that he insisted on having beans for dinner Saturdays. I told her nothing would give me greater pleasure, but that we were all having dinner together. And the mention of beans inspired me to order 'em for dinner later. When Red came in, he asked if they were any good and had some too. The others jeered at us. I remember it all very clearly now."

"Good ole beans," Asey said feelingly. "What did Hat do, havin' lost, or won—just which way you look at it—about the party?"

"I wouldn't know. Probably window shopped or went to a second-hand book store. She picked up so many battered first editions that the van got glutted and we made her pack 'em up and send 'em to a friend of hers in Connecticut who has two attics. It broke Hat up."

"Um. Thanks."

"Look, Asey, what's all this for? What difference does it make where Hat was that afternoon? It was a man who bought the revolver from Satterlee, wasn't it?"

"So he says. But havin' seen Oscar, don't you think a woman dressed up as a man could fool him?"

Edie hesitated.

"An' Hat's acted like a man, ain't she?"

"Mm."

"Good at it?"

"Mm. Not very."

"Well, send her out, anyway."

Hat seemed genuinely distressed when Asey informed her that she had been wrong about the date of the stocking buying.

"I'm sure I'm right. Look, somewhere in the van among my things I think I've still got the slip for those stockings. I'm just one of those people who hangs onto slips and receipts long after the things they came with have worn out. Wait till I see if I can't find it. It should have a date on it."

"That's exactly like George," I said to Asey after she went running off. "George has years and years of files at his house, cramfull of receipts and credit slips and cash slips and all that sort of thing. He worries over my slipshod habit of throwing mine away every week."

When Hat came back with the pink slip of paper she looked distinctly uneasy.

"Asey, I was wrong. We bought the stockings on the third. The fourth must have been the day Ede went to that hen party and I roamed around Nashua wishing that something would happen."

"'Member what you done?"

"Oh, I just wandered about. You know how hard it is to kill time. Looked in shop windows and strolled around a book store. Only they were awfully aggressive. They wouldn't let me browse, they wanted me to break down and buy a new book! I remember standing outside a department store where a lot of people were waiting for other people and pretending that I was waiting too. That's one of my favorite amusements. It's such fun to watch women come up and say, 'My dear, was I really so frightfully late?' And usually they damn well know they are."

"So you can't prove where you was either?"

"Either?" Hat looked sharply at Asey. "No. But it makes no difference, does it?"

"You look like Dan, or would if you took the trouble to dress up."

"Asey, you can't be insinuating that I bought that infernal gun?"

"It's pos'ble."

"Oh, it's possible! But I didn't. Asey, I was fond of Red. If I weren't engaged to a perfectly good professor of mathematics who can't possibly afford to marry me for years till he finishes putting a young brother through school, I really think I might have gone so far as to have fallen in love with Red. But, Asey, granting that this toothpaste business and that my whereabouts Tuesday night are against me, and the afternoon of May fourth, too, still I didn't have any reason to kill Red."

Asey said nothing at all.

"You have to love someone a lot or hate him a lot to kill him, unless you're insane or something," Hat continued earnestly. "I'm not insane, and I neither loved Red nor hated him. We were just good friends, nothing more. When you live with anyone the way we've been living, rolling around from pillar to post, you get to see people's faults. I saw Red's the first week he was with us. I saw then how beastly he could be to women who were attracted by him, without in the least meaning to be beastly at all. I saw how wearing that infectious, oh-what-a-grand-life manner of his could be. It turned out to be a little wearing for us once in a while, too. Edie always said her only criticism of Red was that he never let her have a good gloom. You know everyone likes to be glum and blue and nasty once in a while. Red never gave you a chance to be glum, or serious, either. He was just always bright and shining, and he never hit much more than the surface of things."

I began to see the truth of Punch's statement that Hat had a head on her shoulders, and a man's brain.

"Really," she went on, "though I don't know anything about it, I should imagine he'd never have been such a tearing success in business. He was a wizard with engines and he loved to tinker. But you can't think of him as being constructive. He could mend things, but he couldn't make 'em. As for his sleight of hand—he could copy, but not one of his tricks was original. It was his manner, and even though I detest the phrase, his personal magnetism, that made him seem such a whiz. Somehow I'll always see that boy with his tall silk hat on the side of that red head of his, his wand waving in his hand, changing three purple handkerchiefs into an American flag. Well, that sums it all up, Asey. That's the way I felt about him."

"I see," Asey said.

"And you don't believe me because you think I'm acting. I'm not. I've told you the truth always, except in that matter of May fourth. That was a mistake, and I've admitted it. I could have denied ever seeing that foul tube of toothpaste, or touching it. I could have kept quiet about going out Tuesday night for my cold cream. I greatly doubt if you'd ever have discovered it, either. I could have withheld that stocking receipt and bullied Edie into saying that I was right. It's very easy to sway Edie. But I didn't do any of those things. I told you the truth because you said that if we had nothing to hide, it would all be right no matter how devastating it sounded."

She stopped as a motorcycle roared up the road.

A state trooper dismounted and passed a package and an envelope over to Asey.

"From Boston. About that New Hampshire business. Parker sent them to you."

14

ASEY JERKED open the envelope with his thumb, and Hat and the trooper and I watched him expectantly as he perused the contents.

Somehow the news of the letter's arrival spread; through Rose and Jennie, I suspected. They had been gaping out of the kitchen window all morning long.

Before Asey finished reading, the entire crowd had come out of the house, and sat or stood around him. Everyone pretended to be nonchalant, but the tension was unmistakable.

Punch scratched a match on the sole of his shoe, and the usually controlled Aristene jumped a foot at the sound. Sylly Mayo pulled at his mustache till I thought he would drag it out by the roots.

Overhead great billowy clouds rolled lazily out to sea. There was a smell of pine trees and a scent of wild roses mixed with the sharp tang of the salt air. Had there been a golf course near-by, an airplane observer might have taken us for an interested group waiting for a referee to announce the winner of a handi-cap match. We looked just as festive as all that. But we didn't feel festive one bit.

Asey finished reading and cleared his throat.

"Well," Dan said impatiently, "what's the bad word?"

"From what I been able to gather from this," Asey said grave-ly, "there ain't no p'ticular bad word. It's just all bad news."

"What d'you mean, Asey? Tell us, for Heaven's sakes! Haven't we waited long enough?"

"Yup. Well, after consid'rable trial an' trib'lation, they opened Satterlee's box. There was a loose leaf notebook in it all right. But it didn't have no forms in it about gun buyers."

"You mean that after all this, there wasn't any form with my name there at all?"

"Nope. There wasn't any forms there at all. They looked at this book an' sent it down." Asey picked up the bundle and opened it.

"What is it?"

"Seems, 'cordin' to them New Hampshire fellers, to be Satter-lee's diary an' love letters when he was courtin'."

"Those were in my den!" Satterlee was dumbfounded. "They were in my den! They couldn't have been in my box! How'd they get there?"

He stretched out his hand for the chunky black notebook.

"The rest of you," Asey said wearily, "can go back into the house or somewhere. I want to talk to Mr. Satterlee all by him-self."

"These are my letters. It's my old diary," Satterlee explained. "I had my old letters punched and put them all together. I—"

"Yup," Asey said grimly, "I can see that they're your ole letters an' your diary. I don't care much about 'em. What I want to know is, where's that loose leaf notebook of forms? What you tell us 'twas in your box for an' have us go to all this work? You just do a little hard thinkin' an' make up your mind once an' for all where them forms is. An' make it up quick!"

"But I'm sure I don't know where it can be," Satterlee protested. "I thought I'd put it in my box. You see, it's like this. My old box in the vault got too small and I gave it up and got this newer and bigger one."

"That was what you told us before. Glad you ain't changin' that part of it."

"And I transferred all the papers and things from my old box to the new one. There was a lot of room left over and I thought of all the things I really should keep in a safe place. I made a list of them and put them all together and took them to the new box. Well, on my way to the bank, I stopped in at the store for some additional papers. Now, sometime about there, I suppose that the gun form book must have got mixed up with those things. At least, I couldn't find it the next day, and I decided that was what had happened. I intended to get it out, even though I didn't have much need of it. There were plenty of blanks at the store. But then I lost my box keys."

"In other words," Asey said, "what you told us at first holds true up to here. Your gun forms got mixed with other papers an' got into the vault by mistake. But how—"

"That's it. Now, I had this notebook of letters with me, too. I was going to put it in the box because I didn't want anything to happen to it. It had some of my wife's letters in it and I thought Teen would like to have them when she was older. Well, at the store I remembered I had some more of her letters in one of the pigeon holes of my desk. So I left this book out—or at least I thought I did—and took it and the other letters home. I intended to punch the sheets and put them in the notebook and then put that in the vault. I had some snapshots of Teen when she was a baby and I was going to paste them on pages and put them in too. I thought this book was home in my den. But I guess, since they were both black and both about the same size—"

"That you took the m'mentoes to the vault an' left the gun forms in your den instead. How come you didn't find out before you come here?"

"You know how it is about things like that. You intend to do 'em right off, and then you don't seem to get around to it. Fact is, I didn't even look at the book after I got home, even though it was a week or two ago. You see, Teen was pretty blue, and I didn't know what to do about her—well, that's all."

"So this durn gun book is sittin' in your den right now?"

"Well," Satterlee said lamely, "as far as I can remember, it was on the top of my desk in the den. Of course I might have taken it upstairs to my bedroom, but I don't think I did."

Asey groaned. "Anyone got keys to your house, or we got to get into that with an acetylene torch, too?"

"The cleaning woman, Katy Phelan, she's got keys. She could get in."

"Katy Phelan." Asey wrote it down. "Okay. Now, you just sit an' think of all the places you might of left that book, an' tell me. Then I'll hop up an' phone Nashua an' have the p'lice get hold of Katy an' your keys. An' I'll tell 'em to go hunt in all the places except the ones you mentioned."

"Really, Asey, if it isn't on the top of my desk in the den, then it's on the little table by the side of my bed. I'm sure of that."

"Thank God," said Asey piously, "for small blessin's. It's nice to find you sure about somethin'. Comin', Mrs. Ballard?"

Before I could answer a car drove out to the cottage and Parker walked over to us.

"Not such good news," he said to Asey as Satterlee went back into the house.

"I'll say it ain't. Couldn't even call it tidin's. Humpf. I was plannin' that at least this handwritin' expert could look at that signature an' say like a flash, that nobody in this bunch wrote it or that so-an'-so was the one. An' now see what's happened!"

"But you saw that Satterlee says it's in his house," Parker remarked. "We've just go to get it and have it sent to Boston."

"Yup. That's all. But I got my doubts."

"What d'you mean, Asey?"

"I mean, I got a notion we won't ever find that form at all."

"Why? D'you think Satterlee's destroyed it and that he's deliberately side-tracking us?"

"Couldn't say. But I got a sort of prem'nition that we're never goin' to set eyes on that form at all. You know," Asey grinned, "just the same way Ross Sears used to have prem'nitions about no'theast storms. Fellers used to ask him how he knew a no'theaster was comin' an' he'd snicker an' squeal out in that high-pitched voice of his, 'Can't tell ye, can't tell ye! It's a gift o' God. Gift o' God!' Well, this feelin' of mine is the same thing. Gift of God."

"But do you think Satterlee killed Gilpin?"

Asey shrugged. "After my first dealin's with the feller I set him down as too dumb. He seemed almost too dumb to be true. But you got to have some brains to stick a false clue around, an' still more to leave a thing like that cartridge box with your own name on it. I didn't give Satterlee credit for bein' able to leave a clue behind pointin' to him, so's he could up an' say it was silly *for* him to do any such thing. But now I'm wonderin' if it's pos'ble for him to be as dumb as he seems. It ain't natural."

"I see. I'll go up with you while you phone, Asey. Had lunch?"

"I don't need it now. But Mrs. Ballard does. I'll swallow a glass of milk while she goes through the motions of eatin'."

So, after I'd gone through the motions, Asey, Parker and I set off for the village in the roadster.

"You—er—found out about what I wanted to know?" Asey asked as we sped along.

"Oh, yes indeed." Parker smiled at me. "We checked up on everyone. It's all right."

"Whom are you checking up on now?" I asked.

"On your son an' daughter-in-law an' you," Asey returned.

I looked my amazement. "On *us?*"

"Didn't think I wouldn't look into you an' him an' her an' all your sisters an' your cousins an' your aunts, did you?" Asey asked with a chuckle. "'Course I would, even if you do know Prue an' Denny James an' even if Steve Crump says you're all right. My goodness gracious me, yes!"

"What about us?" I inquired weakly.

It is one thing to speculate over murder suspects. It is still another to find that you and your family have been in the suspect category for some time.

Parker pulled a paper from his pocket. "Really want to know? Well, your son's wife left for Bristol to visit her mother Tuesday morning at eight. Then your son drove her through the heaviest city traffic and stopped at a gas station on Commonwealth Avenue—"

"And had the oil, tires, battery, gas, water and spark plugs looked at," I interrupted. "I know he did. He always does even though his own garageman's always checked up on everything the night before."

"That's just what he did do. Then he took a cab to his office. He lunched at the City Club at one-thirty, went back to his office till six, then went home. After dinner he watched some friends play squash at his club, came home, put his car up and went to bed. I even know the title of the book he read after he went to bed, too."

"How in the world did you find all that out?"

Parker smiled. "He got up at seven, worked an hour in his gymnasium, then had breakfast and went to his office at ten minutes of nine. Wednesday was about the same as Tuesday. Thursday he went to Chicago. Now, his wife reached Bristol safely after lunching with friends in Old Orchard. She's still there with her mother."

"You checked," I remarked, "didn't you?"

"You can see where we rather had to, Mrs. Ballard. I don't think Asey suspected you, but there was that little problem of how you and the troupe should arrive so conveniently at the same place at more or less the same time. The question of why you picked this cottage to convalesce in—"

"I didn't. My son did."

"Yes. We found that out. But why he should have picked it out of all the cottages on Cape Cod was, in a way, just as odd as the troupe's being led to this place, if you see what I mean."

"I don't know why he did," I said rather feebly. I hadn't thought of that side of it before. "But I do remember Mr. Bangs said that he got the wire from the Hendersons the same day he got George's letter asking for a place to rent. That's probably the only reason why we have this particular house. I know that Dr. Burnside recommended Weesit, so that's why George wrote here."

"Bangs told me that, too. And we learned from your son's secretary that he had half a dozen cottages under consideration and took this one on Burnside's advice. Bangs had sent pictures, and your son described the place over the phone to the doctor, who said it was what he should have picked himself and to take you here at once. So you see, all your family are—er—"

"Crossed out. That," I told him, "is a relief. It never entered my head that we might be under suspicion at all. I know all of George and Janet's friends and neither of them ever mentioned Gilpin. I must confess that most of their friends are pretty dull, too."

Asey drew up in front of the telephone office.

"You'd better stage this," he said to Parker, who nodded. "Mind bein' left alone, Mrs. Ballard?"

"Not at all."

I wanted to add that it would be a pleasant relief to be alone, but I thought better of it. Asey, for all his omniscience, might not understand that it was the others whom I meant. In a way, too, it was rather pleasant not to have Asey in the immediate vicinity for a few moments. There had been more than one occasion during the last two days when I'd felt like a slow freight train puffing on a siding while the Century tore by. I hadn't the stamina of a Watson and I was the first to admit it.

I sat back against the soft cushions and watched the automobiles rolling up and down the main street. Several passersby stopped and stared at the roadster and I found myself the target of more curious glances and critical comments than I had been subjected to with the tourists the day before. All Weesit knew Asey's car and, apparently, all Weesit knew about me, too.

It was half an hour before Asey and Parker returned.

"What luck?" I asked.

"A lot," Asey informed me. "They couldn't get hold of this Katy the cleaner at her house an' first off it looked like we was licked right at the beginnin'. Then it turned out Katy was cleanin' the lockers at the station that very minute. They've taken her off home to get the keys an' then they're goin' to Satterlee's. They're goin' to call us here, so we might's well set an' p'ssess our souls with patience."

"I've just had a thought," I said. "D'you suppose Satterlee's lady in the bush and Toby's light were the same? Couldn't they both have been the same campers?"

"I was goin' to see about that," Asey said. "Breck, the traffic cop, an' the Greek that runs the hot dog stand, they ought to know if there's any campers in town. Prob'ly be more likely to know than anyone else."

Parker laughed as Asey strolled across the street.

"That's like him, isn't it? I'd probably have put up a notice saying that anyone who'd given campers permission to camp should report the fact to me. He follows none of the rules, Asey does, but he gets results. I've tried to make him go into the business, but he just chuckles."

"Why won't he?"

"First of all, he doesn't need the money. Old Captain Porter left him very well off. Yet Asey'd go to work as a carpenter if the spirit moved him—and he's a good carpenter, too. When the chef at the Inn quit last fall, Asey filled in till they got another. They tried to make him stay, but he wouldn't. They said he was the best chef they ever had. Sometimes he tinkers with cars at the garage. He's a good mechanic. Sometimes he mows lawns. The rest of the time he looks after Bill Porter. He just putters about."

"It seems a pity."

"Yes. But on the other hand, Mrs. Ballard, it doesn't. He's restless and he loves people. They amuse him no end, and he's just as kind-hearted as they come. But he'd be miserable tied down to one thing. The red tape and the dull routine of private detecting would annoy him. He loathes red tape. I tried to point out the good points of the game to him once, after he'd refused a position in the county. He just snorted at my suggestions and said, 'Parker, I got a lot of respect for you. You're a good arm of the lawr. I even admit they's good points to any p'rfession. I c'n see where there'd be times when it'd be a real pleasure to be a grave-digger or a hang-man.' That," Parker concluded, "successfully squelched me. I've made no further attempts to make him help the police or become a detective."

Asey strolled back. "Breck says all the campers is over to the bay side. He's noticed 'em because the fire warden asked him to. Greek says there ain't no campers in town an' the hot dog business is rotten. Don't see what he's kickin' about. He took in eighty cents cash while I was there. Ho-hum!"

It was another half hour before a girl came out of the telephone office and called Asey in.

His face, when at last he came out, was the picture of calm resignation.

"I'm no prophet," he announced, "an' I ain't got no beard. But I was right, Parker. I was right this time!"

"The form's not there?"

"Not form. Forms."

Parker whistled. "What happened? Did they hunt the whole house over?"

"Listen while I tell you." Asey unwrapped a stick of chewing gum. "It was like this. They bundled Katy into the wagon an' went steamin' off to her place to get the keys. Then they steamed back to Satterlee's an' went in. No black loose leaf notebook on the top of the desk. None up in the bedroom on the little table. Then they begun to tear the house to pieces. In the middle of it, in walks Katy. She'd been lingerin' out in the wagon gettin' her skirts unpinned an' makin' herself presentable. They hadn't given her time b'fore. Anyway, just as they was on the point of slittin' the mattresses, in walks Katy.

"'What you doin'?' says she, or words to that effect. But they're all too busy to tell her. Finally, though, she makes herself heard, an' says if they're huntin' anythin' to tell her what it is an' she'll find it without they go tearin' the place to pieces."

Asey grinned. "Cop I talked with had a brogue. He described this all real vivid, with details.

"Well, they told her.

"'A black book full of papers,' says she, 'papers with printin' an' writin' on 'em?'

"'Where are they?' yells the p'lice force. 'Did you see 'em?'"

"And," Parker interrupted, "I take it that Katy had?"

"Katy had. Said she come in to clean house Monday mornin' an' found the den floor was all littered up with a lot of ole loose papers. Orders about cleanin' in that house was strict. Mustn't touch anythin' on table tops or desk tops or chairs, but on the floor, everythin' foreign was refuse an' to be treated as such. Sure, there was a black book cover there, too, but the papers was still loose papers to Katy. She picked 'em up an' put 'em in the basket an' threw 'em away. In fact, to make it all c'mplete an' final," Asey concluded amiably, "she even burned 'em all up in the back yard incin'rator that same afternoon."

15

"How'd they get on the floor? Who spilled 'em?" I asked.

"Katy wasn't a one to know. I s'pose Aristene or Oscar was in a last minute rush Monday mornin' an' knocked 'em off. Then they hit the floor so hard that the clips snapped open. More likely, the clips wasn't shut in the first place. So the papers spilled anyhow. No matter how they got spilled, fact r'mains that they was."

"Did she burn up the cover too?"

"Nope. She went down cellar an' brought it up for the cops. Prob'ly thought that it was too nice to burn, I shouldn't wonder. Huh!"

"I wonder," Parker said, "if all this just happened, or if Katy was acting on Satterlee's orders?"

"I asked the cop somethin' like that. He said Katy was an honest woman an' no liar. You can't really tell, Parker. Satterlee might of thrown the forms on the floor himself, knowin' Katy'd throw 'em away. No proof. He an' Aristene like as not won't remember knockin' 'em off even if we take the trouble to ask 'em. An' you can be pretty sure that Oscar ain't goin' to tell us he strewn 'em around for Katy to burn up, even if he did. Well, that's an end to that. I had a feelin' that this was goin' to happen, but just the samey I was hopin' hard it wouldn't. With the signature on that form, we could of been pretty sure if any of them fellers an' girls out to the cottage was the murd'rer or not."

"Still," Parker pointed out, "if the form is gone, it's gone. So is the letter that brought the troupe here. I presume the philosophical view to take is to think that it would have made no difference if we'd had them to work with anyway."

"You mean," Asey said, "that even with the Guild letter an' the form signature, we might still be in the dark if the writin' wasn't like anyone else's in the crowd? Yup. That's true enough. Even if the writin' was dif'rent from any of theirs, though, still anyone of 'em could of been behind both. Hired someone else to get the gun or sign the name. Prob'ly wouldn't matter, if you take that side, if we had the things or not."

"Could a handwriting expert have told if the writing were disguised?" I asked.

"Sure, easy. Them fellers is in the same class as Bernsdorf. They look at handwritin' an' get pictures made of it an' enlarge 'em, an' tell you the story the same way he told about the blobs of lead. Don't always have to take pictures. Sometimes a glance'll do. Seems to me I heard tell they can even tell what diseases a feller's got, just by gapin' at his writin'."

"Speaking of the blob of lead," Parker said, "Bernsdorf called me today. He informed this department that thus far he's found twenty-nine points of similarity between the bullets he fired out of the gun Syl found, and the bullets which entered Gilpin's body. Twenty-nine similar markings."

"Stickler for details," Asey commented. "When you get twenty-nine mic'r'scopic likenesses on a couple of little blobs of lead, you can really almost take it for granted they come from the same gun, can't you, now? Well, Parker, what's to be done?"

"Now," Parker told him, "this whole thing is up to you. We can't tell who sent that letter signed by Guild, or if there is one. Or who bought the gun and signed the form, provided that someone other than Satterlee took it, and provided he did sign a form. What ruling out of suspects you make will have to be on a basis of their whereabouts at the time of the murder, I'd say. How do things stand now?"

"Aristene's accounted for at one-fifteen by Nate Hopkins' wife. The Ballards is okay. I'll eliminate Mrs. Ballard on princ'ple."

"I was in the hospital on May fourth," I said, "if that's any help."

Asey laughed. "We won't bother to check up on that, anyway. Well, Rose was drunk. Toby's out of this. An' I b'lieve Judy's story."

"That leaves Punch, Satterlee, Allen and the two women?" Parker asked.

"Just so. Punch ain't come into this a lot as yet. But he admitted right off the bat he was a good shot an' knew a lot about guns. Hat Allen went out to the van sometime after twelve. Punch says he didn't hear Dan go out an' Dan says he didn't hear Punch. Either might of been wrong. Edie Allen says she didn't go out. Satterlee was roamin' around holdin' conv'sations with ladies in bushes that had nice voices. Take your choice!" Asey waved his hand casually. "Take your choice."

He started the roadster. "Well, now that Katy's slipped one over us, we'll have to see what brains'll do. Between you'n me'n the bed post, I got my doubts about brains right now. Ole grey mare's kind of jaded like."

We drove back to the cottage in silence. Parker walked over to his own car.

"I've got to get along, Asey. Carry on. Sing out for anything you need, and if your brain doesn't percolate over this, I'll know it's not possible for anyone else's to. Oh, the papers are a bit wrought up, but pay no attention to 'em. I'll see you later."

"Nice feller," Asey murmured as Parker drove away. "Nice feller. Yup. Just use your brains, Asey. Pick the winner with the ole grey matter. Pick the winner, ladies an' gents. Step right up. Hand's quicker'n the eye. What's the guy think I am, for Pete's sakes? Loco Looey, the mind readin' marvel? An' what he really meant was that the papers was pannin' him an' for me to get someone to hand over to him by t'morrow."

"But he didn't say any such thing, Asey!"

"He don't say. That feller expects. What he wants is someone he can stick in front of a jury. Well, I'll oblige."

"How?"

He smiled. "First off, I want food. Ah. Dan. They ain't nothin' to report, but'll you go ask Jennie for somethin' to eat for us? I'm some hours overdue on this meal problem, an' unlike Syl, I don't forget when I ain't had dinner."

Jennie brought out two trays and placed them on the table under the striped umbrella.

"Been wonderin' about Edie," Asey said when he had finished. "I kind of b'lieve Hat's story about the toothpaste. I think I'll begin this brain drive by worryin' Edie some more."

"You think she might have gone out?"

"Well," he admitted, "I'm goin' to see if I can't make her change her story some more. It's like this: if Hat's tellin' the truth, then Edie put on Hat's coat an' went out an' dropped the tube. God knows what she might of been doin' out, too. But if Edie sticks to her story that she didn't go out under," he grinned, "under what you might call slight pressure, then Hat's lyin'. Int'restin' no matter how you happen to look at it."

Edie came around from the front of the house.

"Isn't it a grand day? I've never seen such perfectly gorgeous clouds."

"More like July than June," Asey said. "Well, Edie, I'm at it again."

"More questions?"

"Still more. Don't want to seem a hard man, but—"

"You're not, Asey. You're one of the most thoughtful gentlemen I've ever met. You've been awfully decent and don't think we're not grateful, either, because we are. We may seem awf'ly flippant and light and all, but we've felt this a lot more than you see on the surface. We've gone through a lot these last three years, but we never hit up against anything as horrible as all this before. We've had to be flippant because things seemed easier that way. The habit's clung even during this. That's why we may seem nasty—playing bridge all the time and bantering around."

She paused to light a cigarette with fingers which were not entirely steady.

"But the fact is, Asey," she continued, "we're utterly terrified and scared. I mean scared, too. I know without any shadow of a doubt that none of us killed Red. I know—but I didn't mean to ramble like this. Ask away, Asey."

"Who's your choice now?" Asey asked unexpectedly.

"You mean—? Well, Satterlee. And at the same time I'm perfectly certain he didn't. He's such a dear, plump, thoroughly helpless soul. Trying to bluster and not quite getting there. Reminds me of Alexander Throttlebottom."

"Who?"

Edie went into detail over the vice-president.

"I see what you mean," Asey said with a chuckle. "Yes—yes. He is that way. Now, back to Tuesday night. You didn't see or hear Hat go out?"

"No."

"How did she an' Red get along?"

"They were pretty good friends, nothing more. Hat wasn't bowled over by him the way so many women were. She's very much in love with Quin, her professor, too. Red treated her the same way he treated Punch."

"An' how did he treat you?"

She flushed. "He used to make silly compliments about me, and there were times when Dan got jealous even though he had no need to. I had as little as I could to do with Red for just that very reason. I'm too fond of Dan to have him jealous even if there's no need of his getting that way. I'm remarkably fond of Dan, even though I admit he's not the world's most perfect male."

Her voice and words were casually flippant, but I knew Asey caught the deep feeling underlying both.

"I'd figgered that out," Asey said. "But there's this." His voice had that purring note again. "Someone seen you goin' out Tuesday night, an' it all ain't so good. No, wait a sec till I get through before you say anythin'. Look at this without takin' sides, same as I sort of have to. Red pays you compl'ments. Dan gets jealous. You go out Tuesday night. No—wait a sec. How do I know Dan didn't find you two together an' shoot Red? How do I know but what you shot him yourself because he was annoyin' you? You just said you loved Dan. How do I know Dan's not guilty an' you been lyin' to shield him, or maybe that he's been lyin' to shield you?"

"But that's not true, Asey! None of it! Asey, will you do just one thing for me? Whatever of all this supposing against Dan and me you really believe, will you believe what I've got to say to you now? That I'd have told you about my going out on Tuesday night if my reason hadn't sounded so incredibly foolish?"

"Why'd you go out?"

"Well, I woke up. I don't know if something waked me, but I woke up in one of those awf'ly wide awake states. Not where you turn over and go to sleep again, but where you stay awake and rearrange the universe and you know you could be another Crœsus if you only started right then. You know what I mean. Anyway, I propped myself up on the pillow and heard the surf pounding away, and all at once I had the most tremendous desire to go down on the beach and hear it. Really, this is true, Asey. I slipped on a coat—"

"Yours?"

"I thought so, but it turned out to be Hat's."

"Tube of toothpaste in the pocket?"

"Yes. I felt it when I put my hands in my pockets after I got outside."

"What then?"

"Well, after slipping on my coat, or Hat's coat, I tiptoed downstairs. The front door was locked and chained and it took ages to undo everything quietly. Then I walked out to the road—"

"How'd you know the lay of the land? An' did you have a light? Must of been dark."

"I had no light. Judy'd told us about the bluff and the steps down to the beach, where they were, and how beautiful the place was in the daytime. It was awf'ly dark. But I groped about parallel to the house till I found the ruts and then followed the road to the steps. My eyes were pretty used to the dark by then. Well, about that time I began to lose some of my desire to go down on the beach. It was terribly cold and I was beginning to jitter. Dan hadn't brought slippers or mules or anything, and I hadn't put on my pumps for fear of making a noise in the house. It never occurred to me to carry 'em an' put 'em on when I got out. Anyway, my feet were simply congealed, and the sea grass seemed full of people rustling about and the wind was moaning dreadfully. It hadn't sounded any-where near that raging in my room. I decided not to go down on the beach."

"Sensible," Asey commented.

"Probably the only sensible thing about the whole affair. I don't think I could have gone very far anyway. The surf was hitting up against the steps at the foot of the bluff. Well, after getting that far, I was determined to listen to the surf, at least, so I sat down on the top step. That must have been where the paste dropped. By that time I was shivering from head to foot. I'd been there about thirty seconds when all of a sudden the most grisly feeling came over me. It was—well, I simply can't describe it. My hair began to feel stiff and on-endy. I got up and groped my way back to the house just as quickly as my frozen feet could carry me."

"Red," Asey began, "was—"

"I know." Edie shivered. "He must have been—have been lying there. Well, it took all my self-control not to yelp this out when Mrs. Ballard told us Wednesday morning and when I saw where Red was lying. I knew that night that something was awf'ly wrong out there. You know. Anyway, if Dan hadn't started to lose his temper and if I'd not had to stop him, I'd have blurted this out to you Wednesday morning then and there. It would have been a tremendous relief. I've wished I had a dozen times since. But it seemed so silly. I didn't think anyone would believe me."

"How'd you get in?"

"I'd left the door unlatched. But by the time I got in and locked it again and put the chain across, I simply collapsed in a heap in the hallway. Finally I pulled myself together and crept up to bed on my hands and knees. Ugh!" She shuddered. "No more of this deep-calling-unto-deep for me!"

"What time was all this?" Asey asked.

"I don't know. But if someone saw me go out and told you as much, they should know."

Asey said nothing.

"Oh! Oh, Asey—you—you—"

"Yup. I lied to you. But I had to."

"And I was so sure," Edie wailed, "that if someone saw me, it would be all right! For they'd have known the time and they wouldn't have heard shots while I was out!" She was almost crying. "And now—oh, I'm worse off than anyone! Asey, why did you? You make me wish I'd tried to brazen this out!"

"If we can fix the time, Edie—"

"How in God's name, Asey, can you fix the time? How? If anyone had seen me, they'd never admit it now, would they? It would only mean that they'd have to explain what they were doing up, or out, at that time themselves."

"Didn't you have a watch?"

"Watch?" Edie laughed grimly. "Watch? The only watch in the crowd is that turnip, the dollar model, out in the van. The boys wear watch chains, but that's just for show."

"We found that out," Asey said. "Doc started to look at Red's watch to see if it'd stopped at any p'ticular time. Found there wasn't any. Punch said his wasn't runnin' when I asked the time. Say, do you twist paper clips?"

"Twist paper clips? Lord, no! We had some in the van once, but lately Dan's been using pins to clip such papers as he wanted put together. Paper clips are luxuries, you see, and we haven't been going in for them. Look." Her voice was desperate. "I might as well tell you right now that the twenty-five dollars we expected to get from Guild is the only money in the crowd. Asey, even if any one of us had wanted to kill Red—and we didn't— we couldn't have afforded to. He was our drawing card. Our meal ticket. When you're as broke as we are, meal tickets mean anything and everything. They're more than all the feuds and hatreds and grudges in the world. If every one of us, Dan and Hat and Punch and I, loathed Red Gilpin with all our souls, if we wanted to kill him, we couldn't have. Without him, well, we wouldn't even have eaten stew!"

"I figgered he was your big shot," Asey said.

"He was. Look, Asey. Dan and Punch and Hat are sitting around a bridge table in the house. Playing cards and pretending that they love it! You may not know it, but the acting— the show we've put on since we came here Tuesday night, since Red was killed, is the greatest show we've ever put on or ever will again! It isn't just that we've lost Red, our friend. It isn't just this grisly, horrible murder. It isn't just that we're scared you may pick out one of us being the murderer. But we don't know what we'll do afterwards. We're washed up. With Red gone, we're nothing. Who'd ever come to see us after all this publicity anyway, even if we were good? No one but curiosity seekers. D'you know," she turned to me, "how much money we had when we came here? One dollar and five pennies. I gave it to Asey when he talked about supplies. He never let on. But we don't know how we're going to live after we get out of this affair, if we *do* get out of it!"

Asey and I were silent. Somehow there was nothing to say. For a moment all was quiet under the striped umbrella.

"Listen, youngster." Asey's voice was gentle. "Were the stars out while you was out on Tuesday night?"

"Some. Very dim." She dabbed at her eyes with a bright checked handkerchief. "Sorry I went on like that. They'll never forgive me. We all knew we could prove to you that Red was our big attraction and that, broke as we are, we'd never have killed him. We couldn't have. But, well. I guess it was pride. And it sounded so alibiing. As Dan said, we had nothing to alibi about."

"How'd the surf sound?"

"It lashed up against the foot of the steps. I could feel the whole flight quivering. I wondered why it wasn't washed away in winter, I remember."

"They take 'em up in the fall an' put 'em down again in the spring, or they would be. Sure the water was hittin' the steps?"

"Positive."

"Then cheer up. Cheer up all around, as a matter of fact. After this is over, I'll see you kids get set up again."

"You—? You'll—"

"Why not? Good Cape Codder always keeps a sock in the corner of the closet just in case the gov'ment bonds fail. Yup, just cheer up."

"But how—?"

"About the time? Well, Edie, you saved yourself. There *was* stars around four o'clock, dim-like, but they was there. I was up with Syl's dog, like I told Mrs. Ballard, an' I know. An' the tide was real high Tuesday. High around four. When I come up the beach Tuesday mornin', I noticed sea weed on the bottom steps out there. Now, if you'd been out around one, before or after the time Gilpin was killed, there'd of been no stars an' you'd never of heard that surf or felt it hittin' the steps. The way I figger it is this. Prob'ly it was long after three o'clock or you'd have heard Judy an' Toby an' Rose roamin' around. Long after three-fifteen, or you'd of heard Toby's truck when it backfired. Now, I figger that prob'ly 'twas his truck backfirin' that waked you up. It must of taken you some time to make up your mind to go out, an' more time to get out, what with creepin' downstairs an' all. So prob'ly you went out around fourish, when the tide was dead high."

"Then—"

"Then it's all okay. Cheer up. You're out of this."

16

"Oh," Edie's voice broke down completely as she jumped up from her chair. "Oh, thank Heaven! Now I must tell the rest!"

"Nun-no. Don't know's I want you to do that now. You can tell Dan that you're safe an' out of this business if you want to, but that's all."

"But Asey! It would make such a difference!"

"Prob'ly would. But I don't want you to play the dove act to this p'ticular ark load just now. Wipe your eyes an' run along."

"Okay!"

Stooping swiftly, she leaned over and kissed him, and then tore into the house.

"That," Asey said without the slightest embarrassment at all, "is the kind of grat'tude I like to see. Huh. I thought that crowd was mighty hard up, but I didn't know they was that bad off. Red *was* their meal ticket, all right. You notice how Jennie an' Mary Peters both remembered him, an' how Satterlee said that Hat was the actor, but then he went on talkin' about Red pullin' the rabbit out of someone's vest? An', bein' as how they're hard up an' bein' as how Red was their drawin' card, I sort of think she's right about their not killin' him even if they'd wanted to. An' she's right they'll have a tough time gettin' goin' again. They will."

"I should think that it might work out the other way."

"I don't think so. Not now. Time's sort of gone when ev'ry second murd'rer went on the vod'vil stage an' folks mobbed the theater to see 'em. The publicity'll draw the tourist trade an' a lot of gapers, but they wouldn't count."

"It seems to me," I remarked, "that this whole affair is solved right now."

"How come?"

"Why, you've eliminated the troupe. And Aristene and Toby and Rose and Judy. That leaves only Squire Satterlee."

"I ain't done with the whole troupe, Mrs. Ballard. Just Edie."

"But you said—"

"I said I thought she was right about their bein' silly to kill Red, an' I do. I been thinkin' that for two days. But still that don't mean that Dan or Hat or Punch wasn't silly. I b'lieve Edie, because she wouldn't of been a one to make up things like dim stars an' a high tide. How'd she of known about the el'ments at four if she killed Red at one? She could of alibied an' said Hat went out first. But she didn't even mention Hat, an' we got Punch's word that for a long time Hat an' Edie didn't get along so good. Yup, Edie's out, but that don't mean I'm through with the rest."

"There's very little to disbelieve about Dan and Punch."

"Uh-huh. Dan just denies he bought the gun or went out Tuesday night. So does Punch. Only we know Punch can handle a gun. You can't get away from that any more'n you can get away from Dan's havin' a temper an' bein' jealous an' fightin' with Red on Tuesday night."

"Punch," I said, "has no motive."

"Only b'cause we ain't had the wit to find him one," Asey retorted.

"Well," I said, "I'm inclined to believe at this point that Satterlee is your man. I didn't think so 'til all this business about the form came up. That he should have put it in his deposit box was not unusual. But his forgetting where the box keys were made it a bit thick. All this business about boyhood love letters and their substitution for the forms, and Katy and the incinerator, it's all too much of a good thing. It seems to me that chance drops out there and good strong conspiring walks in. The first couple of things might have happened. The last few, never. And besides all that, Asey, Satterlee told Aristene he'd like to kill Red. And after all, why should he come down here to visit a cousin he hasn't seen for twenty years? He says it's because of Aristene, I know, but why did he come here? What was he doing roaming around with that lady in the bush?"

"Uh-huh," Asey said, "that's all sort of question'ble. I agree. But you forget the joker, Mrs. Ballard. If Satterlee hadn't been on the Cape for twenty years, why in Christendom should he of sent that gang out here with that letter? How could he of? It takes a lot of knowin' an' surveyin' a place to d'rect folks off on back roads to a place like this. An' Oscar ain't been here for twenty years, an' we know he didn't have no time to do any surveyin' after he got here."

"I'm becoming more and more convinced that the letter was a fake or a joke," I said. "Remember, too, that friend Oscar plays with paper clips."

Syl arrived with more telegrams.

"You're an important person," he said to me. "Folks don't trouble you with letters. They say it short an' snappy an' expensive."

One from George headed the pile and I sighed as I read it to Asey:—

"*Leaving Chicago tonight by plane. Arrive Weesit tomorrow.*'"

"Why 'oh-dear' at that?" Asey asked. "Seems to me like he's sort of cooled off some."

"Cooled off nothing! The very brevity bothers me. The more steam he lets off before he comes here, the less he'll have left when he *does* turn up."

"Maybe there's more from him in the others," Asey suggested cheerfully.

But the other two were not from George. One was from a lurid Boston tabloid, offering me an exorbitant sum for what they termed an original and exclusive story of the Gilpin tragedy. They added that there would be no work involved, "as one of our staff will be pleased to do all writing for you."

The other message was from Janet:

"*Worried to death about you, Vic dear. Coming at once despite George's wires to contrary. Want to come, will come and must see you. Do hope it is over with soon for your sake.*'"

Asey nodded his approval. "Some of your folks ought to be 'round. You're lookin' better than you did Tuesday, but just the samey, I'm glad she's comin'."

"I'm glad too," I remarked. "Undeniably George has wired her not to set foot away from Bristol; he loathes publicity about his family. It will infuriate him all the more if he finds her here. Well, I suppose we'd best let that be till they come."

"No use worryin' about anythin' that's like to be unpleasant,"

Asey said. "You just get twice the dose. Always thought folks suffered a lot more on the way to the dentist's than they did after they got there."

"What are you going to do about Satterlee? And the lady in the bush business? Are you going to try to check that?"

"Yup, I'm plannin' on seein' what I can do about that right now. Think I'll take Syl an' wander around these side roads. Even if Breck an' the Greek don't think they's campers, they still might be. Little late to be doin' this, but I got another thing to look up I didn't think about till now. D'I ever mention Harmon Peters?"

"It seems to me you said something to the officers at the crossroads about him."

"Well, he's an uncle of that woman May Hopkins was talkin' about. Harm's a crazy ole duffer that lives in a shack up this way, between Syl's house an' this, about a mile from the shore. He lives mostly on fish he catches or rabbits he shoots. Once last year he almost blew Syl to Kingdom Come, pottin' at a rabbit that must of been about three inches from where Syl was sittin', *if* Syl had happened to be sittin' at the time."

I smiled. "D'you mean you think that it's possible he might have shot Red, too?"

"Nun-no. I don't think that's pos'ble, though Harm's been known to pot at people kind of reckless. That's one of the reasons why town folks don't use these back roads a lot at night. Young-sters an' summer folks don't seem to care. Anyway, if Harm had happened to be wanderin' around the ice-house turn-off, he might of been the reason for the light Toby saw, though I kind of think that might have come from one of them new camps up around there. Harm might of been the lady in the bush, come to think of it; he's got a high voice. Dunno's you'd call it 'nice', exactly," Asey grinned as he quoted Satterlee, "but if Oscar was tellin' the truth, I'd imagine that most any voice out of the night that give him directions might of sounded nice. Might try to find out if Harm was wanderin' around, anyway. Even if he didn't have a thing to do with all this, just the samey he'd know if anyone had been wanderin' around."

"How?"

"I can't say, but he would. Always been a mystery to me how these crazy hermit-like fellers know so durn much. Reckon it's communin' with nature. I once shipped with a feller named Tonson, out of 'Frisco, 'twas. He b'lieved in this thought carryin' business. He got's many messages as if he'd had a radio tucked away in his pocket. Funny thing about it all was that a lot of it come true. He got a message about the 'Frisco earthquake, f'r example, day it happened. Maybe Harm's like that. I dunno."

"Are you going now?" I got up from the chair.

"Yup. I don't think I'll take you along, Mrs. Ballard. Ain't no tellin' how Harm might be feelin'. Sometimes he's mad an' sometimes he's just plumb crazy. Syl's the chosen one here."

"But I want to go, Asey," I protested, "and if Syl's along, the two of you—"

"Ought to be enough to keep you safe. Uh-huh. But Harm's not nice to look at. You take, Mrs. Ballard, the ugliest person you ever seen in all your born days, n'en you add bleary eyes an' a busted nose, an' what you got looks kind of like Harm. He—"

"Now," I said, "you've aroused my curiosity. I insist on going. I want just to look at him."

Asey sighed. "That's the woman of it! S'pose Harm pots at you? What then?"

"Fiddledeedee."

"All right. Come along if you want to. But Jennie'll fuss somethin' awful."

Jennie did, but in spite of all her remonstrances, and Syl's, too, I set off with the two men in the roadster.

We wove around back roads for twenty minutes before we finally landed up near a small shanty in a clearing among the pines.

Outside the door a man dressed in what appeared to be a gunny sack was playing with a kitten. When I got a full view of his face as he looked up, I realized that Asey had not overstated his description. Harmon Peters was the ugliest man I'd ever seen in all my life. I remarked as much to Syl in a whisper.

Syl nodded and summed him up in a nutshell.

"Bad dream, that's what."

Harm surveyed us thoughtfully for several minutes before he made any move to come over to the car. When he did, I all but howled. What I had taken for a kitten was nothing more or less than a tiny skunk. It wobbled after Harm as he strolled toward us.

"Tame," Asey assured me with a chuckle. "Harm tames 'em. Don't get nervous."

But I was, even though Harm seemed to be in one of his amiable moods—at least, he managed something which would pass for a smile and he greeted Asey amiably enough.

"H'lo, Asey."

"H'lo, Harm. How be ye?" Asey's Cape dialect reached heights.

"I'm so's to be up an' around," Harm admitted.

"That's good."

Conversation languished.

"Y'like t'git out an' set?" Harm suggested. His gesture of invitation did not include Syl and me.

"Thank ye kindly," Asey said, stepping out of the roadster.

"Thank ye kindly. Found I had a few canned goods I didn't want, Harm, an' I asked m'self who c'n I give 'em to? N'en I thought maybe p'raps you might be able to use 'em. S'pose y'c'd?"

Harm allowed that he might be able to. His eyes glittered as Asey produced half a dozen cans of tinned fruit from the trunk on the back of the car; he had forced Jennie to part with those cans only after considerable argument.

"Heaven to him," Syl whispered. "He loves things in cans."

"I might have some more for you some time later," Asey said, passing over the tins. "Bill Porter always sends down a lot. More'n I ever need."

Harm nodded and fingered the labels. "What was it," he inquired gravely, "that y'wanted t'know, Asey?"

Syl and I both chuckled, but Asey's face never lost its grave expression.

"What made y' think I wanted to know anythin'?"

"I kind of been havin' a feelin' for the last hour," Harm said, "that you wanted t'ask me somethin'. Kind of had a feelin' you might turn up. Say, Asey, will y' come'n look t'my pump? It ain't been doin' right lately."

"Sure thing."

Asey and Harm disappeared around the corner of the house. The little skunk trotted after them.

"Will he be all right?" I asked.

"Who, Asey? Sure," Syl said. "Asey's got a way with dogs an' kids an' addled folks. Harm'd have made for me if I'd stepped out of this car, but he likes Asey. Asey knows how to handle him. Y'know," Syl added in a burst of confidence, "sometimes I sort of think Asey's a little addled himself, for all he's so sensible."

"Why, Syl!"

"Yessir. You should see that feller, dressed up in city clothes an' in this car! Looks like a mil'naire. Is, pretty near. An' what's he do? Just putters around in his ole clothes. You can bet if I had his money I wouldn't be messin' around like he does, carpenterin' an' cookin' an' mendin' engines. No sireebob!" Syl sighed. "It's like I always say—them that wants money spends their lives wantin', an' them that has it don't give a hoot."

I clutched his arm as two more skunks, larger and more terrifying, came around the corner of the house.

"Syl, those animals are going to drive me crazy! Are they really tame? Does Harm keep them?"

"Well," Syl said, "he keeps 'em till they sort of suit his purpose. Good market for skunk grease. Ever tried skunk grease for a cough?" he added.

I shudderingly admitted that I never had.

"Best thing in the world for a cold in the chest," Syl informed me. "Y'see, there's a lot of skunks around here. Cape's overrun with 'em these days."

"Why?"

"Well, some feller that 'parently hadn't much experience with 'em got a lot of fancy laws passed about trappin' 'em. So they're all over the place. Must of been the same feller," Syl added bitterly, "that got gull shootin' made against the lawr."

"But gulls are so beautiful—"

"Uh-huh. They're what the summer folks call pitcheresk, but you look out in that inlet near your place some day an' you'll see why clams an' quohaugs an' fish is gettin' scarcer. Millions of gulls feedin' all day long. That's why. The Cape," Syl ended up with a sigh, "ain't what it was, not by a long shot."

Asey appeared around the corner of the shack with Harm. His face was just as grave, his manner just as solicitous as when he left, but there was something about him which made me feel that he was bursting with information. In spite of Harm's attempts to detain him, he made for the car.

"I got to get along," Asey said firmly, with one foot on the running board. "That pump's all right now, an' it'll be all right if you don't jerk it too hard. I'll be back sometime with some more tinned stuff. So long!"

"But, Asey," Harm said, "what was it you wanted t'find out? There was somethin' you wanted t' know. I felt it. You just ask me, Asey, an' I'll tell y' if I can. I got that message an' I know you wanted to find out—"

"Harm," Asey said, starting the roadster, "I'm kind of 'fraid you got your wires crossed. Tuccar!"

"Tuccar," Harm responded blankly, "tuccar!"

"What's that mean?" I asked Syl.

"Take care," Syl translated. "Always used to say it hereabouts. Still do. Asey, what—"

"Exactly," I chimed in. "Asey, what—?"

"What'd I find out? Why, you just heard Harm say he wanted to know what I wanted to know. Never asked him a single thing."

"But you found out just the same. I know. Asey, tell us. You know you're dying to."

"Well, Harm's had a misery in his shoulder an' he ain't been away from these parts for a week. So he wasn't the light Toby seen. That must of been from them new cottages. An' I don't think he was the lady in the bush, because he said he was all doubled up with this misery on Tuesday. B'sides, all he's got in the line of lights is one small home made bayb'ry candle. Satterlee wouldn't have seen that even if Harm'd lighted it."

"But—"

"But why shouldn't he of lighted it? An'," Asey said in mock amazement, "an' use it up? Mrs. Ballard, it's plain you ain't a Cape Codder!"

"Stop jeering at me and tell us what you discovered."

"Okay. There *is* a lady in the bush, an' she ain't far off."

"What?" Syl and I spoke in unison. "How d'you know?"

"While I was fixin' that pump, I sort of cast my eye around. Up in his cupboard he has four tins of S. S. Pierce's peaches."

"Well, what of it?"

"Where'd *he* get S. S. P. peaches? You can bet your boots he didn't buy 'em. He don't buy nothin'. He stole 'em. Who from? Campers. He didn't wander this week, so they must be near."

"But why, even if there are campers, should they turn out to be the lady in the bush?"

"Well, I looked around some more, an' there was a tube of anchovy paste an' a big bottle of olives stuffed with almonds an' a box of long gold-tipped cig'rettes. Ever hear of an able-bodied man takin' stuff like that campin'? It's a woman, or women."

I laughed. "Where d'you expect to find her, or them?"

"I expect to find 'em in about two minutes by the clock. Syl, they're probably beyond your house, in that far clump of pines."

"In the old Poindexter picnic shack?"

"Just so. That picnic shack," Asey explained, "was one some summer folks had to use when they come up here on parties. Fallin' apart, now."

It was just two minutes by the dash clock when we drove up beside a tumbledown log cabin. Near it was a tent.

We were greeted by a series of yelps.

"What on earth?" I asked wonderingly, "wha—"

"Two," Asey said, grinning. "Two girls. Sunbathin'."

In a few moments the two appeared, sketchily clad in beach pyjamas. In a kindly spirit, I attributed the color of their faces to sunburn.

"Sorry to bother you," Asey said, "but have you been here long?"

"Since Monday," the taller of the two said. "I hope we're not trespassing?"

"Nope. Er—you got a car here?"

"The chauffeur brought us and then left. We thought you were Horton bringing us stores."

"Mm. Er—are they from Pierce's? Have you lost any?"

"Yes," the tall girl said, "we have missed some. Did you—"

"Tell me. Did you give anyone directions to the main road on Tuesday night?"

"I did." The short girl spoke up. "Those infernal skunks were out in full force. I got up to make sure the tent was secure. Then I heard this man's voice. I—"

"Do you," Asey interrupted her, "remember the time?"

"Why, yes." She was plainly puzzled by Asey's questions. "Yes, I do. It was just five minutes after one. I remember because Joan asked me and I thought it was loads later. You see—"

"What time is it now?"

The girl stared at Asey before she looked at her wrist watch. "Six-ten," she said, "and may I inquire why you—"

Asey glanced down at the car clock. It was exactly six-ten.

"Thank you kindly," he said, starting the car.

The girls were still staring blankly after us when we rolled out of sight.

"Satterlee," Asey announced with a grin, "is out."

17

"EXPLAIN," I said, "explain!"

"Okay. It'd take fifteen minutes to get from the Henderson place to that tent in broad daylight, goin' as fast as you could, which'd be about fifteen miles an hour. N'en you'd have to know these back roads like a streak. But at night, with some fog to muss things up, it'd take half an hour anyway, maybe an hour. Furthermore, that girl's watch was right by the car clock. Car clock's always right. Chances is if their time's right now, it was right Tuesday. If Satterlee was by the tent at one-five, he couldn't of been at the Henderson place anywhere near the time when Red was killed. See?"

"Yes," I said hesitantly, "I see. But couldn't Satterlee have come by the beach? Or couldn't he just have walked, after leaving his car somewhere around?"

Asey shook his head. "Tide'd of cut the beach off in spots along there even at one. He couldn't of made it by beach, an' there's only thick woods an' a couple of swamps between Syl's an' Henderson's. Take him an hour comin' an' goin' either of them ways even if he knew the place like a book. Am I right, Syl?"

"Yup. Let me tell you, once last summer Jennie an' I went

blueberryin' around here, an' b'lieve it or not, we got lost. Not half a mile from our own back yard! He couldn't of walked it, Asey, an' at night all these roads looks alike. Once in a while I slip up on 'em myself. Say, Asey, whyn't you take the turn-off here an' run up to the house? I been worryin' about Samson. Sam," he threw in for my benefit, "is my dog. I started to bring him over this mornin', but Jennie said Mrs. Ballard might not like it. I thought it wouldn't do no harm to take him over now an' let him run around till we go home. You mind much, Mrs. Ballard? He's been cooped up since Wednesday."

"Of course not," I said. "Get him, Asey."

We cut off on still more sandy roads and finally wound up at Syl's house. Samson turned out to be a beautiful brown and white setter. He promptly made for Asey, licked his hand and fawned all over him.

"Huh," Syl said, "bet he thinks this outin's all *your* idea. Git in the rumble, Sam, an' act like a gentleman. Say, Asey," he added as we started off again, "what you goin' to do now? No one you really ain't checked up on 'cept them two men from the show an' that Hat girl, is there?"

"That's all."

"Well, what you goin' to do?"

"Pray, Sylly," Asey answered briefly.

The rest of the ride was made in silence.

The elimination of Satterlee bothered me, in one sense. I'd pinned all my suspicions on him. On the other hand, I frankly admitted to myself that I was glad he was out. As Edie had said, the Squire was so plump and earnest that you couldn't help liking him.

Jennie had dinner waiting for us when we returned. Before

we sat down, Asey told Satterlee that he had found the lady in the bush.

"Checked the time," he concluded, "so you're all okay, Squire."

"You—you really mean that, Asey?"

"Uh-huh."

Tears of relief rolled down Satterlee's cheeks.

We were just beginning one of Jennie Mayo's mammoth strawberry shortcakes when Syl appeared at the kitchen door. He looked worried and he pulled nervously at his mustache.

"S'matter?" Asey asked. "Don't tell me you gone an' found somethin' else?"

"Well, er—yup. As a matter of fact, I—well, I sort of wish, Asey, that you'd come out here a sec."

Without a word Asey got up and followed Syl out into the kitchen. After I finished my coffee, I excused myself and marched out after them. Syl had aroused my curiosity.

"What's he found?" I asked.

Asey turned around to me "Sort of a queer thing. Syl let Samson loose, an' he wandered off into the woods beyond the van. All of a sudden he set up an awful noise, an' Syl went after him to see what was the matter." He hesitated.

"Well, what was?"

"Well," Asey said, "it was a skunk."

"Oh dear," I said sympathetically, "I do hope that beautiful dog didn't get mixed up with a skunk. Why, it would be awful!"

"It ain't anything like that, Mrs. Ballard. Y'see, it was a dead skunk that Sam found."

"That's a relief! I'd hate to think of poor Sam spending the rest of the summer in seclusion. But, Asey, what *are* you so sober about this for? What is there about a dead skunk to make you look so—so grim?"

"I'll admit," Asey said reluctantly, "that skunks is usually funny. This ain't at all. This ain't no laughin' matter. You see, that skunk didn't just die."

"Don't tell me it was shot with a .45 Colt!"

"Nunno. I guess it would of been sort of better if it had."

"Asey, what *do* you mean?"

"Well, someone killed it, Mrs. Ballard."

"Probably Harmon Peters," I suggested.

"No. No, that's one thing I can be sure of. He don't give a plugged nickel about pottin' at people with that shotgun of his. Kind of amuses him to see 'em jump. Like," Asey smiled faintly, "like Syl jumped. Now, Harm's a little crazy an' he's got a lot of queer notions from livin' too much alone, but Harm wouldn't kill anything, not—well, not like this was killed. When he kills his skunks that he raises, he gets chloroform from the doctor. Yessir, he does. His rabbit snares ain't the kind that hurts the rabbits. He won't shoot birds. Why, I made splints for him once when one of his pet gulls got a busted wing! No, this ain't Harm's work."

"But why," I asked, "pull such a long face about this defunct animal? After all, a skunk is a skunk."

"Uh-huh. But prac'tically no livin' animal in this world," Asey replied with some heat, "d'serves to be treated like this one was. I—well, it don't, that's all."

"Asey, tell me—"

"No, mam! It's too horrid to talk about," Asey said firmly. "N'en besides that, there are durn few critters that'll bother you if you don't bother 'em first. Even skunks. You frighten 'em or hurt 'em, an' you'll be sorry. You leave 'em be, an' they let you be. I never seen one of the things yet that wasn't gladder to get away from you than you was to get away from them."

"Asey, what do you mean? That some one mutilated—"

"Mutilate'll do. Huh." Asey sat down on the wood box. "Huh. Jennie, you get me about a pint of black coffee, will you? Thanks."

Judy came out then and informed me that I was needed to complete the second table of bridge. It was half-past-nine before it occurred to me that Asey had not come back. Rose, out in the kitchen, could give me no information other than that Asey had driven off with Jennie Mayo as soon as the dishes were done. Syl, she thought, had gone off with Kemp to check up on the trooper guard.

I went back to the bridge game, but my mind was anywhere but on the cards. At twelve-thirty, after we broke up for the night, I went out into the kitchen again. Syl was sitting with his feet up on top of the table, reading a magazine with a lurid cover. I saw the title, "Superba Mystery and Detective Stories" before he hastily got to his feet and tried to hide his reading matter.

"Where's Asey?"

"Dunno, Mrs. Ballard. He told me he'd take Jennie home an' that if he didn't come back for a spell, I was to stay here an' hold the fort. He left me his whistle an' said you was to have it."

"But where can the man have gone?"

"Dunno."

"Syl, whom does he really suspect?"

"All I know is," Syl said honestly, "that he told me he b'lieved everybody but that he'd made a lot of mental res'vations."

"What's he up to, Syl?"

"You know just's much's I do, Mrs. Ballard. Asey, he's a deep one."

His tone suggested that Asey was altogether too deep for

common mortals to comprehend. I went back to my room and got ready for bed, feeling that Syl was very probably right. As I slipped into bed, I recalled Asey's translation of Parker's statement about the papers wanting action, and Asey's promise that he would provide Parker with the guilty party by the next day.

I snapped on my bed light again and went over to the desk. I fished around, found my notes of the whole affair and began to make final revisions.

Under the section OUT were Toby, Rose, Judy, Aristene, Satterlee, Edie Allen, Harm Peters—if he could be included—my family and myself.

That left only Dan and Hat and Punch.

We still couldn't prove that Dan hadn't written the Guild letter, bought the gun and killed Red. He was quick-tempered and he had a very good motive, jealousy. Yet as Aristene said when Asey had chided her for playing bridge with the man she thought was a murderer, I knew perfectly well that Dan wasn't.

As for Hat, I believed her story. From the first she had been perfectly honest. She'd admitted to going out Tuesday night when, as she said, she could have withheld the information. I drew a line through her name.

That left Punch. It seemed to me now that Punch was the only person on whom the spotlight of suspicion had not been turned in full. His time on May fourth wasn't really accounted for; he could have bought the gun and written the letter that summoned the troupe to the Henderson place; he had as much chance of going out Tuesday night as Dan had. He was an expert shot. But what motive could he have had? I couldn't think of one.

There was a knock on my door then, and Judy came in. She looked at the papers and laughed.

"At it again, Vic? May I look? Oh! You've eliminated everyone but Punch. Oh, Vic, it's *not* Punch!"

"Why?"

"Oh, it can't be Punch! You're wrong, Vic."

"But why not, Judy?" She turned very pink at my question. "Oh, I see. You like Punch."

"Yes, I do," she said defensively. "I do. You haven't been around so much or had ears or eyes for anyone but Asey, or you'd have noticed. That's, well, that's why I came here just now. I—well, Punch says it was inevitable."

"How, as Asey says, so?"

"Punch and Judy." She blushed.

"My dear," I said, "if you've fallen in love with him and he with you, my blessings!" I picked up the pen and inked out Punch's name. "I intended to do that anyway, Judy."

"Vic, you're a lamb! Well, you can't lose me unless you fire me. Not till Punch gets a job and becomes a wage earner again. But I thought you'd like to know."

After she left I snapped out my light and got into bed again. But I couldn't sleep. As far as I was concerned, everyone had been proved innocent. But what was Asey doing? What did he have up his sleeve?

To my mind the jigsaw puzzle was completed, that is, as much as it could be completed. But I couldn't guess what the picture on the face of it was. Asey had taken me entirely into his confidence. I'd seen everything, been in on everything. I knew all that he knew. In one sense I knew more, because I'd been on the set all the time the play was going on. But I had to confess myself stumped. Even if I was, I somehow felt that Asey wasn't.

Now that I turned the whole business over in my mind, it seemed to me that perhaps Asey had not taken me wholly into his confidence at all. I remembered the numerous occasions during the last two days when I'd caught him peering abstractedly into space. Brooding, to use his own term.

What was there that I had failed to connect? What were the mental reservations Syl said Asey had made?

At three o'clock I stopped puzzling, ceased listening for the sound of the roadster returning, and went to sleep.

Asey had not come back the next morning when Jennie brought me in my breakfast.

"Didn't he even tell you where he was going last night?" I demanded.

"Never even said he *was* goin'," Jennie returned. "Don't you worry none, Mrs. Ballard. He'll be back."

"I almost wouldn't care *when* he got back," I said, "if I only knew where he'd gone, and why!"

Janet arrived around ten o'clock in her own little coupe. She looked very tired and admitted that she was even wearier than she looked.

"I drove to Boston last night," she said, "spent the night at the Ritz and then set off early. I never slept a wink. No wonder I look washed out. But you, Vic, you're yourself again! You don't seem to be the same person I saw last Monday, lying feebly on a couch."

"It's going to be my only comeback to George," I told her, "when he arrives with all his reproaches."

Janet looked around the room at the rest and bit her underlip thoughtfully. "Vic, I'd like to talk with you before he comes. Is there any place where we could go?"

I took her out to the wicker chairs under the striped umbrella.

"It's about George," she said as she lighted a cigarette. "I'd have talked to you before this, but I didn't want to bother you at first, and then you got sick and of course I didn't want to worry you then. I don't know exactly how to tell you even now, Vic, but the truth is, I'm, well, after six years, I've come very near—oh.—There's a car coming out the road. Who is it, Vic?"

"I don't know," I said, annoyed at the interruption. "Probably some county man. That reminds me, how did you get by the troopers?"

"I gave them my name and they said they'd had orders to let me through."

"Probably Asey told them. He knew you—Janet, it's George in that car!"

Both of us rose.

"Something must be wrong with the sedan," Janet said wearily. "Well, here goes. Vic, you and I are going to get what is technically known as ours."

But, to my infinite amazement, George was perfectly calm. He kissed me, commented on how well I looked, and turned to Janet.

"I'm glad you came. Mother shouldn't have been left alone. And I'm sorry, mother, that I got so excited in those telegrams. And I'm even sorrier about Monday, and the vase. The fact is, I've been so worried about business lately that I haven't known what I was doing. But this Chicago trip has settled everything. After I got that load off my mind, I began to realize how nasty I'd been. Didn't mean to be, as I hope you'll realize. Been here long, Jan?"

"About fifteen minutes."

"Too bad I couldn't have driven you down. I wired Jack to bring the car to the airport and he arrived in that hired sedan.

Seemed he hadn't got around to fixing the fender on mine. He'd let it slide because I'd told him before that I shouldn't be back till Tuesday."

Janet looked wonderingly at me. She'd bashed the fender on George's new car herself; that George should have refrained from mentioning the fact was in the nature of a miracle.

Dan and Edie and Hat came out then, but when they noticed George, they started around the corner to the front of the house.

"Are those some of your guests?" George asked, with no word of reproach. "I'd like to meet them."

While I was introducing them, Punch and Judy brought up in the rear.

"I see you've found your perfume," Judy said to Hat. "Rather, I smell that you have."

"But I haven't, really. Mrs. Ballard, I've lost my pet perfume and I simply can't find it. D'you suppose it would do any good to enlist the eagle-eyed Syl?"

"It might," I said.

"Just the same," Judy persisted, "I thought I smelled a new perfume. You know, when I went to business school, all the girls used to spray themselves with perfume out of a slot sprayer in the lobby of the building. You put in a penny and turned a crank. That perfume has haunted me ever since. It was *so* horrible. Working in a room with forty more or less unwashed girls, all sprayed with penny scent—oh, I didn't mean to be funny! Anyway, I've always remembered that smell and it seemed to me I caught a whiff of it when I came out here. The girls at Silverman and Harris used it, too."

"Why didn't you tell me," George said, "that you'd worked with that firm? Harris is a good friend of mine. After you—er— left my office Monday, I wondered if you were the Miss Dunham he was always talking about as being the best secretary he ever had."

Janet and I exchanged another look. George was outdoing himself. By the time that a trooper came roaring up on a motorcycle an hour later, George had become easily the most popular member of the Ballard family.

"I got a call for Mrs. George Ballard," the officer said. "Phone call," he added, "they had to drive down here about it. From Bristol, I think they said."

"It's mother," Janet remarked. "I completely forgot to wire her after I got here and the poor dear's probably worried about me. Don't bother to come, George. I'll take the coupe."

It was nearly an hour before she returned.

"Beastly connections," she explained. "It seemed that they'd held the wire till about five minutes before I got there, and then mother must have given up. All very complicated."

I can't explain why, but I knew she wasn't telling the truth. I'd wondered if what she had been about to tell me before George came was that there was another man in the offing. Now the phone call increased that suspicion. I was a little upset about the situation, but I was far more upset by Asey's continued absence.

He turned up finally at three o'clock, still dressed in his corduroy trousers, blue shirt and canvas jacket. Apparently he had not gone to Boston, as I'd thought at first, for I felt sure in that case he would have worn what he and Syl called his "city clothes."

Asey strolled over to us. "H'lo," he began, then he stopped short and sniffed.

"Asey," I said, "where *have* you been? And what *are* you sniffing like Samson for?"

"Last time I smelled that perfume," Asey said, "was in Calcutta, an' that was a long, long time ago. My, my, that perfume takes me back! Who's got it?" He sniffed again. "Mr. Ballard? I guess you must be Mr. Ballard, ain't you?" He stopped in front of George.

George lost a lot of his amiability.

"Yes," he said stiffly, "I'm afraid that perfume is on me. I stopped off at a barber shop near the airport for a shave this morning. Terrible place. They drenched me with the stuff before I could protest."

"'Tis sort of ripe," Asey agreed. "Tell me, Mr. Ballard, how do you spell your last name? The papers spell it dif'rent from your mother's."

"B-a-l-l-o-r-d. Not 'a.' You see, it was my own name, so much like Ballard that it was never changed."

"Why," I exclaimed, "the strangest thing's just come to me! I never thought of it till George spelled his name out letter by letter. It's nothing important,—just a coincidence. But do you remember, Punch, when you introduced Red to me Tuesday night? He pretended he couldn't understand the name because of your broad 'a' and asked me if I spelled it B-a-l-l-a-r-d? I'm sorry I interrupted, but George's spelling brought it all back."

"Never happened to know Gilpin, did you, Mr. Ballord?" Asey asked.

George shook his head. "No. Tell me, Mr. Mayo, how are you getting along with this case? The papers don't seem to be particularly optimistic."

"Papers," Asey said in his purring voice, "don't know everything. Not by a long shot. Fact is, I found out who *did* kill Red, but I ain't told 'em yet. I guess, though, it's time I told you all. Syl!"

At the summons Syl ran out from the garage.

"Syl, bring me that leather box from the roadster's front seat, will you?"

Syl lugged it out and put it on top of the wicker table. Taking a key from his pocket, Asey unlocked the case and the top snapped open.

We were so quiet that we could almost hear the grass grow. Every eye was on Asey as he drew forth a suit of clothes, a man's grey tweeds. At the odor they exuded, I put my handkerchief to my nose. Whoever had worn that suit had undeniably come in contact with a skunk.

"That suit," Asey said gravely, "was worn by the feller that killed Gilpin Tuesday night. He was a pretty clever feller. He made an awful lot of plans, an' they all worked. N'en somethin' turned up he didn't 'count for. Somethin' you wouldn't take into c'nsid'ration in plannin' a murder. He met," Asey said, "another skunk. Mr. Ballord, no doubt about these bein' your clothes, is they?"

In utter horror I looked at George, sitting there with his face absolutely chalk white. I cried aloud when I looked down at his hands. Between his fingers he was nervously twisting a small wire paper clip.

18

I EXPECTED an instant and furious denial from George in spite of the paper clip—for after all, both Satterlee and Aristene had played with paper clips and it had not been significant. But George said nothing.

"They *are* your clothes, ain't they, Mr. Ballord?" Asey repeated, as Aristene and her father came out of the house.

"They are," George said at last.

"An' you did come down here Tuesday night?"

"Yes, but just to make sure that mother had arrived safely."

"Then why'd you send her that telegram the next day, if you already knew she was okay? An' where's your car you come down in? I know. You're goin' to say it's gettin' a new fender put on it. It's gettin' new upholstery, too. An' I seen the old."

"Look here, Mayo," George began to bluster, "don't be ridiculous. Don't try to pin anything on me. I never knew Gilpin. I—"

"That's true," Asey said. "You *didn't* know Gilpin." He leaned over swiftly and picked up the twisted paper clip George had just dropped on the ground. "But there's other things. There's this. An'," he searched in a pocket and brought out three envelopes, then he spilled their contents out in separate little heaps, "an', these. These clips here was found near where Gilpin was shot. These was found near where a skunk was—was killed. An' these," he pointed to the last pile, "come from your study in your house in Boston."

Before I could digest the fact that Asey had, after all, been to Boston, he continued.

"Here," he said, bringing out a large manila envelope full of papers, "is a statement from Dr. Burnside. You first called him two weeks before you hired this cottage. True, Bangs only knew about the rentin' of this place the same day he got your letter, but it didn't make any difference what cottage you took, really, just so long's you got it, learned the lay of the land an' hired it in time to catch this troupe on its Cape tour. So you got the cottage, lured the troupe out here by a letter signed by the name of Maynard Guild."

"I did not," George returned. "Produce such a letter and I'll prove it."

"I know," Asey returned. "You had someone else sign it. Now here," he selected another paper, "is a statement that you're the head of Chandler, Cobb an' Cross. That's the firm that put Red Gilpin out of the automobile business."

"I'm behind that firm, but I have absolutely nothing to do with the firm's routine business. I knew nothing about any dealings this Gilpin may have had with us. I can prove it."

"Here," Asey went on imperturbably, "is a check out of your file—"

"You've—you've been through my files? I'll have you—"

"Nope, you won't. A check to John Smith for five hundred dollars, dated May first. Here's another for five hundred, dated May sixth. Both come through New Hampshire banks. John was the feller that bought a .45 Colt for you."

"John Smith was given that money," George said, "for—"

"Yup. Services rendered. Here, Mr. Ballord, is a statement that says you're durn good at make-up. Signed by the head of an actin' club you b'long to. You made John Smith up to look like Dan Allen. You was on a business trip around May fourth, wasn't you?"

"Yes. But I never saw Dan Allen till this morning. The whole thing is absolutely absurd!"

"Yup. You never seen Dan in the flesh before this, but you seen his pictures an' you know all about him. Here's your checks to Whitey Weeks's Detective Agency. Whitey's a friend of mine. Used to be cook on a boat for me once. I routed him out of bed the middle of last night. You had him gettin' all the dope, pitchers an' all, on this troupe from January till May first. Told Whitey you thought one of the bunch was a forger your firm was after."

"I paid Weeks to track down a forger, a man who ran away from our office. I thought Weeks was perfectly reliable. It turned out that he was on the wrong track altogether. I—"

"An' here," Asey said, producing a pack of letters, "are some of the letters Red Gilpin wrote your wife."

I understood then why Janet had been called to the telephone. It *had* been a man, but the man had been Asey.

"What!" George said. "What? Jan, did you know this Gilpin?"

"You know I did," Janet replied quietly. "You read the letters yourself even though I locked them up in my desk."

So Janet—Janet was Red Gilpin's only love! It burst on me like a bombshell. It took my breath away. Janet *was* beautiful. She'd been the most beautiful deb of her day. But compared to Edie Allen, she was merely pretty. Hat Allen was far more striking. Judy's hair was lovelier. Aristene's hands made Janet's appear uncouth.

For the first time I realized how much you take for granted the looks of people who are near to you. Janet *was* beautiful. It wasn't the freshly throbbing beauty that had made her so sought after the year she came out. It was rather a weary beauty now. But Janet had more charm than any of the women present.

"I did *not* read my wife's personal letters," George said. "If you think so, I suppose you can prove it by finger prints?"

Asey smiled. "You wore gloves. But I have your wife's word that she never puts letters back in the envelopes in any kind of order. Stuffs 'em back in any which way. You're orderly. After you read 'em, you put the pages back in order. Put the letters in a certain funny way. Same way all the letters in your files is put back."

"The whole thing's absurd," George said. "I don't read other people's letters. I knew nothing about them. I do not see how you can—"

"You," Asey said, "are a planner. You're a durn good planner. Except for what happened after you killed that skunk, or before it, I'd never of got you even though I'd kind of made mental res'vations about you. Somehow it never seemed to me for one minute that you wasn't right here, what with hearin' about you all the time, or seein' telegrams from you. You planned even for groceries here, an' ker'sene oil for the stove if there *was* a stove that'd burn ker'sene oil. You thought of everythin' an' then you went just one better. This was done by a planner. That was certain from the first. You was the only one that seemed planny-like. An' you got a temper. It's takin' most of your c'ntrol right now not to show it. I knew you kept files an' receipts an' such because your mother said so. I knew you knew about guns. She said she'd given you her husband's guns. She wouldn't of if you hadn't known or used 'em. An' that first telegram of yours was the first alibi there was. 'Advise how you stood the trip' an' so on. *You* wanted to make sure *you* was counted out. N'en Punch told us how Red liked good-looking women. N'en I remembered I'd seen your wife's picture in Mrs. Ballard's room the time the doc was lookin' at Gilpin. Things sort of c'nected, Mr. Ballord. You planned almost too hard."

"I admit," George said, "that I make many plans and that I have a temper. But I didn't know John Gilpin. I cannot see how you—"

"Want the story to see just how much I know? All right. From the beginnin'.

"Gilpin met your wife last fall an' fell in love with her. Wrote her letters. You read 'em an' thought the worst—an' as a matter of fact, she was perfectly faithful to you, though from what I dug up about you in the last fifteen hours or so, I don't see how she stood it. I don't see how she stood you. Well, you read the letters an' lost your temper. Looked up Gilpin unbeknownst to him, got your firm, Chandler an' so on, to put him out of business. Out of sight, out of mind, an' all that. But Red's letters kept on comin'. You didn't know that she never answered 'em. Anyway, you got Whitey Weeks to check up on the troupe. Found out just enough to know Dan was the feller you could choose to hold the baby. Hired Mr. J. Smith, a rovin' unemployed, most likely, to buy your gun an' bullets in Nashua. You could of got 'em in a pawn shop, but you wanted somethin' that could be traced easy, back to Dan. An' the signature on the form wasn't yours. Nothin' to be traced to you direct. You told the feller to get an ole gun, an' to make himself remembered. So he dickered. Satterlee said so. Puzzled me, that did. This troupe's too generally free an' easy to dicker. Well, anyway, the feller was made up like Dan an' bought the gun in his name. How's that?"

"You have no proof—"

"Okay. Then you got hold of this house. You already knew the troupe's route. You knew your mother'd need a place to re-coup'rate. Any place'd of done. But you got this. Short run—you're away a lot. Drive a lot. Got yourself a new car after you'd done your rec'noiterin'. That was so 's nobody'd spot your car. You write the troupe a letter to get 'em here. Then you go off to your mother an' pretend it's a new idea. Bully her. She throws your plans out. But you *knew* that even if you or the folks you chose to come with her was here or not, she'd be soft-hearted when the troupe turned up disappointed in not findin' Guild. You knew, in fact," Asey smiled, "you even said she had a horrid habit of pickin' up every Tom, Dick an' Harry. You banked on that. You planned on comin'. All you had to do was to shoot Red, throw the gun away, an' wait for it to be traced back to Dan. Even not bein' able to come yourself wasn't so hard."

"Look here, Mayo—"

"Uh-huh. I know. Parker's report on you said you went up to your room at ten or so. Gave the name of the book you got at the circulatin' lib'ry to read that night. But it didn't say if you really went to bed or really read it. You didn't. You slipped out an' drove down here. You knew what Gilpin looked like even if you didn't know him. Knew all about him, even to his usually sleepin' in the truck. All you had to do was to get hold of him—an' shoot. You got dozens of books on guns at home. You knew them cartridges wouldn't make a lot of noise. You knew enough of this place from lookin' it over to know that there was usually a stiff wind blowin' anyway. An' always the roar of the surf, an' the noise of the waves, even at low tide. Either you got Gilpin out of the truck or else you waylaid him after he got through talkin' with Judy. Or else when he was wanderin' around like he did. You shoot him. Your car's hid in a back road. They ain't no phone. You're safe enough in any case. Even if they found you, you had your alibi: you come down to see your mother. If you'd come with her, well, you'd of been out investigatin' noises. That do?"

"Absolutely false. Circumstantial evidence. You can't prove a thing. You—"

"An' on the way back," Asey went on, "you ran into a skunk. First of all, you stepped into a hole. A skunk hole. The—well, I can prove that. I got your shoes here. Then the mother skunk went at you. You—well, I'll pass over what happened. You'd thrown your gun away. You prob'ly had a flashlight, but you couldn't use it as a club. Needed it to get to your car. You used your bare hands. And you must have one of the most fiendish tempers in this world. That's all I can say. Well, then you went to your car. You didn't have any extra clothes. You had to be back in Boston in time to go through your reg'lar routine the next day. So you went back just as you was. Took off your suit an' put it in a box in a file drawer, an' locked it. You couldn't burn it. No furnace fire. Couldn't have it cleaned. Couldn't let it be seen, even around the house. 'Rouse questions. An' expl'nations'd of come hard. The car? You poured a can of black paint over the front seat, n'en gas. N'en you took the car to the repair shop next day."

Asey paused a moment.

"I don't know what you did about yourself. Carbolic s'lution, I think, an' dis'nfectants. I can smell some on you now under that perfume you had put on. You went to Chicago not b'cause you had any urgent business, but b'cause you didn't dare come down here as you was. Other folks might think just that you'd been usin' a salve or got perfume on you by mistake. Down here, it'd mean somethin' else. Your trip was just to play for time. You had to go. If you'd stayed in Boston, there wasn't no reason why you shouldn't come to your mother. You told your wife to keep away b'cause you was scared she might guess. She did, but she'd stood too much from you to be bullied in a thing like this. When I saw that skunk an' the clip near it—you stood an' wondered what you *could* do, afterwards, I s'pose—then I knew this crowd here was out. I knew they hadn't met up with any skunk. There's the whole shootin' match, from A to Z."

Asey packed the suit carefully and put it back in the big leather case. Gravely he put his various papers back in order, secured them with an elastic band, slipped them in a pocket.

None of us said anything. None of us could. Janet stared fixedly at the ground. Asey looked beyond the pines at a gull which circled and swooped in the blue, blue sky.

I was so dazed that I couldn't think. I couldn't cry. I couldn't speak. The women of my generation and my group were taught to control their emotions, but it was not that training which kept me from going to pieces then. I was too thunderstruck to think of going to pieces.

Jumbled memories raced through my mind. George, a plump, blue-eyed baby, taking the place of young Adin in his crib and in my heart. George in a white sailor suit with a whistle in his pocket, riding in the Public Garden swan boats. George in knickers and a plaid cap, surveying the Atlantic for the first time on the Lusitania. George, head of his class at Harvard. George, the head of Ballard and Company.—I shook my head to try to clear and focus the pictures that flashed together. Then I looked at George, white-faced, still twisting a paper clip between his fingers.

"You know, Mayo," he said, "you have no proof."

"If you came here Tuesday to see your mother, why didn't you see her? Why did you send that telegram? Why did you lock your suit up? Why didn't you say you'd been here when you first heard of this, if your trip was so in'cent? An' there's just one more thing that may make you see this kind of clearer. Steve Crump knows about your mother's money an' about Ballard an' Comp'ny. He's on his way here."

I found my voice. "Asey—there's—there can't be anything wrong with Ballard and Company? Or my money either?"

"Steve says there's left about a fifth of what you give George. He found this all out by himself. He had an idea somethin' was up. It ain't so good about the comp'ny, either."

I began to understand why George had flown into such a rage when I mentioned Steve, and transacting my own business, on Monday. I was beginning to be able to think, now.

"George," I said, "I don't care about my money, but—it's *not* true about the company? Your father's company! He spent his life building it up. An honest company!"

George didn't answer. He avoided my eye. A rush of bitter words came to my lips, but I checked them before they were out. There was no use for words, no need for words. There was nothing to be said, I think, now, that I almost could have forgiven George—at least I should have stood by him—if it had not been for the closing of Ballard and Company.

Janet took my hand. "Don't—don't worry, Vic. Dad'll fix things. He can and he will."

But the reassurance didn't help any. I was trying only to convince myself that things were as they were: George was a murderer. He was a thief. Actually he had not denied either. He couldn't. I didn't want to believe them, but I couldn't help myself. The facts were there. I thought of the time Adin's father had told of a Zulu raid in Africa, where his favorite brother and his family had been slaughtered. I remembered his comment, "It is ridiculous!" I'd never before understood what he meant by that, but now I knew. It wasn't the flippant, callous remark I had thought it was. After the feeling of blankness and the feeling of bitterness had passed, there was only one thing left, to resign myself to what *was,* no matter how incredible it might seem. With that resigned feeling was mixed a wonder that such things could happen—but you knew that they *had* happened. In that sense, this situation was ridiculous. It was what happened to people, other people, in newspaper accounts or novels or moving pictures. It wasn't sensible. It *was* ridiculous.

Yet it was true, and it had to be faced.

I looked up to find only Janet, George and Asey left of all the group. The others must have slipped away at his command, but I'd not been aware of their departure.

From the pocket of his canvas jacket Asey brought out the Colt which Syl had found on the beach, and the buff colored box of cartridges. He took out a cartridge, tossed it in the air and caught it again before he spoke.

"I'm goin' to do a sort of unlawful thing, Mr. Ballord," he said. "But I'm not a reg'lar cop. I don't have to follow reg'lar rules. I think I'll let you go up to Barnst'ble an' give yourself over to Parker. You might, if you want, sign a c'nfession. I—"

"You can't convict me," George said. "You have no proof. I—"

Asey nodded. "Of course, you can take that view if you want to. I'll promise you you'll be mistaken. But in view of Steve Crump an' what he may have to say, I sort of think it might almost be best for you to go along."

He put the big Colt and a single cartridge on the wicker table.

"In one way," Asey continued, "you ain't your mother's son. In another way, you are. You can take these along to Parker, if you figger you can make one honest gesture with 'em."

George looked at Asey and smiled faintly. He flicked the paper clip with which he had been playing and snapped it onto the ground a dozen feet away. There was something final in the act.

As he passed behind me I think he touched my hair for an instant; for the barest second he laid his hand on one of Janet's. Then he pocketed the gun and the single cartridge and walked over to the hired sedan without ever saying a word. I realized, as the car disappeared from sight, that none of us would ever see him again.

"I—I'm—well," Asey's voice broke, "I didn't know what else I could do. I had proof, an' he knew it."

He and Janet caught me as I fell forward.

It was many months before I realized the grim humor of the statement I had made in the beginning—that George was responsible for the whole affair.

THE END

DISCUSSION QUESTIONS

- Did any aspects of the plot date the story? If so, which?

- Would the story be different if it were set in the present day? If so, how?

- Did the social context of the time play a role in the narrative? If so, how?

- If you were one of the main characters, would you have acted differently at any point in the story?

- Did you identify with any of the characters? If so, which?

- What skills or qualities make Asey Mayo such an effective sleuth?

- Did this book remind you of any present day authors? If so, which?

Read on for a preview of
another case for Asey Mayo in
The Cape Cod Mystery,
available now in hardcover,
paperback, and eBook

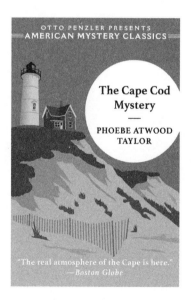

Chapter One
THE WEEK-END BEGINS

" 'Heat wave hits East,' " Betsey read. " 'Prostration record of all time. Mercury soaring.' Well, that's gone and torn our peaceful vacation, that has. By to-night we'll have a stack of telegrams a yard high from city-sizzling friends who want to get cooled off."

I sighed a little. "I know," I said wearily. As a perennial and thoroughly experienced summer cottager on Cape Cod I sat back to await the inevitable deluge.

"You groan as though it were an earthquake or a flood instead of a few visitors, Snoodles," Betsey remarked.

Now my name is not Snoodles, but Prudence Whitsby, and for at least fifteen years I have tried to make my niece drop that absurd name she gave me in her childhood. I feel it is far from appropriate for a respectable spinster of fifty like myself. But Betsey refuses.

"No one knows better than I what nuisances record-temperature guests can be," I told her. "They simply will not be content to sit on the porch and let the cool ocean breezes blow over them. They want violent action every minute of the day and night, and by the time their sunburn has been treated and their aching muscles rubbed with liniment, I feel as though I needed a rest cure myself. And," I added, "I don't see how we can have more than two."

"We can't. And unless we ask a properly married couple, one will have to use the spare bed in my room. The only thing we overlooked in this place was the accommodation of company."

For many summers we had cast covetous eyes on the cottage we now occupied. We would still be envying the Bentleys, who had rented it from time immemorial, if they had not taken it into their heads to see Europe under the guidance of Mr. Cook. We liked our quarters principally because they neither leaked nor squeaked, two virtues which summer vacationists will recognize as paramount. The ship carpenters who had built the place in their spare time declared that Noah himself couldn't have wished for a tighter or a better substitute for the Ark.

We were entranced by the truly spacious living-room and its mammoth fireplace, guaranteed by the agent to draw perfectly. Undeniably the view was the best in town, for the cottage was perched on the flat top of a sandy, bayberry-bush-covered hill from which we could see the greater part of Cape Cod Bay. The Bentleys had bragged that on a clear day they could see Plymouth Rock and the outlines of Boston, but fruitless hours spent with binoculars compelled us to set that statement down to over-enthusiasm on their part.

The bathroom was appallingly palatial. There was an electric light system and an electric pump. To be sure, the lights would and did go out during storms, and sometimes when there was no sign of bad weather, but poking about with feebly flickering candles once in a while was much more preferable than having kerosene lamps all the time.

There was a tiny room for Olga, our cook; a garage more than ample for Betsey's car, and all the space in the world for Ginger the cat to roam about. There were no near neighbors, a fact which delighted us, for many a summer vacation had been spoiled for us by small squalling children who raced under our windows at dawn. Perhaps a hundred and fifty feet away there was the Bentley children's playhouse, now converted into a rough one-room cabin, but we knew it was too small to contain any howling youngsters. It could be seen only from the kitchen window as the agent demonstrated when we objected to it, and we accepted his word that its size and lack of improvements would make it hard to rent.

There were only two drawbacks. One was the absence of a telephone which forced us to make countless trips to town each day. The other was the lack of room Betsey had mentioned. We could have but two extra guests with any degree of comfort.

The sheaf of nine telegrams we straightway received presented us with a task.

"All the old standbys," Betsey said as she ran through them. "The Poors and Jock Ellis and his unspeakable fiancée. I say, Snoodles, here's one from John Kurth. And look. Another from Maida Waring. We haven't heard from those two since they were divorced, have we?"

"No. I had the impression that he was in Sumatra or some such place and she was in Paris."

"That may be," said Betsey, "but these are both from Boston, if the Western Union isn't being funny."

"I should like to see them again, but I understand that they've been at swords' points since they parted. The whole thing was a pity. They were two of the most amusing people we knew."

"Well, that counts them out, unless we want to ask them separately later on. How'll we choose?"

"The usual way will do as well as any"

Betsey took a handful of matches and cut them up into irregular pieces. Then thrusting an end into each telegram so that only the tip protruded, she held them out to me fanwise, like a bridge hand.

"Longer end wins every time. Draw by twos."

I drew. Betsey turned over the winning blanks.

"That's a grand combination. John and Maida, no less. Well, we'll flip a coin."

We flipped a coin, but the same two were again paired.

"I declare," said Betsey crossly, "it's a conspiracy. The fates are against us. That means we'd keep on drawing those two till Kingdom Come. And we can't possibly ask them if they're such sworn enemies."

She tossed the entire bunch into the fireplace.

"Why, Betsey!" I was surprised.

"I don't care. I'm sick of having all the waifs and strays and homeless thrust themselves on us. Let's institute a reform. Let's ask two people we really want to have down, two people who don't fly into a rage at the sight of each other. Let's let all the ex-husbands and ex-wives go hang."

I wondered vaguely why we hadn't done that very thing long before.

"Now," Betsey continued, "take Dot Cram. If the mercury is soaring the way the papers say, that settlement of hers on the East Side of Old Manhattan must be pretty uncomfortable. But does she cry for heat relief like so many politicians crying for drought relief? She does not. So I shall ask her. You know your-self that she's one of my more normal friends, and I haven't seen her half a dozen times since we left college. What do you think?"

"If she can get away, I think it's a fine plan."

"Of course she can get away. You approve of her, don't you?"

I nodded. "I like Dot, and she does have better than average manners for this day and age. I wonder if she still burbles with adjectives."

"You mean," Betsey imitated her, "My dear, it's too simply precious and marvelous for words? That sort of lingering empha-sis as though she were loath to let the next word out? I suppose she does, though it may conceivably have worn off. But I know she's still addicted to dangly earrings, and her hair is just the same."

"It always reminded me of a chrysanthemum."

Betsey laughed. "It is rather like one. At college she claimed that no one really liked her till they found out it was natural-ly blonde and a stranger to peroxide. Who are you going to have?"

"Whom," I corrected her, "and don't say 'No one—they.' It's a mystery to me how you ever acquired an education without gleaning a little knowledge of the English language by the way-side."

"Whom, then, teacher, do you intend to ask?"

"I've been thinking of Emma Manton. She hates the heat, and I don't think she's been away from Boston since Henry Ed-ward died."

"I can well see how she wouldn't enjoy the heat. How much does she weigh?"

"Something over two hundred and twenty-five pounds," I an-swered. "The exact fraction escapes me."

"Funny, but I can't think of her as the wife, or rather the widow, of a clergyman. Not even of such an eccentric clergyman as Henry Edward. She might have been the wife of some robust Englishman out of Dickens, but not the other. She's too addicted to tweeds and jumper suits."

"She'll probably bring some fresh catnip from her garden for Ginger," I said thoughtfully.

"You old plotter! But she'll play Russian Banque with you. And she's met Dot other summers, and they get along together beautifully. And neither one of 'em will want to rip and tear and dash places all the time. Fancy Emma dashing anyway." She snickered. "I'll drive up and send 'em unrefusable telegrams."

The heat-wave head-lines had appeared in Wednesday's paper and our guests arrived Friday on the early morning train. They were promptly dragged off to the beach by Betsey.

From my steamer chair on the porch I could just see the girls on the outer raft. Despite the crowd, holiday size on a common week-day morning, Emma's large black-stockinged legs were exceedingly visible as they protruded from beneath the broad green stripes of my favorite beach umbrella.

I picked up my book, *The Lipstick Murderer,* and prepared to revel with that doughty detective, Wyncheon Woodruff, until luncheon time. But Bill Porter's voice interrupted me as I was gravely considering the value of a strand of red hair as a possible clue.

"Is it blood and thunder, Snoodles, or gin and sawdust? From the title it might be either."

Bill Porter has used my frivolous nickname as long as Betsey, and upon him as upon my niece, persuasion has no effect.

"You know perfectly well," I told him, "that I read mystery stories for the one and simple reason that they exercise my wits. I fail to get any stimulus out of these modern novels full of sordid reminiscences and biological details."

"Hooey," said Bill inelegantly. "Just as if you didn't swipe my entire stock of Old Sleuth in days gone by and force me to read Trollope or something equally wordy. You *said* you did it to make me improve my mind, but I always thought you wanted them yourself. Now I'm sure of it. Think," he sighed as though he were in great pain, "think of your reading that vulgar low-brow volume while a Dale Sanborn masterpiece sits cooling its heels by your elbow." He helped himself to an apple turnover from the plateful Olga had thoughtfully left on the porch.

"Oily," he added with his mouth full. "Very oily."

"Olga said they were particularly good to-day."

"My dear and worthy Snoodles, I am not referring to these toothsome pastries, and you know it. I refer to that Sanborn gent, who is distinctly oily. How'd he ever land in the town?"

"I've wondered at it myself. He told me he thought it would be a good place to rest in before starting another book. What's the name of the purple-covered thing on the table? *Reverence.* Well, that is his latest effort, not available to the general public till next month sometime. We were formally presented with it last night. But whatever his reason for coming, Bill, he has made up his mind to stay."

"That so? Where?"

"He's taken the cabin for the rest of the season. He moved in, bag and baggage, this morning. I should have thought the place was too rough for such a fastidious soul, but he pronounced it enchanting."

Bill made a wry face. "That may be a good two-dollar word, but I know darn few men who'd pronounce that shack enchanting. He's a crazy sort of fellow."

"Crazy?"

"Well," Bill wound himself around a footstool. "Peculiar. He let slip the fact that he went to Harvard, but when I picked him up and asked his year, he hedged like fury. It took a good five minutes of my best Yankee pumping to find out that he was the class of '20. Just for fun I looked him up in an old register at home, but I couldn't find his name in it. Maybe he went incog., like a Student Prince. Maybe he is a Student Prince anyway. He's got all the elements. Looks a little foreign and condescending. Say, do you think he's falling for our Betsey?"

I shook my head. "I don't know for sure. Numerous young men have fallen in love with Betsey at one time and another, and he's shown some of the symptoms. Of course he didn't decide to stay here till after he met her. But the only real peculiarity I've noticed in him is his tendency to say 'Thank-you' in one syllable, as though it were a thing you played billiards with."

Bill chuckled. "I do hope he isn't after Betsey. I always had a sneaking feeling that I'd like to marry the gal myself. Would you mind awfully having the scion of the Porter millions for a neph-ew-in-law?"

"On the contrary, I think I should like it."

As a matter of fact I had always intended Bill to marry Betsey. Not because of the Porter money, for Betsey had enough of her own, but rather in spite of it. As Bill once remarked, it wasn't his fault that his father turned the family carriage business into a prosperous automobile company.

"But would Betsey mind, do you think? At the moment she thinks I'm a wastrel of the worst type. She even has some fantas-tic notion about my going to work. Why," he took another turn-over, "why should I go to work?"

The question was rhetorical. There was no earthly reason why Bill Porter should work. His older brother Jimmy has carried off the business honors of the family since Porter, Senior, died, and Bill has always acknowledged his own incompetence as a business man.

"If," he went on, "I got myself a job with the Porter outfit, Jimmy would put me to work balancing ledgers or filing blotters. And there are plenty of needy individuals in this world who can balance ledgers or file blotters better than I could hope to in a million years. And now that I'm a selectman and on the school committee I find enough to do right here in the town. My taxes swell the local coffers and make for better roads and things. In the city they wouldn't even repair an aged cobblestone."

"If she wants you to go to work," I soothed him, "it's because she thinks about your future and that means she's interested, at least."

"Maybe that's so. I never thought of it in that light. I've been Billy the boy companion so long that I'm dubious of her ever thinking of me as Billy the fond husband. Besides, girls don't want to marry people they know as well as Betsey knows me. She knows how I look when I haven't had a shave and how I like my eggs cooked and everything else."

He turned and looked morosely over the bay. The brilliant July sun flashed over the tiny waves as the tide slid unobtrusively in the harbor. An occasional squawking gull made a brief white dot on the sky of the Cape's own particular blue. The gilt cupola of the house Grandfather Porter had built glittered from the left arm of the bay. Over to the right a group of town boys were diving from the dilapidated wharf that had once been the pride of the town. The oyster-shell lane that led from the cottage down the hill past the tennis courts shone like a piece of white satin ribbon. I remembered that Betsey's impractical underclothing needed new straps. Beyond the road was the sandy strip where the natives and summer people alike made splotches of bright color.

"There's Sanborn now," Bill said suddenly. "Talking with Betsey and your visitors down by the bath house. I saw Dot and Mrs. Manton at the station this morning. Dot looked tired."

"She says New York is simply a boiling steaming cauldron."

Bill laughed. "You know, the more I look at your friend Emma the more she reminds me of that mammoth bronze Buddha, the resigned one in Japan somewhere. It's fifty feet high and about double that in girth."

"You say she's like a Buddha and Betsey says she's like the wife of someone out of Dickens."

"She's a combination of both. Did you ever read any of Sanborn's books, Snoodles?"

"Not exactly. I started one of them once. That one they called *The Greatest Exposé of Married Life in America*. It was all about a man—no; about a girl who loved a man who was married to a girl—I think this is straight—who loved a man who loved the first mentioned girl. It confused me to such an extent that I left off on page forty. It was a little nasty, too. I am not convinced that his characters bear any resemblance to human beings, though I am given to understand that he takes his stories from life."

"Most authors," Bill commented, "love to call their works the creation of a fertile imagination. I had an idea that it was a law of the author's union or something to disclaim any connection with real life at all."

"So did I. But he gloats over the fact that his tales are true. I haven't tackled the new one yet. I haven't had time, but I very much doubt whether I'll read it at all. I'm sure that *The Lipstick Murderer* is vastly more entertaining."

"Better not let your niece hear any such heresy. She thinks he's got Dreiser and those lads all sewed up in a sack." He grinned.

Except when he grins, no one would accuse Bill Porter of being good-looking. For one thing, his nose is far too hawk-like and his ears protrude more than is permissible for masculine beauty. He has the Porter face, too, which my father used to describe as being double-breasted in shape. There is a long scar on his forehead where an enthusiastic hockey opponent thrust several inches of skate. But when Bill grins, one forgets these details and sees only that his eyes are gray and honest and his chin is firm.

His ensemble of dungarees and a faded blue shirt were not what one expects to find the well-dressed man wearing. Dale Sanborn, I reflected, would probably not care to be seen in Bill's outfit at the proverbial dog-fight. Sanborn was always so perfectly dressed.

Bill rose from the stool as Betsey came up on the porch with Dot and Emma bringing up the rear.

"The water was too perfectly gorgeous, Miss Prudence," Dot's earrings jangled as she bobbed her head to emphasize her statement. "Wasn't it just, Mrs. Manton? Wasn't it absolutely divine? And why didn't you tell me that Dale Sanborn was here? I thought he was out on Long Island, or some other island."

"I didn't know you knew him," I said mildly. Almost any remark seems mild after listening to Dot flow on.

"But I do, really I do. And I think it's too utterly splendid to find him down here."

"If you have anything," Emma interrupted, "that I could read, I think I'll take it up-stairs and browse till luncheon."

She looked at the collection on the table.

"Take your choice," I said.

"Don't you have anything but murders?" she asked plaintively. "Haven't you anything in a calm restful story where the hero and the heroine end up happily in each other's arms?"

"Betsey goes in for the moderns and I specialize in murder," I said. "But here's Dale Sanborn's latest. I don't know what it's about, but I feel sure it's nothing so commonplace as murder. And it's autographed."

"I'll take it." She stopped at the threshold. "Is lunch at one?"

"At two. It's dinner to-day because Olga has the afternoon and evening off instead of Thursday. It's inconvenient, but we have a pick-up supper. You can browse over Mr. Sanborn for two hours or so."

"Is it his very newest?" Dot inquired. "How too wonderful."

"Simply precious," Bill teased her. "You know, just too truly splendiferous. You girls want to get the mail? If you do, I'll take you up to the post-office in Lucinda. To prove my sterling worth, I'll even take you to the grocery and let you do the family marketing for Snoodles."

"Oh!" Dot squealed. "Do you have Lucinda even now? Do you still drive it?"

"Even now," Betsey answered for him. "And he still drives the thing, though one of these fine days it's going to disintegrate like the One Hoss Shay. Jimmy sent him a sixteen-cylinder roadster this spring. It's got a special body, silver fittings and a lalaque radiator ornament, a trick horn and Lord knows what all else. It's even got a radio tucked away somewhere. But does he use it? He does nothing of the kind."

"Why, Bill, how utterly insane of you!"

"It scares me to death," he confessed. "And the town would think I was putting on side. And Lucinda understands me like a brother."

"She ought to," Betsey returned; "you've certainly driven that wreck for ten years at least."

"Eleven," said Bill placidly. "If you're bound to malign her, give the lass her due."

"Eleven then. And do you expect us to ride with you in those awful clothes?"

Dot found a slicker in Lucinda's capacious tool chest and together they forced Bill into it.

He put his yachting cap at a forty-five degree angle, wrapped the slicker around him and struck an attitude.

"'My own convenience counts as nil,—it is my duty and I will!'" he declaimed. "Be good, Snoodles, until this here Light Brigade gets back, when and if it does."

They wedged themselves into Lucinda's worn front seat and drove off to town.

I wondered as I watched them down the hill if there were a front seat in existence into which at least four modern young people could not wedge themselves. I doubted it. Picking up my thriller, I went back to the clue of the strand of red hair.

To be continued in...
THE CAPE COD MYSTERY

All titles are available in hardcover and in trade paperback.

Order from your favorite bookstore or from
The Mysterious Bookshop, 58 Warren Street, New York, N.Y. 10007
(www.mysteriousbookshop.com).

Charlotte Armstrong, *The Chocolate Cobweb*. When Amanda Garth was born, a mix-up caused the hospital to briefly hand her over to the prestigious Garrison family instead of to her birth parents. The error was quickly fixed, Amanda was never told, and the secret was forgotten for twenty-three years ... until her aunt revealed it in casual conversation. But what if the initial switch never actually occurred? **Introduction by A. J. Finn.**

Charlotte Armstrong, *The Unsuspected*. First published in 1946, this suspenseful novel opens with a young woman who has ostensibly hanged herself, leaving a suicide note. Her friend doesn't believe it and begins an investigation that puts her own life in jeopardy. It was filmed in 1947 by Warner Brothers, starring Claude Rains and Joan Caulfield. **Introduction by Otto Penzler.**

Anthony Boucher, *The Case of the Baker Street Irregulars*. When a studio announces a new hard-boiled Sherlock Holmes film, the Baker Street Irregulars begin a campaign to discredit it. Attempting to mollify them, the producers invite members to the set, where threats are received, each referring to one of the original Holmes tales, followed by murder. Fortunately, the amateur sleuths use Holmesian lessons to solve the crime. **Introduction by Otto Penzler.**

Anthony Boucher, *Rocket to the Morgue*. Hilary Foulkes has made so many enemies that it is difficult to speculate who was responsible for stabbing him nearly to death in a room with only one door through which no one was seen entering or leaving. This classic locked room mystery is populated by such thinly disguised science fiction legends as Robert Heinlein, L. Ron Hubbard, and John W. Campbell. **Introduction by F. Paul Wilson.**

Fredric Brown, *The Fabulous Clipjoint*. Brown's outstanding mystery won an Edgar as the best first novel of the year (1947). When Wallace Hunter is found dead in an alley after a long night of drinking, the police don't really care. But his teenage son Ed and his uncle Am, the carnival worker, are convinced that some things don't add up and the crime isn't what it seems to be. **Introduction by Lawrence Block.**

John Dickson Carr, *The Crooked Hinge*. Selected by a group of mystery experts as one of the 15 best impossible crime novels ever written, this is one of Gideon Fell's greatest challenges. Estranged from his family for 25 years, Sir John Farnleigh returns to England from America to claim his inheritance but another person turns up claiming that he can prove he is the real Sir John. Inevitably, one of them is murdered. **Introduction by Charles Todd.**

John Dickson Carr, *The Eight of Swords*. When Gideon Fell arrives at a crime scene, it appears to be straightforward enough. A man has been shot to death in an unlocked room and the likely perpetrator was a recent visitor. But Fell discovers inconsistencies and his investigations are complicated by an apparent poltergeist, some American gangsters, and two meddling amateur sleuths. **Introduction by Otto Penzler.**

John Dickson Carr, *The Mad Hatter Mystery*. A prankster has been stealing top hats all around London. Gideon Fell suspects that the same person may be responsible for the theft of a manuscript of a long-lost story by Edgar Allan Poe. The hats reappear in unexpected but conspicuous places but, when one is found on the head of a corpse by the Tower of London, it is evident that the thefts are more than pranks. **Introduction by Otto Penzler.**

John Dickson Carr, *The Plague Court Murders*. When murder occurs in a locked hut on Plague Court, an estate haunted by the ghost of a hangman's assistant who died a victim of the black death, Sir Henry Merrivale seeks a logical solution to a ghostly crime. A spiritual medium employed to rid the house of his spirit is found stabbed to death in a locked stone hut on the grounds, surrounded by an untouched circle of mud. **Introduction by Michael Dirda.**

John Dickson Carr, *The Red Widow Murders.* In a "haunted" mansion, the room known as the Red Widow's Chamber proves lethal to all who spend the night. Eight people investigate and the one who draws the ace of spades must sleep in it. The room is locked from the inside and watched all night by the others. When the door is unlocked, the victim has been poisoned. Enter Sir Henry Merrivale to solve the crime. **Introduction by Tom Mead.**

Frances Crane, *The Turquoise Shop.* In an arty little New Mexico town, Mona Brandon has arrived from the East and becomes the subject of gossip about her money, her influence, and the corpse in the nearby desert who may be her husband. Pat Holly, who runs the local gift shop, is as interested as anyone in the goings on—but even more in Pat Abbott, the detective investigating the possible murder. **Introduction by Anne Hillerman.**

Todd Downing, *Vultures in the Sky.* There is no end to the series of terrifying events that befall a luxury train bound for Mexico. First, a man dies when the train passes through a dark tunnel, then it comes to an abrupt stop in the middle of the desert. More deaths occur when night falls and the passengers panic when they realize they are trapped with a murderer on the loose. **Introduction by James Sallis.**

Mignon G. Eberhart, *Murder by an Aristocrat.* Nurse Keate is called to help a man who has been "accidentally" shot in the shoulder. When he is murdered while convalescing, it is clear that there was no accident. Although a killer is loose in the mansion, the family seems more concerned that news of the murder will leave their circle. *The New Yorker* wrote than "Eberhart can weave an almost flawless mystery." **Introduction by Nancy Pickard.**

Erle Stanley Gardner, *The Case of the Baited Hook.* Perry Mason gets a phone call in the middle of the night and his potential client says it's urgent, that he has two one-thousand-dollar bills that he will give him as a retainer, with an additional ten-thousand whenever he is called on to represent him. When

Mason takes the case, it is not for the caller but for a beautiful woman whose identity is hidden behind a mask. **Introduction by Otto Penzler.**

Erle Stanley Gardner, *The Case of the Borrowed Brunette.* A mysterious man named Mr. Hines has advertised a job for a woman who has to fulfill very specific physical requirements. Eva Martell, pretty but struggling in her career as a model, takes the job but her aunt smells a rat and hires Perry Mason to investigate. Her fears are realized when Hines turns up in the apartment with a bullet hole in his head. **Introduction by Otto Penzler.**

Erle Stanley Gardner, *The Case of the Careless Kitten.* Helen Kendal receives a mysterious phone call from her vanished uncle Franklin, long presumed dead, who urges her to contact Perry Mason. Soon, she finds herself the main suspect in the murder of an unfamiliar man. Her kitten has just survived a poisoning attempt—as has her aunt Matilda. What is the connection between Franklin's return and the murder attempts? **Introduction by Otto Penzler.**

Erle Stanley Gardner, *The Case of the Rolling Bones.* One of Gardner's most successful Perry Mason novels opens with a clear case of blackmail, though the person being blackmailed claims he isn't. It is not long before the police are searching for someone wanted for killing the same man in two different states—thirty-three years apart. The confounding puzzle of what happened to the dead man's toes is a challenge. **Introduction by Otto Penzler.**

Erle Stanley Gardner, *The Case of the Shoplifter's Shoe.* Most cases for Perry Mason involve murder but here he is hired because a young woman fears her aunt is a kleptomaniac. Sarah may not have been precisely the best guardian for a collection of valuable diamonds and, sure enough, they go missing. When the jeweler is found shot dead, Sarah is spotted leaving the murder scene with a bundle of gems stuffed in her purse. **Introduction by Otto Penzler.**

Erle Stanley Gardner, *The Bigger They Come.* Gardner's first novel using the pseudonym A.A. Fair starts off a series featuring the large and loud Bertha Cool and her employee, the small and meek Donald Lam. Given the job of delivering divorce papers to an evident crook,

Lam can't find him—but neither can the police. The *Los Angeles Times* called this book: "Breathlessly dramatic … an original." Introduction by Otto Penzler.

Frances Noyes Hart, *The Bellamy Trial*. Inspired by the real-life Hall-Mills case, the most sensational trial of its day, this is the story of Stephen Bellamy and Susan Ives, accused of murdering Bellamy's wife Madeleine. Eight days of dynamic testimony, some true, some not, make headlines for an enthralled public. Rex Stout called this historic courtroom thriller one of the ten best mysteries of all time. Introduction by Hank Phillippi Ryan.

H.F. Heard, *A Taste for Honey*. The elderly Mr. Mycroft quietly keeps bees in Sussex, where he is approached by the reclusive and somewhat misanthropic Mr. Silchester, whose honey supplier was found dead, stung to death by her bees. Mycroft, who shares many traits with Sherlock Holmes, sets out to find the vicious killer. Rex Stout described it as "sinister … a tale well and truly told." Introduction by Otto Penzler.

Dolores Hitchens, *The Alarm of the Black Cat*. Detective fiction aficionado Rachel Murdock has a peculiar meeting with a little girl and a dead toad, sparking her curiosity about a love triangle that has sparked anger. When the girl's great grandmother is found dead, Rachel and her cat Samantha work with a friend in the Los Angeles Police Department to get to the bottom of things. Introduction by David Handler.

Dolores Hitchens, *The Cat Saw Murder*. Miss Rachel Murdock, the highly intelligent 70-year-old amateur sleuth, is not entirely heartbroken when her slovenly, unattractive, bridge-cheating niece is murdered. Miss Rachel is happy to help the socially maladroit and somewhat bumbling Detective Lieutenant Stephen Mayhew, retaining her composure when a second brutal murder occurs. Introduction by Joyce Carol Oates.

Dorothy B. Hughes, *Dread Journey*. A bigshot Hollywood producer has worked on his magnum opus for years, hiring and firing one beautiful starlet after another. But Kitten Agnew's contract won't allow her to be fired, so she fears she might be terminated more permanently. Together with the producer on

a train journey from Hollywood to Chicago, Kitten becomes more terrified with each passing mile. Introduction by Sarah Weinman.

Dorothy B. Hughes, *Ride the Pink Horse*. When Sailor met Willis Douglass, he was just a poor kid who Douglass groomed to work as a confidential secretary. As the senator became increasingly corrupt, he knew he could count on Sailor to clean up his messes. No longer a senator, Douglass flees Chicago for Santa Fe, leaving behind a murder rap and Sailor as the prime suspect. Seeking vengeance, Sailor follows. Introduction by Sara Paretsky.

Dorothy B. Hughes, *The So Blue Marble*. Set in the glamorous world of New York high society, this novel became a suspense classic as twins from Europe try to steal a rare and beautiful gem owned by an aristocrat whose sister is an even more menacing presence. *The New Yorker* called it "Extraordinary … [Hughes'] brilliant descriptive powers make and unmake reality." Introduction by Otto Penzler.

W. Bolingbroke Johnson, *The Widening Stain*. After a cocktail party, the attractive Lucie Coindreau, a "black-eyed, black-haired Frenchwoman" visits the rare books wing of the library and apparently takes a head-first fall from an upper gallery. Dismissed as a horrible accident, it seems dubious when Professor Hyett is strangled while reading a priceless 12th-century manuscript, which has gone missing. Introduction by Nicholas A. Basbanes

Baynard Kendrick, *Blind Man's Bluff*. Blinded in World War II, Duncan Maclain forms a successful private detective agency, aided by his two dogs. Here, he is called on to solve the case of a blind man who plummets from the top of an eight-story building, apparently with no one present except his dead-drunk son. Introduction by Otto Penzler.

Baynard Kendrick, *The Odor of Violets*. Duncan Maclain, a blind former intelligence officer, is asked to investigate the murder of an actor in his Greenwich Village apartment. This would cause a stir at any time but, when the actor possesses secret government plans that then go missing, it's enough to interest the local police as well as the American government and Maclain, who suspects a German spy plot. Introduction by Otto Penzler.

C. Daly King, *Obelists at Sea*. On a cruise ship traveling from New York to Paris, the lights of the smoking room briefly go out, a gunshot crashes through the night, and a man is dead. Two detectives are on board but so are four psychiatrists who believe their professional knowledge can solve the case by understanding the psyche of the killer—each with a different theory. **Introduction by Martin Edwards.**

Jonathan Latimer, *Headed for a Hearse*. Featuring Bill Crane, the booze-soaked Chicago private detective, this humorous hard-boiled novel was filmed as *The Westland Case* in 1937 starring Preston Foster. Robert Westland has been framed for the grisly murder of his wife in a room with doors and windows locked from the inside. As the day of his execution nears, he relies on Crane to find the real murderer. **Introduction by Max Allan Collins**

Lange Lewis, *The Birthday Murder*. Victoria is a successful novelist and screenwriter and her husband is a movie director so their marriage seems almost too good to be true. Then, on her birthday, her happy new life comes crashing down when her husband is murdered using a method of poisoning that was described in one of her books. She quickly becomes the leading suspect. **Introduction by Randal S. Brandt.**

Frances and Richard Lockridge, *Death on the Aisle*. In one of the most beloved books to feature Mr. and Mrs. North, the body of a wealthy backer of a play is found dead in a seat of the 45th Street Theater. Pam is thrilled to engage in her favorite pastime—playing amateur sleuth—much to the annoyance of Jerry, her publisher husband. The Norths inspired a stage play, a film, and long-running radio and TV series. **Introduction by Otto Penzler.**

John P. Marquand, *Your Turn, Mr. Moto*. The first novel about Mr. Moto, originally titled *No Hero*, is the story of a World War I hero pilot who finds himself jobless during the Depression. In Tokyo for a big opportunity that falls apart, he meets a Japanese agent and his Russian colleague and the pilot suddenly finds himself caught in a web of intrigue. Peter Lorre played Mr. Moto in a series of popular films. **Introduction by Lawrence Block.**

Stuart Palmer, *The Penguin Pool Murder*. The first adventure of schoolteacher and dedicated amateur sleuth Hildegarde Withers occurs at the New York Aquarium when she and her young students notice a corpse in one of the tanks. It was published in 1931 and filmed the next year, starring Edna May Oliver as the American Miss Marple—though much funnier than her English counterpart. **Introduction by Otto Penzler.**

Stuart Palmer, *The Puzzle of the Happy Hooligan*. New York City schoolteacher Hildegarde Withers cannot resist "assisting" homicide detective Oliver Piper. In this novel, she is on vacation in Hollywood and on the set of a movie about Lizzie Borden when the screenwriter is found dead. Six comic films about Withers appeared in the 1930s, most successfully starring Edna May Oliver. **Introduction by Otto Penzler.**

Otto Penzler, ed., *Golden Age Bibliomysteries*. Stories of murder, theft, and suspense occur with alarming regularity in the unlikely world of books and bibliophiles, including bookshops, libraries, and private rare book collections, written by such giants of the mystery genre as Ellery Queen, Cornell Woolrich, Lawrence G. Blochman, Vincent Starrett, and Anthony Boucher. **Introduction by Otto Penzler.**

Otto Penzler, ed., *Golden Age Detective Stories*. The history of American mystery fiction has its pantheon of authors who have influenced and entertained readers for nearly a century, reaching its peak during the Golden Age, and this collection pays homage to the work of the most acclaimed: Cornell Woolrich, Erle Stanley Gardner, Craig Rice, Ellery Queen, Dorothy B. Hughes, Mary Roberts Rinehart, and more. **Introduction by Otto Penzler.**

Otto Penzler, ed., *Golden Age Locked Room Mysteries*. The so-called impossible crime category reached its zenith during the 1920s, 1930s, and 1940s, and this volume includes the greatest of the great authors who mastered the form: John Dickson Carr, Ellery Queen, C. Daly King, Clayton Rawson, and Erle Stanley Gardner. Like great magicians, these literary conjurors will baffle and delight readers. **Introduction by Otto Penzler.**

Ellery Queen, *The Adventures of Ellery Queen*. These stories are the earliest short works to feature Queen as a detective and are among the best of the author's fair-play mysteries. So many of the elements that comprise the gestalt of Queen may be found in these tales: alternate solutions, the dying clue, a bizarre crime, and the author's ability to find fresh variations of works by other authors. **Introduction by Otto Penzler.**

Ellery Queen, *The American Gun Mystery*. A rodeo comes to New York City at the Colosseum. The headliner is Buck Horne, the once popular film cowboy who opens the show leading a charge of forty whooping cowboys until they pull out their guns and fire into the air. Buck falls to the ground, shot dead. The police instantly lock the doors to search everyone but the offending weapon has completely vanished. **Introduction by Otto Penzler.**

Ellery Queen, *The Chinese Orange Mystery*. The offices of publisher Donald Kirk have seen strange events but nothing like this. A strange man is found dead with two long spears alongside his back. And, though no one was seen entering or leaving the room, everything has been turned backwards or upside down: pictures face the wall, the victim's clothes are worn backwards, the rug upside down. Why in the world? **Introduction by Otto Penzler.**

Ellery Queen, *The Dutch Shoe Mystery*. Millionaire philanthropist Abagail Doorn falls into a coma and she is rushed to the hospital she funds for an emergency operation by one of the leading surgeons on the East Coast. When she is wheeled into the operating theater, the sheet covering her body is pulled back to reveal her garroted corpse—the first of a series of murders **Introduction by Otto Penzler.**

Ellery Queen, *The Egyptian Cross Mystery*. A small-town schoolteacher is found dead, headed, and tied to a T-shaped cross on December 25th, inspiring such sensational headlines as "Crucifixion on Christmas Day." Amateur sleuth Ellery Queen is so intrigued he travels to Virginia but fails to solve the crime. Then a similar murder takes place on New York's Long Island—and then another. **Introduction by Otto Penzler.**

Ellery Queen, *The Siamese Twin Mystery*. When Ellery and his father encounter a raging forest fire on a mountain, their only hope is to drive up to an isolated hillside manor owned by a secretive surgeon and his strange guests. While playing solitaire in the middle of the night, the doctor is shot. The only clue is a torn playing card. Suspects include a society beauty, a valet, and conjoined twins. **Introduction by Otto Penzler.**

Ellery Queen, *The Spanish Cape Mystery*. Amateur detective Ellery Queen arrives in the resort town of Spanish Cape soon after a young woman and her uncle are abducted by a gun-toting, one-eyed giant. The next day, the woman's somewhat dicey boyfriend is found murdered—totally naked under a black fedora and opera cloak. **Introduction by Otto Penzler.**

Patrick Quentin, *A Puzzle for Fools*. Broadway producer Peter Duluth takes to the bottle when his wife dies but enters a sanitarium to dry out. Malevolent events plague the hospital, including when Peter hears his own voice intone, "There will be murder." And there is. He investigates, aided by a young woman who is also a patient. This is the first of nine mysteries featuring Peter and Iris Duluth. **Introduction by Otto Penzler.**

Clayton Rawson, *Death from a Top Hat*. When the New York City Police Department is baffled by an apparently impossible crime, they call on The Great Merlini, a retired stage magician who now runs a Times Square magic shop. In his first case, two occultists have been murdered in a room locked from the inside, their bodies positioned to form a pentagram. **Introduction by Otto Penzler.**

Craig Rice, *Eight Faces at Three*. Gin-soaked John J. Malone, defender of the guilty, is notorious for getting his culpable clients off. It's the innocent ones who are problems. Like Holly Inglehart, accused of piercing the black heart of her well-heeled aunt Alexandria with a lovely Florentine paper cutter. No one who knew the old battle-ax liked her, but Holly's prints were found on the murder weapon. **Introduction by Lisa Lutz.**

Craig Rice, *Home Sweet Homicide*. Known as the Dorothy Parker of mystery fiction for her memorable wit, Craig Rice was the first detective writer to appear on the cover of *Time* magazine. This comic mystery features two kids who are trying to find a husband for their widowed mother while she's engaged in sleuthing. Filmed with the same title in 1946 with Peggy Ann Garner and Randolph Scott. **Introduction by Otto Penzler.**

Mary Roberts Rinehart, *The Album*. Crescent Place is a quiet enclave of wealthy people in which nothing ever happens—until a bedridden old woman is attacked by an intruder with an ax. *The New York Times* stated: "All Mary Roberts Rinehart mystery stories are good, but this one is better." **Introduction by Otto Penzler.**

Mary Roberts Rinehart, *The Haunted Lady*. The arsenic in her sugar bowl was wealthy widow Eliza Fairbanks' first clue that somebody wanted her dead. Nightly visits of bats, birds, and rats, obviously aimed at scaring the dowager to death, was the second. Eliza calls the police, who send nurse Hilda Adams, the amateur sleuth they refer to as "Miss Pinkerton," to work undercover to discover the culprit. **Introduction by Otto Penzler.**

Mary Roberts Rinehart, *Miss Pinkerton*. Hilda Adams is a nurse, not a detective, but she is observant and smart and so it is common for Inspector Patton to call on her for help. Her success results in his calling her "Miss Pinkerton." *The New Republic* wrote: "From thousands of hearts and homes the cry will go up: Thank God for Mary Roberts Rinehart." **Introduction by Carolyn Hart.**

Mary Roberts Rinehart, *The Red Lamp*. Professor William Porter refuses to believe that the seaside manor he's just inherited is haunted but he has to convince his wife to move in. However, he soon sees evidence of the occult phenomena of which the townspeople speak. Whether it is a spirit or a human being, Porter accepts that there is a connection to the rash of murders that have terrorized the countryside. **Introduction by Otto Penzler.**

Mary Roberts Rinehart, *The Wall*. For two decades, Mary Roberts Rinehart was the second-best-selling author in America (only Sinclair Lewis outsold her) and was beloved for her tales of suspense. In a magnificent mansion, the ex-wife of one of the owners turns up making demands and is found dead the next day. And there are more dark secrets lying behind the walls of the estate. **Introduction by Otto Penzler.**

Joel Townsley Rogers, *The Red Right Hand*. This extraordinary whodunnit that is as puzzling as it is terrifying was identified by crime fiction scholar Jack Adrian as "one of the dozen or so finest mystery novels of the 20th century." A deranged killer sends a doctor on a quest for the truth—deep into the recesses of his own mind—when he and his bride-to-be elope but pick up a terrifying sharp-toothed hitch-hiker. **Introduction by Joe R. Lansdale.**

Roger Scarlett, *Cat's Paw*. The family of the wealthy old bachelor Martin Greenough cares far more about his money than they do about him. For his birthday, he invites all his potential heirs to his mansion to tell them what they hope to hear. Before he can disburse funds, however, he is murdered, and the Boston Police Department's big problem is that there are too many suspects. **Introduction by Curtis Evans**

Vincent Starrett, *Dead Man Inside*. 1930s Chicago is a tough town but some crimes are more bizarre than others. Customers arrive at a haberdasher to find a corpse in the window and a sign on the door: *Dead Man Inside! I am Dead. The store will not open today.* This is just one of a series of odd murders that terrorizes the city. Reluctant detective Walter Ghost leaps into action to learn what is behind the plague. **Introduction by Otto Penzler.**

Vincent Starrett, *The Great Hotel Murder*. Theater critic and amateur sleuth Riley Blackwood investigates a murder in a Chicago hotel where the dead man had changed rooms with a stranger who had registered under a fake name. *The New York Times* described it as "an ingenious plot with enough complications to keep the reader guessing." **Introduction by Lyndsay Faye.**

Vincent Starrett, *Murder on 'B' Deck*. Walter Ghost, a psychologist, scientist, explorer, and former intelligence officer, is on a cruise ship and his friend novelist Dunsten Mollock, a Nigel Bruce–like Watson whose role is to offer occasional comic relief, accommodates when he fails to leave the ship before it takes off. Although they make mistakes along the way, the amateur sleuths solve the shipboard murders. **Introduction by Ray Betzner.**

Phoebe Atwood Taylor, *The Cape Cod Mystery*. Vacationers have flocked to Cape Cod to avoid the heat wave that hit the Northeast and find their holiday unpleasant when the area is flooded with police trying to find the murderer of a muckraking journalist who took a cottage for the season. Finding a solution falls to Asey Mayo, "the Cape Cod Sherlock," known for his worldly wisdom, folksy humor, and common sense. **Introduction by Otto Penzler.**

S. S. Van Dine, *The Benson Murder Case.* The first of 12 novels to feature Philo Vance, the most popular and influential detective character of the early part of the 20th century. When wealthy stockbroker Alvin Benson is found shot to death in a locked room in his mansion, the police are baffled until the erudite flaneur and art collector arrives on the scene. Paramount filmed it in 1930 with William Powell as Vance. **Introduction by Ragnar Jónasson.**

Cornell Woolrich, *The Bride Wore Black.* The first suspense novel by one of the greatest of all noir authors opens with a bride and her new husband walking out of the church. A car speeds by, shots ring out, and he falls dead at her feet. Determined to avenge his death, she tracks down everyone in the car, concluding with a shocking surprise. It was filmed by Francois Truffaut in 1968, starring Jeanne Moreau. **Introduction by Eddie Muller.**

Cornell Woolrich, *Deadline at Dawn.* Quinn is overcome with guilt about having robbed a stranger's home. He meets Bricky, a dime-a-dance girl, and they fall for each other. When they return to the crime scene, they discover a dead body. Knowing Quinn will be accused of the crime, they race to find the true killer before he's arrested. A 1946 film starring Susan Hayward was loosely based on the plot. **Introduction by David Gordon.**

Cornell Woolrich, *Waltz into Darkness.* A New Orleans businessman successfully courts a woman through the mail but he is shocked to find when she arrives that she is not the plain brunette whose picture he'd received but a radiant blond beauty. She soon absconds with his fortune. Wracked with disappointment and loneliness, he vows to track her down. When he finds her, the real nightmare begins. **Introduction by Wallace Stroby.**